THE MURDERS at ASTAIRE CASTLE

A Mac Faraday Mystery

By

LAUREN CARR

The Murders at Astaire Castle

Published by Acorn Book Services

For information call: 304-995-1295
or Email: writerlaurencarr@gmail.com

Designed by Acorn Book Services

Publication Managed by Acorn Book Services
www.acornbookservices.com
acornbookservices@gmail.com
304-995-1295

Cover designed by Todd Aune
Spokane, Washington
www.projetoonline.com

ISBN-10: 0-9891804-2-5
ISBN-13: 978-0-9891804-2-9

Published in the United States of America

To Story-tellers and Writers of Ghosts and Goblins, and Things That Go Bump in the Night.
This one's for you. Enjoy!

A Note From the Author

Fans of the Mac Faraday Mysteries may notice a slight difference in *The Murders at Astaire Castle*. While this mystery does contain some supernatural elements, I would not classify it as a paranormal.

Halloween has always been a fun time. It is the time to break out and be someone else. As a child, I would pretend to be one of the Bobbsey Twins searching for clues to lead me to a secret treasure. If I was lucky, it was made up of chocolate. As a teenager, I was Nancy Drew. Always, when October rolled around, I craved mysteries with something extra added—something beyond the normal—something *supernatural.*

As an author, I couldn't resist taking this one Mac Faraday Mystery on a scary Halloween adventure. I hope you enjoy this ride as much as I enjoyed writing it.

For you, my dear readers, *The Murders at Astaire Castle* is my Halloween trick or treat goodie to you! Enjoy!

Happy Reading!

Lauren Carr

Author of the Mac Faraday Mysteries

The Murders at Astaire Castle

A Mac Faraday Mystery

The Murders at Astaire Castle

Cast of Characters

(in order of appearance)

Rafaela Diaz: Housekeeper at Astaire Castle. She thought it was a dream job cleaning an actual castle for a world famous horror author. She was wrong.

Damian Wagner: World-Famous Horror Author. After years of writer's block, he hides out at Astaire Castle to pen the final chapter in his horror series. Mysteriously, both Damian Wagner and his final book disappear.

Genevieve Wagner: Damian Wagner's daughter.

Bill Jansen: Damian Wagner's editor.

Mac Faraday: Retired homicide detective. His wife had left him and took everything. On the day his divorce became final, he inherited $270 million and an estate on Deep Creek Lake from his birth mother, Robin Spencer.

David O'Callaghan: Spencer police chief. Son of the late police chief, Patrick O'Callaghan. Mac Faraday's best friend and half-brother.

Deputy Chief Arthur Bogart (Bogie): Spencer's Deputy Police Chief. David's godfather. Don't let his gray hair and weathered face fool you.

Archie Monday: Personal assistant, editor, research assistant to world-famous mystery author Robin Spencer. She is now Mac Faraday's lady love.

Gnarly: Mac Faraday's German shepherd. Another part of his inheritance from Robin Spencer. Gnarly used to belong to the United States Army, who refuses to talk about him.

Robin Spencer: Mac Faraday's late birth mother and world famous mystery author. An unwed teenager, she gave him up for adoption. After becoming America's queen of mystery, she found him and made him her heir. Her ancestors founded Spencer, Maryland, located on the shore of Deep Creek Lake, a resort area on Western Maryland.

Police Chief Patrick O'Callaghan: David's late father. Spencer's legendary police chief. The love of Robin Spencer's life and Mac Faraday's birth father.

Jeff Ingles: Manager of the Spencer Inn, the five-star resort owned by Mac Faraday. His therapist is on speed dial.

Hector Langford: Spencer Inn's chief of security.

Riley Adams: Friend of David O'Callaghan. Disappeared during a Halloween party at the castle.

Reginald & Gwen Astaire: Built Astaire Castle on the south side of Spencer Mountain in the 1920s.

Nathan Hindman: Retired Army Colonel. Bought Astaire Castle in the 1940s.

Gisselle Hindman: Nathan's World War II war bride.

Nigel: Nathan Hindman's white German Shepherd, who he had rescued in Germany during the war. Is he still protecting Astaire Castle and Spencer Mountain?

Iman: Spencer Inn's head chef.

Ed Willingham: Mac Faraday's lawyer. Senior partner at Willingham and Associates. He chased Mac Faraday for three city blocks to tell him that he had inherited a fortune beyond his dreams. First lawyer Mac ever met who he actually liked—maybe because he works for him.

Stan Gould: Billionaire. Wants to purchase Astaire Castle as a wedding gift for his new wife Lacey. He won't take no for an answer.

Lacey: Stan Gould's wife. International lingerie super model.

Kyle Finch: Vice President of Gould Enterprises.

Raymond Hollister: Damian Wagner's literary agent.

Chelsea Adams: Riley's sister. David O'Callaghan's first love.

Molly: Chelsea's service dog, trained to sense and warn of seizures.

Karin Bond: Lacey's assistant.

Tonya: Spencer Police Department's desk sergeant.

Dr. Dora Washington: Garrett County Medical Examiner.

Ben Fleming: Garrett County prosecuting attorney. He's one of the good guys.

Officers Brewster, Zigler, and Fletcher: Spencer police officers.

Where there is mystery, it is generally suspected there must also be evil.-- **Lord Byron 1788-1824, British Poet**

Prologue

November 2002 – Astaire Castle, top of Spencer Mountain, Deep Creek Lake, Maryland

Shivering, Rafaela turned up the fan for the heater in her old Plymouth. The weather channel was calling for snow. With an eye on the storm clouds heading straight for Spencer Mountain, she picked up the speed a notch. Her car bumped along the worn road forged through the trees and rock to take her to Astaire Castle.

The notion of being trapped at the castle by a winter storm made her curse the day she had accepted the job as housekeeper at the Astaire estate. The young immigrant thought her prayers had been answered by landing the job at the luxurious home. Not only was it prestigious to work in a castle, but lucrative since Damian Wagner was paying almost twice her normal hourly wage.

What a gem to put on my housekeeping resume—to clean an honest-to-goodness castle for one of the world's most famous authors of horror books! So what if the Astaire Castle has a repu tation of being haunted? I'll be making a bundle for cleaning five days a week in the daylight. Besides, I don't believe in no ghosts.

Rafaela regretted her decision the first time she walked into Astaire Castle.

At first, she dismissed her cleaning supplies moving from where she had left them as forgetfulness. Then there was the time she kept hearing someone whispering her name. She had looked around, but had never seen anyone. Similarly–with doors closing or opening, or footsteps coming up behind her, and the old-time music and party noises in empty rooms when no one was there—she tried to tell herself that it was all her imagination.

None of that was anything compared to the Wolf Man she had seen in the dining room mirror while she was cleaning it.

She had heard all about the Wolf Man who lived in the woods surrounding Astaire Castle. The woman with two teenagers who lived in the apartment next to hers was quick to tell her about him. Rafaela had dismissed it all as ghost stories made up by her neighbor's kids to scare her—until she had seen him with her own two eyes.

That day she ran out of the castle. She returned only after Genevieve, Damian Wagner's daughter, had promised that her father would finish his book and be moving out of the castle by the end of the year—at which time he would pay her a handsome bonus that would give her enough money to visit her family in Brazil for Christmas.

Rafaela caught her breath when her Plymouth entered through the gate at the end of the road to pull into the front courtyard and fountain.

The fountain was off. Damian Wagner had never bothered to turn it on. He wouldn't notice if it was. He spent his time banging away on his computer in the study on the top floor. He wouldn't eat if it weren't for his daughter bringing food to him.

Then there was the editor—Mr. Jansen.

He reminded Rafaela of a bird with his bony frame, high cheekbones over a pointy chin, and thick eyeglasses with his blinking eyes magnified behind them. He even sounded like a squawking bird with his high-pitched voice, no matter what his mood or what he was saying. Ready to pounce in anticipation of any need from Damian Wagner, he was always lurking nearby.

Damian's daughter, Genevieve, was as charming as she was beautiful. She often asked Rafaela about her family in Brazil and about her life in Deep Creek Lake. For the new immigrant to America, Rafaela felt as if she was making a friend who would give her good references for more housekeeping jobs in the resort town of Spencer—more millionaire estates to clean—estates that weren't haunted.

Rafaela pulled her car around the circular drive and parked at the bottom of the steep steps that led to the front door. When she got out of her car, the wind howled and whipped her long dark hair around her head. The wind actually seemed to want to rip her thin coat off her body. Grabbing her box of cleaning supplies, she squared her shoulders, and sucked up her nerve to go inside.

Need to make this quick. They don't have enough money to make me stay here during this storm.

The wind yanked the heavy wooden door from her grasp to slam it against the side of the house.

"Stupid door!" Rafaela set the box inside the foyer and went outside to grab the door and pull it shut. "Mr. Wagner! Mr. Jansen! Genevieve! It's me, Rafaela! Hope I'm not disturbing you." She picked up the box and made her way through the foyer.

"Raf-aela …"

She stopped. With wide eyes, she peered up the staircase to the second floor balcony. "Is that you, Mr. Wagner?" She paused to listen. "Genevieve?"

"Get out. Now."

Has to be my imagination. She reassured herself. "There's no such thing as ghosts. There's no such thing as ghosts," she muttered over and over to herself while hurrying to the back of the castle. "I don't suppose you had any trick-or-treaters last night, did you?" she called out to ease her nerves with the sound of her own voice. "Not up here I suppose."

She waited for an answer. She heard footsteps on the floor up above.

The smell of burnt meat came to her nose. It smelled like steak that had been left on the grill for too long.

They must have grilled steaks last night.

"Lots of little children stopped by my apartment." Feeling braver as she rattled on, Rafaela set the box of cleaning supplies on the kitchen table and gathered together her duster and furniture polish.

Best to start in the living room. The antiques, wood, and silver take the longest.

Admiring the decades-old priceless china encased in the china closet, she went through the dining room. With her cleaning lady's eye, she gauged what needed to be addressed on this visit that she might have missed before. She stopped when the blotch of red on the kitchen door frame caught her eye.

What's that? Catsup?

It wasn't until she saw a spot on the floor that she first considered that it wasn't a condiment, but something much more sinister. She spotted another. Bigger this time … and another.

There was a red pool in front of the kitchen door that opened out onto the back patio and deck that projected out over the rocks to provide a massive view of the valley down below. The drops, splatters, and pools led to one common source—the fire pit outside.

She saw the flames and smoke wafting in the wind whipping around her where she stood in the open doorway. She stared at the blackened objects in the pit. What at first appeared to be a burnt log projecting out of the flames took shape.

The hand and fingers reached out to her.

The index finger was pointing at her.

Through the rapid beating of her heart, Rafaela could hear the footsteps behind her coming closer.

"Get out!"

His image was reflected in the glass pane of the door. The wild hair. The crazed eyes.

It's the Wolf Man!

Chapter One

Present Day—Late-October

The two ATVs shot through the shrubbery that had overtaken the south side of Spencer Mountain's top. The occasional sunray that managed to peak through the clouds above would catch on the gold trim of the black all-terrain vehicles.

To the left side of the road, Police Chief David O'Callaghan scoured the landscape littered with bare trees for any sign of the old woman they were seeking.

Behind him, Mac Faraday searched the right side of the road. A retired homicide detective with more than twenty-five years of police work under his belt, Mac had looked for more than one missing person. His experience, plus his availability, made him a regular volunteer for the Spencer police department when extra manpower was needed—whether it be a missing person or a major murder case.

This search was for an elderly woman with Alzheimer's who had wandered away from her family at the Spencer Inn. She had been missing for five hours. The sun was starting to set. Soon, the chilly day would turn into a freezing night.

Snow was expected and that wasn't a good thing in the mountains.

They were running out of time.

David held up his hand in a fist to signal a stop and slowed down his vehicle. While waiting for Mac to halt behind him, the police chief removed his helmet and ran his fingers through his blond hair. "Any idea where you are now?" He shot Mac a wicked grin.

Guessing, Mac shot a thumb over his shoulder to indicate the road they had just traveled. "The Spencer Inn is about three miles back that way."

The police chief nodded his head. "The Spencer Inn is on the north side of the mountain top, looking down on the lake and the valley to the north."

"But the Spencer Inn owns the whole mountaintop," Mac said with a question in his voice.

"And you own the Spencer Inn. Therefore, you own this whole mountaintop." David pressed the button on his Bluetooth to check in with the search party. "Hey, Bogie, we're up on the southern side of the mountain top. Nothing's up here. Any luck in your area?"

"Nothing, Chief," the deputy chief responded.

"We're going to head back toward the Inn," David said.

"But we haven't searched to the end of this road." Mac pointed further up the trail.

"She's not up there," David said in a tone so sharp that it startled him. The police chief shifted his ATV into reverse and backed up.

Even though David O'Callaghan was the chief of police, Mac Faraday was one of Spencer's wealthiest residents. Descended from the town's founders, he was unofficial royalty in the small town of Spencer, located on the shore of Deep Creek Lake.

Several years younger, David O'Callaghan had much less law enforcement experience than Mac. Being David's older half-brother added another level of respect to make the police chief tread softly when issuing orders to the retired homicide detective. With the same tall slender build, their familial relationship was evident to the few who were aware of it. The only notable difference was in Mac's dark hair with a touch of gray showing at his temples.

"We won't know unless we look," Mac argued for going further out the tattered road. "We've searched for her in all of the usual areas. You can't—"

"She's not there." David's hard expression ordered him to drop it.

"We won't know unless we look," Mac said in a steady tone.

"Check it out," David said. "Do you see any sign of humans being in this area in recent years? This road is completely overgrown. No sign of hikers. No one comes over to this side of the mountain. We're talking about an eighty-six year old woman with Alzheimer's. She's fragile and on foot. She'd never be able to make it this far." With a wave of his finger, he ordered Mac to turn around. "We're going back."

The order only served to make Mac more suspicious. "What's up that road?"

"Nothing."

"Then why are you afraid to go up there?"

David whipped off his sun glasses as if to show him the glare in his blue eyes, which were identical to his. "Drop it, Mac. Forget about this road. Forget about this side of the mountain. Now turn your vehicle around and go back to the Spencer Inn and forget about coming back here ever again. Got it?"

Mac met his glare. "And what if I don't? Like you said, it's my property. You can't stop me from going up there to search … or whatever."

"Don't make me shoot you, Mac."

"Shoot me?" Laughing, he shook his head. "Are you serious?"

Any shred of humor that David had when they started talking was now gone. "If you go out that road, there's nothing I can do to help you. Have I made myself clear?"

The corner of Mac's lips curled while he studied the intense nature of David's order. "Very clear."

⁂

They were halfway back to the command post set up at the Spencer Inn when the call came in from Deputy Police Chief Art Bogart: Mac Faraday's German shepherd, Gnarly, and Archie Monday, Mac's housemate and "lady love" as he liked to call her, had found the woman.

Gnarly had followed her scent down the mountain trail. He had zig-zagged through the ski slope to the service shed that managed the electronic chair lift. The elderly woman had forced her way into the shed and fallen asleep in the dark corner.

Gnarly was hero of the day, which was why Mac thought it suspicious when he found the German shepherd hiding in the backseat of his SUV.

"We need to go," Archie whispered in a hurried voice to Mac. "We need to go now." There was fear in her deep emerald green eyes. Her pink cap was pulled down to cover her pixie blonde hair and ears. With her petite features, the cap made her resemble Tinker Bell in Peter Pan.

"Why?" Mac received part of his answer when he saw the dog lift his head to peer out of the back window. Mac caught a glimpse of what appeared to be a cigar in the dog's mouth.

Seeing Mac, he laid his pointy ears back to rest flat on his head and ducked back down.

Mac heard a crackling voice yell from the open back of the ambulance. "I'm telling you, one of you robbed me. How dare you rob an old woman! You should all be ashamed of yourselves—all of you." He turned around to peer through the window at where Gnarly was crouched.

Hurrying up to them, David asked, "Mac, Gnarly was the one who found her, wasn't he?"

Mac hung his head.

The police chief turned to Archie. "That scent that Gnarly was following—we assumed it was her, but could it have been the scent of beef jerky?"

"He did find her," Archie said. "Whether it was her or the beef jerky she was carrying in her purse doesn't matter."

"Thieves! You're all thieves!" They heard the impact of her purse hitting one of the EMTs.

"Mother, calm down," her daughter said to her. "I'll buy you another package of beef jerky on the way to the hospital."

"What kind of people are you to steal beef jerky from an old woman?" the mother demanded to know.

"Is she going to press charges?" Archie asked David.

"We'll replace the jerky," the police chief said.

"Oh, a cover up?" Mac replied.

"Only because it's Gnarly," David said. "Bogie is going to buy a pack of jerky on the way to the hospital and slip it into her purse while she's being treated so they'll think she missed it."

"Sounds like you've been down this road before," Mac said.

"Only since Gnarly came to town." David paused before telling him in a soft voice, "Sorry I was so hard on you out there."

"How were you hard on him?" Archie wanted to know.

"He threatened to shoot me," Mac said.

"Well, you must have done something to deserve it," she said.

"It was nothing." To change the subject, Mac glanced at his watch. "Hey, it's late and I'm starved. How about dinner here at the Inn? My treat."

"I'm meeting Finnegan at her place," David replied. "But you two go ahead. I have to stop by the cottage to shower and change. I'll take Gnarly back home to Spencer Manor and drop him off."

Mac wrapped his arms around Archie. "I guess it's just you and me, kid."

☙ ❧ ☙ ❧

Mentally, Mac Faraday would often have to pinch himself when entering the Spencer Inn. Before his inheritance from his birth mother, he would never have been able to afford to set foot in the elegant mountaintop resort.

With its five-star rating, the Spencer Inn was the place to go for romance and luxury. There were a dozen other little out of the way places around Deep Creek Lake that couples could patronize to explore the intimacy of love. For those blessed with wealth, and who desired the best in fine food, drink, and romance, then the Spencer Inn was the place to go.

Two years later, Mac was still getting used to receiving the royal treatment. Doors were opened for him. Trying to anticipate the inn owner's every need or desire, clerks would race to get his favorite cognac or predict what type of dinner he might be in the mood for. If Mac and Archie were dining at his table in the gourmet restaurant at sunset, the host would ensure the blinds were set to perfection to block the sun from his eyes, while still allowing him a view of the mountains and the lake below.

Mac Faraday was forty-seven years old when he had learned that the teenaged girl who had given him up for adoption had grown up to become Robin Spencer, an internationally famous murder mystery writer. She had come from a long line of blue bloods, who had founded the upscale resort town of Spencer, Maryland. For an underpaid homicide detective, the whole experience was still surreal.

Mac didn't think he would ever get used to it.

The hosts of both the lounge and the restaurant opened their cut-glass doors when they spied Mac and Archie crossing the lobby. Unsure of where they wanted to eat, the couple paused. Glancing down at their coats and gloves and dirty boots and jeans, Archie suggested the lounge where they would not appear so out of place—even if they did own it.

The host hurried in ahead of them to signal for a server to prepare the corner booth where Mac usually sat when visiting the lounge. By the time they crossed the bar area, the bartender was getting a bottle of Archie's favorite white wine from Mac's private collection—2008 Domaine Leflaive Puligny-Montrachet Les Folatières. He also fetched two wine glasses.

"What happened between you and David?" Archie asked after they were settled in the booth.

"Nothing happened," Mac insisted in a low voice.

"Liar."

The bartender showed the gold bottle with the white label to Archie, the wine expert of the couple. He uncorked and served a single swallow for her to approve before filling their glasses. "Have you decided on what you would like for dinner this evening?"

Mac turned to Archie for her choice. Dining with Archie Monday was an adventure. As Robin Spencer's assistant, she had traveled all over the world. Fearless when it came to exotic food, she loved to test the culinary skills of the chief chef.

"What does Iman feel like trying this evening?" she asked. "Tell him that I'm drinking a 2008 Domaine Leflaive Puligny-Montrachet Les Folatières and to surprise me with something to complement it." With a wicked glance in Mac's direction, she added, "Make it a dinner for two."

The bartender went back to the kitchen to deliver her message.

After a toast, Archie took off her cap and ran her fingers through her hair to revive the circulation to her scalp before urging Mac to continue. "You had to do something to make David threaten to shoot you."

"David wasn't going to shoot me," Mac said. "He only threatened to."

"He's been down lately," she said. "He tries to hide it, but I can see it. You do know that Finnegan is leaving for Quantico tomorrow."

"Yeah, that's right." Mac confessed that he had forgotten about David's latest girlfriend, a former U.S. Marshal, was starting a new career with the Federal Investigative Agency. She was moving to Quantico, Virginia. After her training was completed, she would be transferred to her first assignment, which would definitely not be western Maryland.

"How long do you think that relationship is going to last?" Archie asked with a frown. "It's like Yvonne all over again. It's all hot and heavy. She gets a big job offer. They say they'll make it work long distance. After less than six months, she's sleeping with someone else and dumps David."

Mac was only half listening. He was remembering the determination, with a hint of something else, etched on David's face when he turned around and ordered that they were coming back. They were going no further.

Fear. "Something scared him," Mac said more to himself.

"Do you mean like a bear?"

"David had a weapon," Mac told her. "We were both armed. If it was a bear, we could have shot it if we had to. No, he didn't—"

"Mac, they didn't tell me that you were here." Jeff Ingles, the manager of the Spencer Inn, was hurrying across the lounge in their direction. "I am so glad they found that lady." He trotted at a quick pace, while trying to maintain the dignity befitting the manager of one of the country's most elegant resorts.

"Gnarly found her," Archie said.

The manager's grin quivered at the thought of the rambunctious German shepherd. "I'm glad." He turned to Mac. "Hector is debriefing the Inn's security team to find out how these types of incidents can be avoided in the future."

"The woman has Alzheimer's," Mac said. "I didn't get any vibes from her family that they intended to hold us responsible for her wandering off."

"Well, you never can be too safe," Jeff said. "If you want to have a word with Hector before—"

Shaking his head, Mac took a sip of his wine. "Tell him to go home and enjoy his evening. We'll talk about it later." Jeff was about to turn away when Mac interrupted his departure with a question. "What's on the Spencer Inn property over on the south side of the mountain?"

Mac didn't miss Jeff's posture straightening. It was like a rod had been rammed down his back. Standing up straight, his shoulders tense, the manager turned to face him. "Pardon me?"

"What's at the end of the road leading over to the other side of the mountain?" Mac asked again. "David and I went out there, and I saw signs saying, 'No Trespassing, Spencer Inn Property.' But I don't know what's out there." He shrugged. "I can't believe I've never gone—" He recalled, "*You* took me on a tour of this whole resort when I inherited it, but you never took me out there."

"Because there's nothing out there," Jeff said firmly.

Mac turned to Archie, who shrugged. "I've never been out that way either. The further you go, the more overgrown the road gets—nothing but rocks and trees. I assumed there was nothing."

"She's exactly right," Jeff said. "There's nothing."

Mac narrowed his eyes at the manager. "What are you not telling me?" Beyond Jeff, he saw the man whom he knew would be truthful with him.

Hector Langford, the Inn's chief of security, was a straightforward Australian who had been working for the Spencer Inn for over twenty-five years. He would know what was on the south side of the mountain that could spook David O'Callaghan, the chief of police and Marine officer. After serving two tours overseas, David wasn't easy to spook.

Mac waited for Hector to stop at the bar to pick up a beer, served in the bottle, and take a seat across from them—all under Jeff's warning gaze—before he asked, "What's at the end of the road leading to the south side of Spencer Mountain."

While helping himself to a handful of peanuts from the middle of the table, Hector laughed at Jeff's glare. "Oh, do you mean the castle?"

Mac's and Archie's mouths dropped open. "Did you say 'castle'?" Mac asked.

Hector nodded his head. Jeff rubbed his face.

"As in moat and alligators and drawbridge … castle?" Mac leaned across the table at him.

"Well," Hector drawled, "this one doesn't have any moat or alligators or drawbridge, but it is an honest to goodness castle."

"Castles are kind of big," Archie said. "Why can't we see it from the lake?"

"Because it's on the other side of the mountaintop, facing the valley to the south," Hector said. "Used to be—back in the old days—that you could see it from the valley below. After about a decade of no one going near it, it's all overgrown and everyone has forgotten about it. In the winter, when all the leaves are down, if you know it's there, you can see from the valley floor if you look for it. It's made of stone. So, if you don't know about it, with the trees and rocks, you could miss it."

"Why don't I know about it?" Mac asked. "I got a list of my holdings and property that I inherited from my mother, and I don't recall seeing any castle on that list. I would have noticed if I owned a castle."

Jeff answered, "Because it was listed as a vacation rental property under the Spencer Inn. It's identified as a luxury mountaintop vacation cabin."

"There's a big difference between a castle and a cabin," Archie said.

"Why has everyone been keeping this castle a secret from me?" Mac asked. "Why all the secrecy? Even David refused to go out there this afternoon."

"He had a bad experience out there," Hector said with a wave of his hand. "We used to have a devil of a time keeping kids, looking for ghosts and scaring each other, out of there."

"There was that boy who disappeared out there," Jeff said with all seriousness. "David knew him."

"The Adams kid," Hector said with a nod of his head. "David was there the night he disappeared."

"What happened?" Archie asked.

"It was back in 2000," Hector recalled. "A bunch of young people, David and some of his friends, wanted to have a Halloween party out at the castle. He had just gotten out of college and was going into officer training with the Marines. There were between twenty to thirty guests—all in costume.

We're not talking high school kids that were out of control. They were responsible young people. After the party, one of his guests was missing. He never made it home."

"Maybe something happened to him after he'd left the party," Mac said.

Jeff and Hector shook their heads in unison. "No one saw him leave," Jeff said.

"It wasn't an open party," Hector said. "David knew everyone who was there. None of them did anything to him."

"He disappeared in that castle?" Mac asked.

"Riley Adams," Jeff recalled the name. "The whole state was looking for him."

"He was dressed in a werewolf costume," Hector recalled. "A lot of the guests believed that he was killed or captured by a ghost. We had no trouble keeping kids out after that. He was never found, but unofficially, it was believed that he got drunk or was on something—witnesses said he was acting very strange that night—and wandered off into the woods or fell off the cliff—died—and his body was never found. If he had fallen off the cliff, his body could have been caught in some deep crevices of the rocks where searchers couldn't find it."

"I think the ghosts got him," Jeff said.

"Ghosts?" Mac laughed. "Seriously?"

"Seriously," Jeff responded without humor. "Look it up. The Astaire Castle is one of the ten most haunted houses in America."

Excited, Archie tapped Mac's arm. "I've heard of Astaire Castle. I knew it was in Maryland, but I never knew it was here." She hugged him and squealed. "And you own it!" She dug into her bag to extract her computer tablet to look it up on the Internet. "This is totally wicked!"

Jeff uttered a hollow laugh. "Yeah, congratulations," he said with heavy sarcasm.

"It's haunted?" Mac still laughed.

"Not a week goes by that some paranormal expert doesn't want to come film it," Jeff said. "The answer is always the same. No. After the last murders, Robin ordered the place boarded up and to never let anyone inside it ever again."

His attention piqued, Mac sat up straight in his seat. "The last murders?"

Hector locked his gaze on Mac and said in a sinister tone, "The last of several."

Chapter Two

"Two suicides, three mysterious disappearances, and four murders have taken place at Astaire Castle." Archie leaned against Mac to show him the tablet on which she had found a website about the most haunted places in the Unites States.

"Really?" Mac took the tablet from her to read the article.

Jeff groaned and sank into the booth next to Hector. "Why did you have to tell him?" he chastised the security manager.

"He had a right to know, don't you think? Considering that he owns the place ..."

"Don't tell me that you believe in ghosts." Mac laughed at the two men across from him.

"You've never been to that castle," Jeff said. "You didn't see what happened there."

The corners of Mac's lips curled when he asked, "What happened?"

"The Wolf Man is on the prowl!" Hector let loose with a ghoulish cackle.

While Mac joined in, Jeff groaned and glared at all of them. Seeing that he wasn't reading the tablet, Archie took it back to read for herself.

"It all started in 1919," Hector said. "Edward Spencer, your great-grandfather, had met Reginald Astaire while fighting over in Europe during World War I. They became good friends—both coming from money and all that. While in Europe, Reginald had developed affection for castles. When he came back, he determined to have one here in the states. While visiting his old war buddy here in Spencer, he decided that the top of Spencer Mountain was the perfect place to build his castle. At the time, construction was already underway for the Inn. So Edward agreed to sell the south end of the mountaintop to his pal. Reginald had an architect draw up the plans based on the design of a Scottish castle."

"It took seven years and over two million dollars to build," Archie interjected. "Can you imagine how much it would cost to build that today?"

"Astaire's money came from railroads," Jeff said, "plus stock market investments."

"When the castle was finished, Reginald and his wife Gwen, a New York socialite, moved in," Hector said. "This was the heyday of the Roaring 20's and Prohibition. The castle was a major showplace then—parties every night, twenty-four-seven. Then ..." He paused for dramatic effect, "it happened."

Mac didn't want to reveal how close he was to the edge of his seat.

"The stock market crash of 1929," Archie said.

"Reginald Astaire lost everything," Hector said.

Archie read, "Reginald and Gwen Astaire, dressed in their party finest, stood up on top of the stone wall lining the cliff behind their castle. Looking down on the valley below, they joined hands, and jumped off the wall to their deaths on the rocks below."

"Deaths number one and number two," Hector said. "Move forward twenty years. Nathan Hindman, a retired Army Colonel from World War II, buys the castle for him and his German war bride, Giselle, to spend their golden years. Now, he was not as sociable as Reginald Astaire. On the contrary, he was a complete recluse."

"He had been captured by the Nazis during the war and spent close to a year as a POW," Archie read from the tablet.

"They say Hindman was closer to his dog than people," Hector said. "He had a beautiful white German shepherd that he had brought back from Germany."

"A German shepherd?" Archie melted. "Like Gnarly."

"This was a white German shepherd," Jeff said. "Gnarly is a black and tan beast."

"Hindman's dog's name was Nigel," Hector said. "I've seen pictures of him. He was a gorgeous animal—all white—he looked like a wolf. Hindman was heard to say Nigel was the most compassionate living creature he had encountered over in Europe."

"How sad," Archie said.

"It's amazing how uncivilized man can become in wartime," Mac said. "I've heard people who have served overseas in war say that animals can be more civilized than man in some circumstances."

"I believe it." Hector nodded his head. "Anyway, Hindman had some issues moving into the castle. Giselle got lonely, of course. Hindman tried to help her, I guess, by letting her take tennis lessons from the pro here at the Inn. Then rumors started about her having an affair with the pro. Things didn't end well."

Beads of sweat were forming on the hotel manager's forehead. Jeff took out the linen kerchief that he always carried to wipe his face.

"One afternoon," Hector reported, "Giselle had invited the tennis pro to the castle for a private lesson. Afterwards, they sat down for a glass of iced tea on the back patio looking out across the valley. In the middle of their drink, Hindman came out with an ax and hacked them both to death. The police found them a couple of days later when the Inn reported the pro missing. Hindman had disappeared. Neither he nor his body was ever found."

"Those are the first two murders and the first mysterious disappearance," Mac said.

Hector chuckled. "You'd never guess what came out after the murders."

"What?"

"Giselle Hindman was discovered to have been a Nazi spy during the war," Hector said. "She had used her sexual talents to extract information from high-ranking U.S. officials and identified allied undercover agents. She was responsible for the execution of many American spies during the war. You wouldn't believe the stories that came out about her. This was one cold-hearted woman. When Giselle saw that her side was losing the war, she played the poor little German girl to get an American serviceman to marry her and whisk her out of Germany."

"Maybe Hindman found out the truth and that's why he killed her," Mac said, "to avenge the deaths of his comrades during the war."

"That's not all," Hector said. "The tennis pro ..."

"What about him?"

"Years later, it was discovered that he was a Russian spy in the new Cold War," Hector said. "As you know, Deep Creek Lake and the Spencer Inn are hot vacation spots for big wigs from the nation's capital. After this news was uncovered, it is believed that Giselle and the tennis pro were involved in more than a love match."

"What about the dog? Nigel?" Archie asked.

"Disappeared, too." A slow grin crossed Hector's face. "Technically, that makes it four, not three, mysterious disappearances connected with the castle. Legend says Hindman's spirit entered the dog, they became one and went off to live in the wild. But then, by now, Nigel would have died, wouldn't he?"

Archie and Mac exchanged glances.

"What are you saying?" she asked.

"A dog has been heard to howl late at night over on that side of the mountain," Hector said.

"A lot of people around Deep Creek Lake own dogs," Mac said. "Even Gnarly howls regularly—especially when there's a full moon over the lake."

Hector leaned forward in his seat. "In June 1964, a five-year-old little boy, named Ethan, wandered off from his parents' campsite down on the lake. An all-out search was called. Campers, park service, police from Spencer, Garrett County, and even state came in to look for him. Night-time rolled around. Ethan still was not found. The temperature got down into the twenties."

Archie clutched Mac's arm. "How awful."

Hector held their gaze. "We have bears, wild cats, snakes—there was no telling what could have happened to a little boy during the night."

"What happened to him?" Mac asked.

"As soon as the sun was up the next morning, the search resumed," Hector said. "A park ranger was driving along a trail in his jeep when he saw a white German shepherd blocking the road. He slowed down and the dog turned and ran. He drove on, went around a bend and there he was again. The same dog blocking the road. He looked right at that ranger, turned, and ran back into the woods. On a hunch, the ranger decided to follow the dog. He claims this dog kept stopping and looking over his shoulder at him, as if to see if he was following. He came to realize that the dog wanted him to follow. The dog led this ranger right to the boy, who was asleep in a pile of fallen leaves under a tree in a clearing. After making sure the boy was okay and calling it in, the ranger looked up—the white dog was gone."

"Nigel," Archie said in a breathy voice.

Hector chuckled. "Ethan told his parents and authorities that a white wolf took care of him. The wolf made the bed in the pile of leaves and kept him warm the whole night so that he wouldn't get cold."

"Seriously?" Mac asked. "A ghost wolf? Named Nigel?"

"Dog," Archie corrected him. "A ghost dog. And he's a friendly ghost dog."

"Nigel?" Mac chuckled. "If you're going to have a ghost dog, can't you give him a tougher name than Nigel? What kind of name is that for a legendary ghost dog?"

"Hey," Hector said, "I didn't name him. The dog had that name before he became a ghost."

"Well, I'm just saying that if I had the name of Nigel—" Mac said.

"What's wrong with the name Nigel?" Archie asked.

"It makes me think this ghost should be wearing a pocket protector, glasses, and haunting the library in Oakland."

"I'm just saying what has been reported." Hector shrugged his shoulders with a shake of his head. "That's not the only case of a white dog or wolf, depending on who you ask, who has disappeared into thin air before their eyes."

"Are they sure it's not Gnarly?" Mac asked with a grin. "When this dog disappeared, did their beef jerky disappear with him?"

Hector and Archie joined in his laughter.

"Do we really have to do this?" Jeff asked with a choked voice. He glanced around to see if any of the Inn's guests were listening.

"I'm sensing a theme here," Mac said. "This young man who disappeared from the party was dressed as a werewolf, and this dog that disappeared and turned into a ghost is a German shepherd—"

"German Shepherds are said to have some wolf in their genes," Archie said.

"It's been speculated that this young man who had disappeared was possessed by Nigel's spirit," Jeff said.

"Because he was wearing a werewolf costume," Mac laughed.

"I really think that this isn't the time or the place to be telling Mac about all this," Jeff said in a hushed voice.

A grin crossed Hector's face. "Oh, but we're getting to the best part."

Led by Iman, the chief chef at the Inn, two servers carried in trays filled with Mac and Archie's dinners. A tubby Indonesian man, Iman almost climbed over Mac to take Archie's hand and kiss it. In his tall white chef's hat, and double-breasted white jacket, his position as the chief chef was evident. Those customers who hadn't noticed his entrance into the lounge, with the flair of his clothes and manner, now noticed when he announced in a loud voice filled with his thick accent:

"Ah, Miss Archie, my favorite victim—I mean, customer—never afraid to try new things." He noted Mac's apprehensive expression.

His eyebrows arched, Mac tried to peer through the metal covers over their plates to see what Iman had prepared for them. While he was excited by Archie's occasional order for the chef to surprise them, he was also apprehensive.

Not long after Mac had inherited the Spencer Inn, Iman had surprised the new owner by serving him a grilled stuffed whole bluefish—complete with its head and tail still on it. When Iman removed the cover to reveal the fish, its eyes seemed to jump out of the plate to glare accusingly at Mac, who recoiled away from the plate. Unable to eat something that was looking at him, Mac had ordered the chef to remove both his and Archie's plates from the table—even though she found it to be quite delicious.

A jokester, Iman never let the tough former police detective forget it. The chef was not afraid to say, or do, things to Mac that drenched the Inn manager's clothes with nervous sweat.

"Do not fear, Mr. Mac," Iman assured him, "no fish heads tonight. For tonight's dinner," he picked up a covered plate, "we have a wonderfully exciting new dish that I happen to be experimenting with, which I am sure you and Miss Archie will love. You two, Mr. Mac and Miss Archie, will be the first here at the Spencer Inn to experience this delicious delicacy."

Mac could feel Archie's excitement permeating from where she sat next to him.

When Iman grasped the cover, Mac held his breath. He was afraid to look.

"I, Chef Iman, present to you," He snatched off the top. "Htapothi sti Skhara - Flame-Grilled Octopus."

Archie gasped with delight.

"No!" Mac almost jumped out of his seat at the sight of a plate filled with octopus tentacles, arranged in a spiral design, covered in a golden sauce.

"Doesn't it look delicious?" Iman brought in the plate to give him a closer look. While Mac backed away, Archie was pressing forward to see and smell it.

"No!" Mac replied.

"The Spencer Inn will be the only resort in the state to serve it. People will come from states away just to taste my octopus."

"No, no, and hell no!" Mac shouted.

"Iman, stop it!" Jeff ordered.

Next to Jeff, Hector was rolling with laughter at what he knew was a joke.

With a toothy smile, Iman returned the plate to the tray. "Just a little joke, Mr. Mac. No octopus for you tonight. This is a new dish that I am trying. It is my dinner. I thought I would have a little fun at Mr. Mac's expense."

Archie sighed when she saw the cover return to the plate. "What about me?"

"If you want octopus, you're going to have to eat it over there." Mac pointed to a table on the other side of the lounge.

Iman took up another plate from the tray and removed the cover for them to see an elegantly arranged dinner. "Tonight, to go with your delicate white burgundy, I have prepared a glamorous roast chicken and porcini mushrooms in a white truffle paste." The meal was accompanied with broasted potatoes and grilled asparagus.

The sight of the golden brown roast chicken breast made Mac sigh with pleasure and relief.

Laughing heartily at his joke, Iman grasped Mac by the shoulder while freshening both of their wines. After giving Mac a good-natured slap on the back, Iman and the servers returned to the kitchen.

"This chicken is a downer after seeing that octopus," Archie whined, looking at her plate.

"Do you want to go eat in the kitchen with Iman?" Mac asked.

"For someone who can face killers without blinking," she said, "you can be quite a coward when it comes to food."

"Allow me some comfort when it comes to what I put inside my body." Mac picked up his fork and poked the chicken as if he feared it would attack him.

While Jeff was horrified by the chef's joke played on their boss, Hector couldn't stop chuckling. "You should have seen your face when you saw that octopus."

"Just when I think Iman has topped himself …" Mac smiled at the prank played on him.

Jeff brought them back to their previous topic of discussion. "Well, I strongly recommend that you forget all about that castle."

"I think I have a right to know about it," Mac said, "considering that I'm paying the property taxes on it. How much property tax is there on a castle?"

"More than on a manor house on Spencer Point," Archie said.

"You haven't heard about the best part," Hector said.

"Only you would call it the best part." To convey his displeasure, Jeff shifted in the seat in the booth to turn his back to the security chief sitting next to him.

"What's the best part?" Mac asked. "Don't tell me. The gateway to hell is in the basement?"

While Archie and Hector laughed at the quip, Jeff grumbled.

"Have you ever heard of Damian Wagner?" Hector asked Mac.

"Who hasn't?" Mac replied. "I've read all of his books."

"You've read all of Damian Wagner's books but not your mother's?" Almost dropping her fork, Archie shot a glare at him from where he was sitting next to her.

"I've been reading Damian Wagner since I was in high school," Mac said. "Robin wrote mysteries. Damian Wagner's books are really scary horror masterpieces—keep you up all night, unable to sleep, type of scary. Really bizarre."

"Like the author himself," Jeff said.

"Then you know Damian Wagner did not end well," Hector told Mac.

"He disappeared," Mac said. "I seem to recall—"

"His daughter and editor were killed—hacked to death, dismembered, and set on fire," Hector said in a sullen tone. "Damian Wagner disappeared. Some say the killer, or the Wolf Man, got him. But his body was never found. Others say he did it himself and is living abroad under another identity. No one knows. Thing is, he spent four months living at the Astaire Castle, which Robin had bought for a song."

"She felt sorry for him," Jeff said.

"Why would Robin feel sorry for such a big name as Damian Wagner?" Mac asked.

"Damian Wagner had written over two dozen books," Hector said, "all big, best sellers going straight to the New York Times list and blockbuster movies. Besides being a big time author with a huge following, he was also a drunk and heavy into drugs. In 1990, he got into a car accident. His wife was killed. His daughter was in the back seat, but not badly hurt. Damian was driving drunk. His wife's family sued for custody of the daughter. He gave her up and they took her to Canada. That was where her mother's family was from. Damian went into rehab and got sober." He added in a sad note, "Only problem was, he couldn't write while sober."

Mac recalled, "That's right. His main character, Hagar, hunted all of these creatures, zombies and aliens and werewolves and vampires. But he was after this one alpha werewolf, Santos, who had turned Hagar's sister into a werewolf, forcing Hagar to kill her."

"The final showdown between Hagar and Santos was to be his last book," Hector said, "but Damian couldn't write it and was about to lose his contract with his publisher. He had the general outline done when he was in the car accident, but—After he had spent ten years with writer's block, Robin thought that if he had the right setting, the castle, that he might be inspired to write it. So she offered to let him stay there during the summer of 2002."

Archie interrupted, "You said his daughter was murdered?"

"Right before he came here, his daughter came back," Hector said. "She was twenty-two, had graduated from college, and came to live with him to help him write his book."

"You know," Jeff said with a shake of his finger, "now that I think about it—David knew her, too." He told Mac, "I never realized that. David was friends with Riley Adams; plus, if I remember correctly, he had a fling with Damian Wagner's daughter, Genevieve."

"A fling?" Archie asked. "Are you sure?"

Hector was nodding his head. "I remember that, too. The swimming pool at the castle was closed up. It had been for a few years and it was too expensive to repair it for just one season. So Genevieve came over to use the Inn's pool and would hang out at the outdoor lounge. David was home on leave after his first tour overseas, and I remember seeing them together. From what I saw, they were hot and heavy."

"But David was back out on his next tour when they were killed," Jeff said.

"Damian also brought his editor along to stay at the castle with them," Hector said. "That Halloween, Damian either went berserk or someone broke in—the next day, when the housekeeper went to clean the castle, she found a fire in the pit on the back patio and body parts in it."

"And Damian Wagner was gone," Mac mused. "And his book—"

"Some speculate that he went mad trying to break through his writer's block and he never did write it," Hector said.

"Robin said that he had told her that his book was done," Jeff insisted.

"I think he was lying," Hector said. "Because if Damian Wagner had written that last book, with the final showdown between Hagar and Santos, then there's no way he would have stayed hidden this long. That book would have been published somehow. As many people were waiting to read it—it was a gold mine—no way could he sit on it."

"Unless he preferred poverty to going to jail for murder." Mac washed down his last bite of the chicken with the wine before asking, "All right, you told me about the murders in the castle, a long string of bad karma, but what about the haunting part?"

"After the murders in 1950," Hector said, "the castle sat abandoned for over thirty years. When Robin returned to Spencer, after becoming a famous author, she decided to have it renovated and turned into a luxury bed and breakfast—an American castle in the country."

"She sank over a million dollars into updating the electric and plumbing," Jeff said. "Not to mention the décor."

"A haunted American castle," Archie said.

"It was a disaster," Jeff said.

Hector explained, "You see, up until then, anyone who lived or stayed there died. Kids, young people, used to say things, but everyone dismissed it as stories to scare each other. When Robin opened up the castle, and paying customers were staying there—"

"And came running back here demanding their money back," Jeff said.

"There were people who got off on staying in a haunted castle," Hector said, "but even some of them came back here with only the clothes on their backs. Most of them refused to go back inside that castle for their things. They just wanted out."

"What kind of things were they saying?" Mac asked.

"The sounds of parties on the main level in the middle of the night," Hector said, "or they'd see a couple holding hands, standing on the stone railing and then jumping into thin air."

"The sound of a couple laughing and playing tennis on the court when no one was there," Jeff said.

"Then, there's the Wolf Man," Hector reminded Jeff. "Remember that couple who said he chased them all the way down the upstairs hallway and out the front door." He turned to Mac. "That was before Riley Adams disappeared, by the way."

"Robin stopped trying to rent the place out," Jeff said with a shudder. "But then, it was a few years later, she said Damian Wagner was going to move in and stay there. She thought with him being into that type of thing, that he could handle the castle's peculiarity." He frowned, "Obviously, he couldn't, which proved to be bad news for his daughter and his editor."

Chapter Three

Next Morning – Spencer Manor

In the heart of Maryland, the cedar and stone home known as Spencer Manor rested at the end of the most expensive piece of real estate in the resort area of Deep Creek Lake. The peninsula, known as Spencer Point, housed a half-dozen lake houses that grew in size and grandeur along the stretch of Spencer Court. The road ended at the stone pillars marking the multi-million dollar estate that was the birthplace and home of the late Robin Spencer.

In her will, Robin Spencer had stipulated that her research assistant and editor, Archie Monday, was permitted to live in the stone guest cottage tucked away in the rose garden for as long as she wanted.

The beautiful green-eyed blonde had come with the house and Mac Faraday had been in no hurry for her to move out, unless it was to relocate to the master suite in the main house. Now, Archie having done that very thing, the stone cottage was being renovated to reflect the masculine nature of its new occupant, David O'Callaghan, Mac's half-brother by their late father, Patrick O'Callaghan.

David's mother had recently been sent to live in the nursing home. While the rundown home where he had grown up was being revamped to put on the depressed housing market, David was making his home at Spencer Manor.

It felt like Indian summer. The morning sun was warming the Point to brighten up what had been a dreary fall. While playing a game of fetch with Gnarly, Mac was thinking about removing his jacket when David drove his police cruiser through the stone entrance and around the circular drive to park it in the six-car garage.

When Mac paused in throwing the ball, Gnarly jumped up on him and barked as if to demand he continue playing. His master obliged. "Did you see Finnegan off?" Mac called over to David when he came out of the garage.

"She's on her way to Quantico as we speak." David urged Gnarly to bring the ball to him for a round of fetch.

Mac searched David's face for a sign of emotion, in particular remorse over the possible demise of his relationship with the former U.S. Marshal. "How are you doing?"

David threw the ball across the yard to send it over the flower bed and roll down toward the lake. Gnarly gave chase. "Fine. Why wouldn't I be?"

"Well … I kind of thought you cared about Randi."

"I do care about her," David said. "I'm also realistic about getting involved with women like her, and Katrina and Yvonne, and all the rest of them—women passing through Spencer on their way to the next chapter in their lives. I cared about every one of them. Maybe even loved some of them—but I've learned that the likelihood of any of them giving up their dreams of seeing the world to be a small town police chief's wife is nil." With a shrug, he tossed the ball that Gnarly was pawing at him to throw. "So I just suck it up when they say it's been fun and I hope we can still be friends. No hard feelings? Sure, no hard feelings."

Mac took the ball when Gnarly brought it back to him. "That's no way to have a love life." He tossed it to David.

"Of course, you'd say that." David caught the ball. "You've got the perfect woman."

Mac laughed. "Don't tell her that. It'll go to her head."

"I wouldn't dream of it," David said. "I can't expect Randi to put her romantic life on hold in hopes of the unlikely possibility that she'll be assigned back here." He threw the ball back to Mac. Before Mac could catch it, Gnarly intercepted the ball and ran off into the bushes with it.

"I'm going in to get some sleep," David said. "What are you and Archie doing today?"

He was turning around to take the stone walkway around to the rose garden when Mac answered, "Hector's taking us up to Astaire Castle."

David stood up straight. His shoulders tensed. He turned back around to Mac. The only time Mac had seen that expression on his face was when the police chief was directing it at suspects whose cocky demeanor had pushed him over the edge. "Tell me that's a joke."

With his ball clamped in his jaws, Gnarly jumped up onto the porch and scurried under a chaise.

"No," Mac replied, "Hector should be here any minute. Archie's inside getting ready."

"You're taking her with you?" David stepped in so close that Mac could feel the heat of his breath on his face. "Listen, if you want to do something stupid, do it alone. Don't be dragging Archie in on it with you."

Mac stood up tall to push David back with his own forceful demeanor. "I'm not dragging anyone. Archie wants to go. Turns out Robin never told her about the castle either. We want to see it. Forgive us for being curious. It isn't every man who owns a castle. If it was—"

"Did it ever occur to you that no one told you about the castle for a reason?" David's face screwed up with emotion. "This is all a game to you! A joke! Well, it's not some scare each other and scream and laugh later type of fun house. Real people, nice people, people with hopes and dreams for the future have disappeared up there. Damian Wagner lost his mind and killed two innocent people—and then he disappeared. Robin had the good sense, and was responsible enough, to order that the castle be shut down—the doors locked and allow no one else near it again. She wouldn't even sell it—and she had lots of offers, but she knew that as long as she owned it, she could protect anyone else from getting hurt."

Mac was gazing at David's face. He tried to recall any other time that he had seen such earnestness in his face. *Riley Adams was at the party—David's party. Of course, he would feel responsible for his friend's disappearance. Not to mention Genevieve—Damian's daughter. How close was he to her?*

"I'm ready to go!" Archie trotted down the porch steps and crossed the driveway to join them. For the outing in the abandoned, and most likely filthy, castle, she was dressed in worn jeans and a sweater under a jean jacket. She had put on leather gloves with a matching cap.

Seeing his favorite lady, Gnarly ran to escort her to them.

David whirled around and grasped Mac by the arm. "Listen to me." His fingers dug into his bicep. "If you truly love and care about Archie, don't let her go with you. Order her to stay here."

"I can't order Archie to do or not to do anything," Mac hissed back at him.

"What are you two talking about?" When she saw David glaring at Mac, she planted her hands on her hips. "Are you threatening to shoot Mac again?"

"Still." David didn't take his eyes off him.

"What's going on?" Archie asked Mac.

"David doesn't think you should go up to the castle." She laughed.

"I'm inclined to agree with him," Mac said in a quiet voice.

Now it was Archie's turn to glare at him. "I thought you didn't believe in ghosts."

"I don't."

"Then we have nothing to be worried about."

"Do you believe in evil?" David asked them. "Damian Wagner wasn't a monster until he lived up there inside those castle walls. Then, evil consumed him and he did a really horrible thing. That's why I'm begging you two not to go up there—or—at the very least, Archie, you stay here and let Mac, if he insists on going, check it out first."

Archie regarded David before turning to Mac for his reaction. Seeing that he was considering it, she said, "You can't order me—"

"I can tell Hector not to let you in the jeep," Mac said.

She turned to David. Her voice dripped with sarcasm. "Thanks a lot, David." She whacked him in the arm with all her might, before storming back into the house. The force of her blow was so hard that in spite of his effort, David stumbled and grabbed his arm.

Mac waited for the echo of the slamming door to stop ringing in his ears before he asked David, "Are you going to tell me what you experienced up there? What happened to your friend Riley?"

"There are two theories going around," David said. "Some of my friends who were there that night believe he was possessed by Nigel's ghost, that's the dog that disappeared after the Hindman murders in 1950." David paused. "They say that because Riley came to the party dressed as the Wolf Man.

Others say he's dead and his ghost, still in the character of the Wolf Man, is up there on that side of the mountain."

"What about Damian Wagner?" Mac asked.

David said, "I wasn't involved in that investigation."

"But you did know Genevieve Wagner."

"Is there a list of my sexual conquests published somewhere?" David asked.

"I've been hearing that it's quite a list," Mac said. "I'm beginning to think that you've developed a bad habit."

"You're just now beginning to think that?" David replied. "Yes, I did know Genie Wagner in the biblical sense, but it was a fling. I was home on leave for a couple of months after my first tour to Afghanistan. She was hanging out at the pool at the Inn. We got together like two ships passing in the night and going in opposite directions. When her father was through with his book, she was moving to California. I was back at Quantico the Tuesday after Labor Day."

"Was she afraid of what was going on in the castle?"

David slowly shook her head. "She was afraid for her father. That summer was his last chance to write his book. The publisher had advanced him another one hundred thousand dollars on top of his original advance. If he didn't get the book written by the end of the year, he was going to have to pay it all back to the publisher, and he didn't have it. She told me that she was afraid of what he would do if he didn't get over his writer's block."

"Desperation," Mac said. "It's driven more than one man to kill."

"Desperation mixed liberally with evil," David said. "Listen, Mac. If you insist on going up there, then I can't say anything to stop you, but I can tell you this, I can't protect you when you're up there."

The two men paused to watch Hector pull in through the gate in his beat up four-wheel drive jeep, which was built for rough riding across the mountain terrain.

"I'm not asking you to," Mac said.

଍ ଎ ଍ ଎

They had passed the Spencer Inn resort and continued until they had run out of smooth road. Trees gave way to boulders, which formed a natural gateway to the south side of Spencer Mountain.

Hector announced what Mac had already observed, "We're being followed."

Mac's eyes narrowed while he studied the black police chief's cruiser marked with gold trim. "Is he escorting us or trying to stop us?"

"You're the boss," Hector said. "Tell me what you want me to do."

"Pull over. Let's ask him."

Hector pulled the jeep over to the side of the road.

Recognizing the cruiser, Gnarly stood up in his seat in the back and wagged his tail, which, in the tight confines of the jeep, beat Hector along the side of his bald head.

Mac climbed out of the passenger seat of the jeep and met David along the road between the two vehicles. "I thought you said you couldn't protect me." Mac noted that David was wearing his utility belt, complete with his gun, radio, and baton.

"Well," David drawled, "even if I can't, it's my job to at least try. I assume you brought your gun, and Hector has his."

"Always," Hector called back from the front seat of the jeep.

Gnarly barked as if to give his answer. His weapon was the hundreds of pounds of force built into his jaws.

"Follow me," David ordered before climbing back into his cruiser, which had four-wheel drive to take them across the rough terrain. He led them deep into the rustic area filled with trees sprouting up out of boulders and brush. The paved road dissolved into broken slabs of cement with deep ruts in between the slabs. In some places, the road was so rocky that it was smoother for the vehicles to go off the road and plow through the five-foot tall brush that lined the trail.

Concluding that there couldn't be anything worth seeing this deep into the wilderness, Mac was starting to regret his decision when they broke through the brush to come up to a stone wall with a thick wooden gate that blocked their access to the other side. It was locked shut with a rusty thick chain and padlock.

Hector picked up a large key from the center console of the jeep and a pair of bolt cutters from the floor in the back. "Just in case," he said while showing the bolt cutters to Mac.

Staring straight ahead, David remained behind the wheel of the cruiser to wait for Hector to open the gate. As the security guard had predicted, the lock was rusted shut, so he broke the chain with the bolt cutters. With great effort, he pushed the heavy gate back off the road to allow enough room for the cruiser and jeep to make their way through.

"Oh, wow," Mac muttered upon the sight.

It was like something he had only seen in movies. A big old rundown castle rose up from the stony landscape. Only sky was visible from the front. In the back, the valley stretched out below.

Hector had been correct. The castle wasn't noticeable from the valley floor. The walls, built into the edge of the mountaintop, had been constructed of stone. It was further camouflaged by vines that had grown up to engulf and kill off the trees. The centerpiece of the circular driveway was a fountain, covered with green mold, with a statue of two winged nymphs holding a giant urn between them.

Cracked and broken steps led up from the edge of the driveway to the main doors, which were caked with dirt and grime. Off to the other side of the driveway was a separate building, a four-car garage that appeared to have a second floor.

Speechless with awe, Mac turned around in a full circle to take in the sight. He had never expected there to be anything like this on the other side of the brush that he and David had been traveling in the day before. Imagining what the castle would have been like in its heyday, he could see that Reginald Astaire had created a whole world separate from the rest of Deep Creek Lake.

"Well, we're here." Hector produced a key ring filled with keys from his jacket pocket. "Do you want to go inside to meet the Wolf Man?" he asked with a mockingly evil laugh that reminded Mac of Vincent Price, a popular horror movie actor from back in the 1940s and 50s. Certain of Mac's answer, he climbed the steps to the main door.

"That's not funny, Hector." David had his arms folded tightly across his chest.

"I don't believe in ghosts," Mac said. "In over twenty-five years of police work, I never encountered a murder that had been committed by a ghost or vampire or wolf man. I want to see inside." He added to David, "You don't need to babysit me. If you're afraid to go in—"

"I'm going where you're going."

Gnarly leapt out of Hector's jeep, ran up the steps, and beat them to the front door.

"Hey, are you guys coming?" Hector unlocked the door. "I don't have all day." When David and Mac came up the steps, he chuckled at Gnarly racing in ahead of all of them. "Gnarly ain't 'fraid of no ghosts."

"He takes after his master," David said.

After turning on his high-powered flashlight, Hector stepped inside. "We had a couple rent out this place for a weekend. Their sheltie never came out from under the bed."

Mac had thought the foyer of the Spencer Manor was huge. The foyer for the castle stretched up three floors to reveal an oak ceiling and log beams that stretched across the width of the entrance hall. A suit of armor stood guard next to the double doors.

Gnarly quickly lifted his leg to mark the suit of armor as his.

To Mac's surprise, the foyer was furnished with dust-covered solid wood chairs, paintings, and tables complete with brass and crystal bowls.

"Robin didn't allow us to take the time to remove it," Hector said. "She wanted as few people coming in here as possible. As soon as the crime scene was released for the Wagner murders, she ordered the place locked up."

His hackles up, Gnarly uttered a low growl while sniffing his way around the foyer. Periodically, he would stop to mark tables or corners.

"Gnarly, stop it," Mac said.

Instead of being horrified, Hector snickered. "The Wolf Man isn't going to be happy about you marking his territory, Gnarly."

"Cut it out, Hector," David ordered.

"There's no such thing as a Wolf Man." Mac lifted the face piece for the suit of armor and peered inside.

"People down in the valley have claimed hearing him howl from up this way," Hector said.

"I thought you said that was Nigel's ghost." Mac let the metal face piece drop in place, which produced a puff of dust.

"A couple of years before you moved out here," David told Mac, "a couple claimed to have seen Bigfoot up here, too." He turned to Hector. "But that doesn't mean he's living here in the castle."

Gesturing at Gnarly who was marking the bottom step of the stairs leading up to the second floor, Mac said, "Before Gnarly has time to petition for homesteading here in the castle, can we move on?"

Directing them with the beam of his flashlight, Hector led the way through the entrance hall and the game room in the back. They stepped off the granite floors onto what had to be an Oriental rug. The layers of filth made it difficult to determine the design. A pool table rested in the middle of the rug. A bar was at one end of the room. A dart board was at the other. Hunting trophies filled the walls and display cases.

"Reginald Astaire considered himself a hunter," Hector said.

"Bar," Mac said. "Wasn't this castle built during the Prohibition?"

"They drank iced tea," the security manager said with a smile.

Mac noticed David staring at a display of what was supposed to be two battle axes on the wall. The outline of the two axes, one crossing the other, was still evident, even though both were missing.

Hector led them through a cut-glass door to a verandah. Outside, the wind whipping up from the valley below tore at their jackets with chilling fingers. As soon as the wind hit Gnarly in the face, he backed up to return inside and went over to the pool table to mark one of the legs.

The patio below was made up of granite plates out to the edge of the cliff, which was blocked off with a stone wall. "That was where Reginald and Gwen Astaire leapt to their deaths," Hector told them.

In the center of the patio was a huge fire pit.

Seeming to sense Mac's thoughts, David said in a low tone, "That's where Wagner's daughter and editor were burned up after being hacked to death." He turned to Hector. "Let's go inside."

"Want to see Damian Wagner's study?" Hector offered to Mac. "Since you're a fan."

Inside, Hector led the way up the circular stairs lining the inside of one of the turrets to the top floor. At the top of the stairs, he handed his flashlight to Mac to hold while he lifted a wooden plank from where it rested in brackets on either side of the door to hold it shut. Then, grasping a huge brass ring, he pulled the door open to reveal a grand room with windows providing a bird's eye view of the valley below. The room was furnished with bookcases, paintings, and artwork. Mac noticed a hole in the layout at the end of the room where a desk seemed to have once rested. "Someone stole his desk."

"Robin had—I mean you have—the desk," Hector said. "The day before Wagner killed his daughter and editor, he gave it to Robin. It was his. A big fancy heavy thing. He had brought it from his place in Washington State."

Shivering, David stomped his feet. Mac couldn't tell if it was anxiety for them to leave or cold. He felt a chill in the stone lined room himself. He envied Gnarly's fur coat. The German shepherd was sniffing along the bottom shelf of the bookcase at the end of the room.

"Okay, Mac, you've seen the place," David said. "Let's go." As if he expected them to follow his order, David turned to the door leading into the turret only to have the heavy wooden door swing shut. A split second after the slam of the door, they heard the wooden plank fall into place on the other side of the door.

"No!" David raced to slam his shoulder into the door to force it open. "Don't just stand there looking like a couple of doofuses. Help me!"

The three men lined up and pressed against the door until David gave up with a sigh. "It's useless. The bar came down on the other side."

"No problem." With a shrug of his shoulders, Mac took his cell phone off his belt. "All we have to do is call the Inn to have one of the security personnel come to let us out." He frowned when he read the screen on the phone: *No Service*. Seeing that he had no bars to indicate a signal, he held up the phone closer to the window.

Hector did likewise with no success. "That's weird," he said. "The tower is right over on the next mountain."

"I'll use my radio." David took his radio out of his utility belt and turned it on. "Dispatch, this is Police Chief O'Callaghan. Can you read me?" The only answer he received was static. "Dispatch," he said into the radio. "Come in, Dispatch."

They all strained to hear any sign of someone responding to the call.

"That doesn't make sense," Mac said. "Even with the stone walls, that radio should be able to pick up and project a signal." He gestured at the sky outside the window. "And we're on top of a mountain. There's nothing to block either signal. We should have the strongest cell phone signal in the area."

With a devilish grin, Hector laughed. "Unless it's because we're in a real and authentic *dead zone*."

Chapter Four

David slid down from where they were peering out the window to the valley and freedom to the granite floor of Damian Wagner's study. "Mac," he said, "there's something you need to know ... in case we die."

"What?" Mac asked him in a soft voice. He suspected it had to do with their father or a great family secret.

"If we die here, it's your fault." David pointed his finger directly at Mac.

As if to signal that he was taking David's side, Gnarly trotted over to paw at the police chief. After receiving a pat on the head, Gnarly returned to the last section of the bookcase to sniff along the bottom shelf.

"I didn't ask you to come here with me," Mac argued with David.

"I wouldn't have had to come if you had listened to me yesterday and forgot about this whole side of the mountain."

"Archie will notice when we don't come back," Hector said. "She'll call someone and come looking for us."

"If she cools off before we freeze or starve to death." David wrapped his arms around himself and shivered.

"Is Gnarly dark meat or white meat?" Mac joked.

"Don't even talk like that," Hector said. "We're going to get out of here."

"David's right," Mac said. "It's cold in here." Standing at the far end of the room, in the corner where the windows and the last bookcase met, he looked around the long grand room. With fifteen-foot high ceilings, he estimated that it was one of the biggest rooms he had ever been in. Maybe that's why it's so cold. "It could be the stone walls, but we're inside. That should block the wind."

"Cold spots," Hector said from where he was peering out the window. "Another complaint we got from renters. Here and down in the pantry." He pointed to Mac. "They used to say it was in that corner where you're standing. Folks speculated that it was the ghost of Nathan Hindman, standing there watching Giselle playing tennis with the pro. Notice that you can see the tennis court perfectly from there."

Mac shivered when a cold chill hit him in the back of the neck and traveled down his spine. *This is not a cold spot. It's a draft.* He noticed that Gnarly was now trying to dig through the granite with his paws.

"I have a plan," Hector said. "We break one of these windows and throw Gnarly out. He'll go for help."

"What if he dies from hitting the cement patio three stories below?" David asked.

"He'll land on his feet," Hector said. "Dogs always land on their feet."

"That's cats that land on their feet," David said.

"Dogs, too. Everyone knows that." Hector continued, "Gnarly will run all the way back to the Inn, go inside. Jeff will throw a fit upon seeing Gnarly in the Inn. He'll call Archie to bitch. Archie will realize that we're in trouble and call Bogie, who will bring the cavalry to the rescue."

"That's the dumbest idea I've ever heard," David said.

"Do you have a better idea?" Hector asked.

"We throw Mac out the window and, if he survives, he can go get help," David said. "If he doesn't survive …" With a wicked grin, he shrugged.

"How about if we go out the other way?" His back to them, Mac was studying the bookcase in the corner that had captured Gnarly's attention. It was set at a slight angle off from the other bookcases.

"What other way?" Hector asked.

Mac ran his fingers along the edge of the case. "There's a draft blowing in from behind this bookcase. That's why Gnarly keeps digging at it." He pointed to the other end of the room. "This castle has four turrets. This room is the length of the castle. There's a turret on the other side of this bookcase."

They looked out the windows and along the building.

David displayed the most excitement he had shown since entering the castle. "There's probably another staircase behind that bookcase. It's a secret entrance."

They yanked the books from the shelves.

"There has to be a way to open it," Mac said, "like a secret lever. In the movies, it's usually a book."

After yanking all of the books off the shelves, they studied the edges and shelves for any sign that it was more than wood. They had made their way to the last shelf when David noticed hinges connecting the bottom shelf to the case. He stood up and pressed his foot against the shelf. They heard a click before the case popped back a couple of inches. All three men pressed their full weight against the book case to push the door back into the dark room on the other side. As they pressed, it gave way to allow them entrance.

Uncertain of what was inside, they stood in silence. Hector and David shone their flashlights around the dark room. As they had concluded, the opposing turret was circular like the one they had climbed up on the other side of the study. However, this turret appeared to have not been used in nearly a century. Sealed up, they could smell the mold and dank walls. The wind whipped the cobwebs that hung from the walls.

In contrast to the scary atmosphere, Mac chortled. When Hector and David glanced at him as if he had lost his mind, he pointed up to the ceiling at the top of the turret. One quarter of the top was missing. "There's your cold spot. The wind has been coming in from up there and blowing down through this turret. How much do you want to bet this turret has another secret entrance down in the pantry, which is where people have complained about another cold spot?"

"I never said I believed in these ghosts," Hector claimed. "I'm just saying what others say."

Noting that Mac didn't have a flashlight, David ordered for him to follow him. "Keep Gnarly close." Hector was to bring up the rear while they made their way down the stairs to the bottom. Even with their flashlights, they had to feel their way along the wall to the stairs leading down. They had only just entered the turret when David stumbled. The only thing to prevent him from tumbling down the stone steps was Mac grabbing the back of his belt to pull him back up to his feet.

"What happened?" Hector asked.

"I tripped over something—something big." David shone his light to the floor to reveal a human skull with an ax embedded in the back of its head.

"Make that five murders associated with this place," Hector said.

Chapter Five

"Damian Wagner," Hector said in a low voice.

"Let's not make any assumptions." Mac knelt down to study the skeleton. "It could be David's friend Riley."

Gnarly sniffed at the body and its clothes.

In the dark, Mac could not see David and Hector both shaking their heads. "That ax disappeared when Damian's daughter and editor were killed," David said. "Both Dad and Robin were fixated on what happened because only one of those two axes was found in the fire pit."

"He's wearing a blue cardigan." Hector shone the light on the torso of the skeleton. "Damian Wagner always wore a blue cardigan when he was writing. It was his lucky charm. I used to see him wearing it when he'd come to the Inn for lunch."

His curiosity about the dead body satisfied, Gnarly turned his attention to the stairs leading down to freedom. Once again, his hackles were up. He shifted from growls to low barks and back to growls.

Checking to see if there was any signal yet on his cell phone, Mac rose to his feet. It still read No Service. "We can't do anything about this body until we get someplace to call it in."

Mac grabbed hold of Gnarly's collar to keep him from tumbling down the stone steps. Hugging the wall, they inched their way down the stairs lining the inside wall of the turret. Each of the men put on a brave mask when the cobwebs blowing in the wind tickled their faces or necks or a rat would scurry across their path when a flashlight beam would frighten it.

Mac found it increasingly difficult to hold onto Gnarly as they neared the bottom. The German shepherd lunged to break free of his hold on the collar. Mac wondered what prey he had picked up. At the bottom, they found a door not unlike the one at the top of the stairs in the opposing turret, only there was no wooden beam to block the entrance. But it did have a giant brass ring which Hector grasped and pulled out to open.

As soon as it was open enough, Gnarly charged through the opening into the light.

"Gnarly! No!" Mac ran after him.

Barking his alarm to announce his presence, Gnarly stood in the middle of an abandoned kitchen pantry littered with rusted and rotten cans that had been opened. The room smelled of decayed food and feces. They gingerly watched their steps while Gnarly sniffed the garbage.

"Looks like raccoons hit the mother load," Hector said.

Finding that it was not good enough even for him, Gnarly followed the scent he had picked up out of the pantry.

Mac examined one of the cans. "I've seen some smart raccoons, but never one intelligent enough operate a can opener." He picked up an old hand crank can opener.

David grabbed the can opener from him. "It's not animal—"

Gnarly's barks cut him off. His bark was joined by the bark and growl of another. The three men were still piecing the noises together when Gnarly's snarling bark was cut off by a yelp.

Mac was the first out the door. In the two years that he had Gnarly, Mac had never seen the dog cry out for help. Later, he would struggle to recall if he had ever heard Gnarly yelp. He was certain of the fact that this was the first time he had seen Gnarly downed by another animal.

At first glance, he thought Gnarly was being attacked by a giant white dog that was more than twice his size. The animal had Gnarly pinned down on his back by his throat. Gnarly was yelping in terror while the thing tried to shake him to snap his neck.

Mac drew his gun, took aim, and was firing a shot when David slapped his arm down to send the bullet into the floor. Before Mac could object or take aim again, David charged forward with his baton and swung it at the thing to make him let go of Gnarly.

The beast released Gnarly and fell aside. Mac dove in to throw himself on top of Gnarly to shield him from another attack.

As quickly as the beast fell, he was back up and charging at David, who blocked his attack with the baton. Hector ran up behind the beast to deliver a shot from his Taser to the neck to drop him down to the floor. The animal did not go down gently. With the shock, he whirled around to whack the side of Hector's head, which knocked the security manager against the kitchen counter. While the beast's attention was directed at Hector, David struck a blow with his baton across its back. When the beast turned his attention back to David, Mac kicked him in the back of the knee, which dropped him down to all fours. By then, Hector recovered to shoot him with the Taser gun once again.

It was only after it was unconscious that they all saw what it was.

His head, face, and chest were covered in thick long blond hair, which gave him the appearance of an animal. The growling and snarling added to his animalistic nature. But resting motionless at their feet, they could see beneath the thick hair of his head, face, and chest that made a direct path down his stomach to his naked lower body and exposed genitals.

"Is that …" Mac cradled Gnarly in his lap. The big dog was still trembling from the attack.

"I believe it is," Hector said.

"Don't say he's Bigfoot," Mac said.

"No, not Bigfoot." David moved in closer. "It's a man."

Chapter Six

Archie sped her royal blue Escalade SUV through the gateway into Astaire Castle, climbed out, and slammed the door shut. “Mac Faraday, what did you do to Gnarly?”

Her stern voice tore Mac’s attention from where he was stroking Gnarly, who was curled up in the back seat of David’s cruiser. “I did nothing to him.”

“Oh, yeah?” She ran past the line of cruisers, EMT trucks, ambulance, and medical examiner’s van to get a look at the injured German shepherd. “I couldn’t come with you because you were afraid something bad would happen to me, but Gnarly—it was anything goes for him.” She squeezed by him to check on the dog.

Seeing his mistress, Gnarly’s ears fell to the side of his head and he let loose with a loud mournful cry while pawing at her coat.

“Oh, Gnarly!” She wrapped her arms around him in a hug. “What happened to you?”

“He was bitten,” Mac answered for the dog. “The teeth broke the skin and drew blood. The EMT suggested that we take him to the vet to get him a shot of antibiotics.”

Archie tried to stand up, but Gnarly's cry brought her back to take him into her arms. "What bit him?"

"A werewolf," Hector called out to her. He had strolled over from where David was supervising the EMTs' examination of the man they had taken down in the castle's kitchen.

"Werewolf!" Archie jumped up and out of the back of the cruiser. Her glare fell on Mac. "You let a werewolf attack Gnarly? What's going to happen to him? Do you know what happens to dogs that get bitten by werewolves?"

"They turn into men," Mac answered with a straight face. Seeing Hector and Archie's puzzled expressions, he said, "If a man is bitten by a werewolf, he turns into a wolf. So, it seems only logical—"

"That's crazy," Archie said. "I never heard of a dog turning into a man after being bitten by a werewolf."

"Then you tell us," Mac said. "What does happen to dogs after they're bitten by werewolves?"

Archie had to pause to think before answering slowly, "Men turn into wolves. Dogs would turn into ..." She shook her head.

"Men," Hector said. "Gnarly's going to turn into a man." He gave into a hearty laugh. "Watch him turn into a cat burglar!"

Mac joined in his laughter while Archie fought the grin fighting its way to her lips. "This isn't funny. Gnarly's been injured."

A slow grin crossed Mac's face. He folded his arms across his chest. This was one area where, if there were such an expert, he was. Archie Monday was not a fan of horror movies or books. She would only tolerate the horror films Mac and Gnarly would watch together and half of the time she hid her face and covered her ears. "Calm down," Mac said, "Gnarly was not bitten by a werewolf."

"Then what do you call him?" Hector pointed up the sidewalk to where the EMTs were wheeling out the unconscious, hair-covered man on a gurney. The EMTs had to sedate him in order to strap him down for transport to the hospital in Oakland. David was following close behind. "He was growling and snarling and he bit Gnarly."

In the back seat of the cruiser, Gnarly sat up and howled loud enough to draw everyone's attention. When finished with one howl, he let loose with another and another until the gurney had been loaded into the back of the ambulance and the doors shut.

Archie's eyes grew wide with both curiosity and fright. "Has that creature or man or whatever he is had his shots? Maybe he's got rabies."

"Gnarly's had his rabies shots," Mac assured her before turning to answer Hector's question. "I would call him a wolf man."

"What's the difference?" Hector and Archie asked in unison.

"A werewolf is a man who changes completely into a wolf," Mac said. "A wolf man is a man who takes on the characteristics of a wolf without actually changing into one." He pointed at the man in the back of the ambulance. "He's not a wolf. He was only acting like one."

Mac didn't miss the remorse on David's face while watching the ambulance turn around to go out through the heavy wooden gates.

"Well," Archie said, "I'm taking Gnarly to the vet. There's no telling what that guy had that he passed on to him." She called to Gnarly to climb out of the back of the cruiser. "Come along. We're going to see Dr. Lee." She paused to give Mac a quick kiss on the lips. "I'm glad you're okay."

He grabbed her by the waist to pull her back when she attempted to turn away. "Forgiven?"

"No." With a naughty grin, she whispered in his ear, "I'll be expecting make-up sex later."

Mac watched her saunter back to her SUV with Gnarly. He noticed that Gnarly's tail was tucked down against his butt. The attack had served to take the wind out of his cocky canine sails.

"Bogie and Doc Washington are examining the body up in the turret," Hector reminded Mac after Archie turned her SUV around to head back down the mountain. "Want to go see what they've uncovered?"

"After I talk to David," Mac said. "Did either of you get a name from the wolf man?"

Hector shook his head. "Only barks and growls and snarls. He was really acting like a wolf. Extremely weird. The guy's a real wacko."

Overhearing Hector, David said, "He's sick," as he came up to them.

"Is he—" Mac dared to ask.

"Riley Adams," David said. "I recognized him under all that hair after we brought him down.

"I'm sorry," Hector said. "I didn't realize."

"It's not your fault," David said. "Riley was always different. Most people avoided him. When we were teenagers, he became even stranger. It got to the point that I was his only friend and even I was ashamed of him at times." He looked down at his feet.

"I'm sorry," Mac said.

"Our people are searching the castle and grounds," David said. "They found where he's been living on the ground floor of the castle. Old blankets filled with fleas, mites, and human waste where he's been sleeping. Garbage stolen out of what had to be trash bins that he's been feeding on for Lord knows how long. He's been living like an—"

"Animal," Mac said. "That's what he'd turned into."

After a long silence, David looked up at the castle. "I should have realized what had happened."

"How could you?" Mac asked.

"Riley became fascinated with werewolves," David said. "He must have seen *The Howling* I don't know how many times. That night that he came to the party, he was acting weird."

"That's what a lot of the witnesses said," Hector recalled.

"But it was how he was acting weird," David said. "He wouldn't talk to people. I thought, he was in character for his costume. He was acting like a dog—like a wolf." He shook his head. "I didn't put it together until now—until we came out of that pantry and I saw that he had Gnarly down—wolf—man—Riley had run away to be a wolf. ... If I had put it together sooner—"

"How could you?" Mac asked. "I've been a detective for more than twenty-five years and I've never heard of someone running away to live like a wild animal—thinking he was a wild animal. Don't beat up on yourself. There's no way you could have figured that out."

"I should have," David argued.

"Let me ask you a question," Mac said. "Suppose Riley had cancer?"

"What do you mean?"

"I mean," Mac said, "suppose instead of Riley running off to live in the woods like a wild animal, he had cancer and had spent all these years in the hospital getting chemo. Would you blame yourself then?"

"No," David said, "but it's not the same thing."

"It is the same thing," Mac said. "If your friend had cancer, he'd be ill. He'd be sick. You'd feel sympathy for him, but you wouldn't be beating yourself up like you are now. Riley is mentally ill—ill, just like he had cancer. Only in this case he's sick in his head. I'm not a shrink, but it doesn't take one to see that there's something wrong with him and he needs help." He concluded, "It's not your fault."

"Unless you were the wolf man that bit him and turned him into one," Hector said.

"Exactly," Mac agreed.

Hector said, "The important thing is that Riley has been found. Now he can get the help he needs."

"You stopped me from shooting him," Mac said. "If you hadn't have hit my arm, Riley would be dead now. You saved his life."

"Gnarly's okay," Hector said, "So Mac here won't have to sleep in the guest room for the rest of his life."

"If everything turned out so good," David asked, "why don't I feel better about this whole thing?"

"Because it's your job to figure out who buried an ax in Damian Wagner's head, before or after killing his daughter and editor," Mac said. "Believe me, once that news gets out, you're going to have a lot of eyes watching this case.

☙ ❧ ☙ ❧

"Well, this proves Robin was right." Chuckling, Deputy Chief Art Bogart, known as Bogie, stood up tall, stuck his thumbs in his belt while scrutinizing the corpse with the ax stuck in the back of his skull. The silver-haired deputy chief possessed the solid build of a wrestler. It was not uncommon rookies to underestimate the older deputy based on his silver hair and bushy gray mustache. Some had even goaded him into a challenge in the gym, only for them to be eating the mat in less than thirty seconds.

"She was outright fixated on that second ax that was missing from the display downstairs," Bogie said. "She claimed it proved that Damian Wagner wasn't a killer, but a victim; and swore that we would eventually discover his body along with that ax." He shook his head. "I can see her and Ol' Pat up at the Pearly Gates laughing at me right now."

The abandoned turret was now brightly lit with portable lights and sealed off with crime scene tape.

Bogie stood over the body while the medical examiner, Dr. Dora Washington, a stunning woman with long blue black hair worn in a ponytail spilling down her back, examined the skeleton. Dr. Washington was searching the corpse's pockets for further evidence.

"I expected to have Damian Wagner show up in a country that didn't have extradition," Bogie said. "I have to admit, this is an odd twist."

"Who swung this ax to kill him?" Mac asked.

"Maybe your wolf man," Dr. Washington said.

"It wasn't him," David said.

"This is where he disappeared before the Wagner's murders," she said. "It's also where he was found. Maybe he considered this his territory and objected to them trying to evict him."

"I'll be the first to accept that Riley has a problem with the elevator going all the way to the top," David said, "but he's not a killer."

"From what I hear, he tried to kill Gnarly," Bogie said. "He bit a dog—a big dog—a big strong dog."

"Bit," Mac said. "Riley thinks he's a wolf. Wolves don't attack people with murder weapons like axes."

"If you try to pin this on Riley, I'm going to fight you," David told Bogie.

"Settle down, Chief," Bogie said. "There's more to this case than a sick boy thinking he's a wolf. It's plain to see that this was a much more sophisticated murder. Most likely, whoever did this is the same perp who wiped out Wagner's account of seventy thousand dollars on the same day he was killed."

In response to Mac and David's stunned expressions, Bogie said, "That's a piece of information your father and I kept under our hats. On October 31, Damian Wagner's bank account was emptied out, and the funds transferred to an off-shore account. After that, it disappeared entirely. The house-keeper told us that Wagner had been arguing with his literary agent because he was having trouble finishing the book. That money was all that was left of his advance. If he didn't have a completed manuscript by December 31, he would have had to give everything, including the agent's portion, back to the publisher."

"When he disappeared and you had no body, you assumed he killed his daughter and editor in a rage, took the money, and ran," Mac said.

"Made sense until now," Bogie said.

"That's why whoever killed them hid Wagner's body," David said. "They wanted you to assume that."

"Did the agent have access to Wagner's account in order to transfer the funds out?" Mac asked.

"Wait a minute." From where she was kneeling next to the decomposed body, Dr. Washington held up her hand. "Let's get a positive ID on this body first, and then you can start looking for suspects."

"How long will that take?" Mac asked her.

"We have Damian Wagner's dental records on file," she said. "All we need is a comparison to this corpse."

❧ ❧ ❧ ❧

David's silence during the drive down the mountain and across the lake to the hospital in Oakland to check on Riley's condition proved that Mac's attempt to alleviate his guilt had been futile. He wondered if he would have been able to shake the guilt if it had been him. *Survivor's guilt. Not unlike surviving a shootout while the cop next to me got gunned down. David said they had been friends all through school. What's the saying? There, but for the grace of God, go I.* Mac cleared his throat.

"What?" David asked without taking his eyes from the road.

"Does Riley's family still live in the area?"

David gave only one shake of his head. "His father died when he was real young. His mother passed away less than a year after Riley disappeared. She hadn't been sick a day in her life, but after he was gone … She died of congestive heart failure."

"Broken heart." Mac glanced out the passenger side window at the passing countryside.

"Riley had a sister a couple of years behind us," David said. "Last I heard, she was in law school. I'll have Tonya look her up. We'll need to contact her."

As they drove south on Garrett Highway, the countryside gave way from farms to rural homes to shopping plazas until they were in Oakland, Maryland. David made a right turn at a traffic light to take them into the hospital parking lot. In comparison to the metropolitan hospitals that Mac had been accustomed to in the city, Garrett County Memorial Hospital appeared to be more of a medical center. It certainly wasn't equipped to deal with men who thought they were wolves.

"I doubt if they're going to be able to keep Riley here for long," David said. "As bad off as he is, they'll be shipping him off to a psychiatric hospital as soon as possible."

"They can do a lot with meds." Mac unclipped his seat belt. "Don't assume the worst. With treatment and medication, he may be able to get to the point where he can function like a normal person."

David cocked his head at him. "Mac, the guy thinks he's a wolf."

"And Gnarly thinks he's a cat burglar."

ꕥ ꕥ ꕥ ꕥ

A police chief's gold shield can get a lot of action and information that those without can't get. As far as the hospital staff was concerned, David was looking for information about a murder suspect, not a long lost friend. While he wasn't allowed to speak to Riley, who was in no condition to talk to anyone who wasn't of the canine species, he was able to ask the chief nurse practitioner about his condition.

She was as bewildered by Riley Adams as everyone else. "He's under heavy sedation," she told David. "He became violent when we tried to bring him out from under it after he was brought in. We had to strap him down to sedate him again. Before that, the only talking he did was in the form of growling and barking. Do you know if he has a history of drug use?"

"No," David said with certainty.

She went on. "We're doing a full medical workup on him. We'll be able to give you more information later, but as far as his physical medical condition—he's malnourished. We can see signs of nerve damage on some of his fingers and toes—possibly brought on by frost bite. Healed over bite wounds—" She stopped to look from David to Mac and then back to the police chief. "The EMTs said he's been living in the wilderness with no human contact. Is that true?"

"For at least a decade," David told her. "You've seen him."

"Judging by the way he smells, I'd believe it," she said.

"Not too long ago," Mac said, "I heard of authorities arresting a guy for breaking and entering who'd been living in the wilderness with no human interaction for thirty years. He had set up a tent that was green, so it blended into the wood surroundings. He lived off of food that he stole from campers during the night and homes near the woods where he lived."

"Did he think he was a wolf?" the nurse asked Mac.

"No," he answered.

"Then this case takes the prize," she said.

"What's going to happen to Riley?" David asked her.

"We'll only keep him here long enough to determine if he has a physical ailment that needs to be addressed," she said. "Once we determine that he's fine physically, he'll be shipped off to a psychiatric facility. Hopefully, he has family who can make arrangements for him at one of the better hospitals where he'll get treatment. If he ends up on the government dime, all they'll do is keep him drugged and locked up."

"I'll find his sister," David said. "Hopefully, she can afford to take care of him."

"If she can't, I will." Mac was as surprised by his offer as David and the nurse.

"Mac, you don't—" David objected.

"He's your friend," Mac said. "That makes him my friend. The Forsythe Foundation is set up to do this type of thing."

"Forsythe Foundation?" the nurse asked. "Is that a government agency?"

"No, it's a private foundation and I'm the chair." Mac dug a business card out of his wallet. "It's named after Mickey Forsythe, a fictional multi-millionaire who helped people by solving murder cases. But this is a real foundation set up by Robin Spencer. We provide legal representation for those who need it, but can't afford it; we pay for medical care; we provide investigative services; and we've even awarded a full scholarship to send a young man to college whose father was a police officer killed in the line of duty." He tapped the card in her hand. "Give that to your business office to put in Riley Adam's file. You'll get a call from Ed Willingham to arrange payment for his treatment."

For the first time since the start of the conversation, a smile came to the nurse's lips. "Anything you say, Mr. Faraday."

When she walked away, David turned to Mac. "Mr. Faraday," he muttered in a mocking tone.

"That's my name," Mac said. "Don't wear it out."

Slyly, David said in a low voice, "Thank you, Mac. I do appreciate you helping Riley."

Embarrassed by the expressed gratitude, Mac shrugged. "It's the least I could do after trying to shoot him."

Chapter Seven

They rode back to Spencer in silence. Mac usually didn't mind silence, except in this case, he could see that David had something weighing heavy on his mind. He had assumed that it was guilt or concern for Riley until David broke the silence at the red light where Garrett Highway intersected with Route 495.

"Can I ask you a question?" David peered into the rear view mirror at the car behind them to avoid looking directly at Mac. The casualness in his tone was forced.

"Sure."

The light turned green. David eased the cruiser forward and turned right to cross the bridge. "Do you know anyone ..." His voice trailed off.

Mac had begun to think that David had changed his mind about asking him whatever it was he was going to ask when he turned onto Spencer Drive to take then along the lakeshore toward Spencer Point.

David waited until after making the turn before starting again. "Is there anyone in your past ... someone who you have hurt so badly that you're afraid—too ashamed to see them?"

"By hurt, I'm assuming you're not talking about shooting them," Mac replied.

"No." David failed to smile at his attempt at humor.

"Is this Riley you're referring to?"

Instead of answering, David glanced over at Mac while checking the traffic before turning left onto Spencer Point. "Is there?"

"David," he replied, "I think anyone who has ever gone through their teens and high school has something or someone in their past that they're ashamed of."

David drove through the stone pillars marking the entrance to Spencer Manor. In silence, he rolled the cruiser into its stall in the garage and turned off the engine. Without a word, he unclipped his seat belt.

"Want to talk about it?" Mac asked.

"Not really," David said in a quiet tone. "I'm tired. I'll probably feel better about everything after a good night's sleep." He opened the door before turning back to Mac. "Thanks." Without further explanation, he went straight to his guest cottage.

Mac got a good laugh when he stepped through the front door to see a white plastic cone sticking up above the top of the loveseat, which was positioned with its back to the front door. It resembled an upside down dunce cap.

In spite of Mac's efforts to keep him off the furniture, Gnarly had taken possession of the living room loveseat. Gnarly marked the sofa as his with three of his toys: a stuffed green gecko, a yellow rubber duck and a bone filled with peanut butter. It was the one piece of furniture that he was able to climb up on in Mac's presence without provoking a stern glare. Though he couldn't prove it, Mac suspected Gnarly of climbing up onto other pieces of furniture when he wasn't around to police him—and that he did so with Archie's approval.

Like a child having a bad day, Gnarly hugged the gecko between his two front paws, rested his head on it, and watched his parents discuss his latest misadventure.

Seeing the white cone, Mac came around the loveseat to find Gnarly staring straight ahead as if he was unsure of what to do. "So they put the white cone of shame on you, huh?" he said as if Gnarly could respond to tell him the whole story.

"Don't make fun of him." Carrying two wine glasses, Archie came out of the kitchen and climbed up the steps from the drop down dining room. She handed one of the drinks to him.

"It was only a bite," Mac said. "Why the cone?"

"They had to lance the bite and clean the wound," she said. "There's no telling what that wolf man was carrying."

"That still doesn't explain the cone."

Gnarly hung his head. He was such a proud dog. Big and strong, he ruled everywhere he roamed—including the general store across the bridge where Mac had an account to cover the dog toys and treats that he regularly went in and lifted.

"After cleaning his wound, they stitched it up and had to put on the cone to keep him from tearing the stitches," Archie said.

"It was only one bite," Mac argued. "I've been more seriously hurt doing some of that stupid gardening that you drag me into every spring and I've never had to wear a cone on my head."

Gnarly let out a bark as if to voice his agreement.

"It broke the skin," she said. "This man that attacked Gnarly has been living in the wild—Probably the last time he bathed was a decade ago—"

"True," Mac agreed.

"Not to mention brushing his teeth," she continued. "I'm sure he hasn't been brushing his teeth—It's surprising he even had any teeth to bite Gnarly. Did you know that a couple hundred years ago the number one cause of death was tooth decay?"

"I knew that," he said.

"Well, it isn't Gnarly turning into a werewolf or whatever it is dogs who get bit by wolf men turn into," she said. "It's lime disease or rabies or any number of germs and bacteria that this man was carrying in his mouth when he bit Gnarly. Dr. Lee said that the best thing they could do was to clean out the bite wound really good and hopefully the get rid of the germs so he doesn't get sick and possibly die."

Narrowing his eyes, Mac cocked his head. "I think Dr. Lee saw you and Gnarly coming and decided to gouge you—me—to help pay for that fancy addition he built onto his animal hospital."

"Why are you so suspicious?"

"Because I'm usually right."

Gnarly interrupted with a bark. Whining, he pawed at the cone.

"Not only am I out however many hundreds of dollars this is costing," Mac said, "but Gnarly is being humiliated in the process." He let out a breath filled with disgust. "I hope Elvis didn't see him."

"Since when do you care about what the Schweitzer's little Chihuahua thinks about Gnarly?"

"Since he looks so pathetic."

Unable to remove the cone, Gnarly hung his head with a long mournful whine.

Beaten by Gnarly's depressed state and Mac's feeling of being taken, Archie took a sip of her wine. "Does this mean I'm not going to get makeup sex?"

"After seeing what you did to my dog, I think I'm the one deserving of makeup sex." Unable to look at his dog anymore, Mac went into the kitchen for a stronger drink.

ଔ ଓ ଔ ଓ

"There's no sex like makeup sex." With a contented sigh, Archie brushed her fingertips down the length of Mac's lower arm. When she came to his hand, she entwined her fingers with his and bought his hand to her lips to kiss.

Mac kissed the top of her head. "We need to fight more often."

"Just try to keep me at home next time you go to Astaire Castle and find wolf men," she said, "and dead bodies of famous horror authors."

"If this is what I get for leaving you home, there's no way I'm taking you with me."

Holding her against him, the feel of her warm back perfectly fitting against his chest and stomach, Mac marveled at how in sync they were. It felt as if his mother, sensing how perfect Archie would be for him, had this moment in mind when she had dictated in her will that she was to be allowed to live in the guest cottage. It was like she knew that they belonged together.

He pulled her in closer to smell her hair. The floral scent made him want to kiss her again. Pressing his lips against the nape of her neck, he mouthed her flesh until the sound of the phone made her jolt away from him. "Ignore it." He wrapped his arms around her.

"It might be David with more news about the wolf man or Damian Wagner's murder." Clutching the covers against her naked chest, as if he had never seen her breasts before, she checked the caller ID on the phone. "It's Ed Willingham." Before Mac could stop her, she pressed the button for the connection. "Hello, Ed."

While she continued to make small talk with his attorney, the senior partner of one of the most prestigious law firms on the east coast, Mac dropped back down onto the pillows in the king-sized bed.

The moment was gone.

This assessment was cemented when Gnarly managed to open the door and come in with his teddy bear, stolen from some unknown place. Somehow, Gnarly had gotten the cone off. Mac had wanted to remove it earlier, but Archie insisted that Dr. Lee had said no. While they were in bed, the shepherd had taken matters into his own paws.

A dog's got to have some pride. If Elvis, that cocky little pipsqueak at the other end of the Point, ever sees Gnarly wearing that cone, he'll never let Gnarly live it down.

It must have been nine o'clock and time for Gnarly to go to bed. He had a mental clock that refused to be changed. Nine o'clock to bed. Six o'clock in the morning was his time to rise and check the perimeters around Spencer Point for any invaders—mainly squirrels, low-flying birds, and aircraft. A big fat squirrel, whom Archie had named Otis, was notorious for invading Gnarly's territory. Now that it was fall, Otis had been particularly bothersome to the dog while gathering nuts for winter.

With his teddy bear clutched in his jaws, Gnarly crawled on his belly under the bed where he kept his den.

"Sure, Ed, he's right here."

Archie held out the phone to Mac, who pulled the covers up to his chest. Even though the high-priced lawyer was on the phone and couldn't see them, Mac felt odd taking the phone to talk business while naked in bed with Archie next to him. Somehow, it felt sordid. "Yeah, Ed," he finally said on the phone.

"Are you okay?" Ed came back.

"Sure, why do you ask?"

"You sound strange."

Mac sniffed. "I think I'm coming down with a cold." Ignoring Archie's raised eyebrow, he asked, "What's up?"

"Well, I just got off the phone with a lawyer in New York who had an offer that you would never believe," Ed said. "I couldn't wait to call to tell you because it's so unbelievable."

"Try me."

"Well, I never went into this when going over your estate with you, but have you ever heard of Astaire Castle?"

Mac glanced over at Archie, who had lain back down on her side next to him. She draped one of her legs across his thigh. "Yeah," he said. "Up on top of Spencer Mountain. It falls under the property of the Spencer Inn, vacation rental, but they never rent it."

Ed sounded surprised when he responded, "So you heard."

"Kind of. What about it, Ed?"

"Billionaire Stan Gould wants to buy it," Ed said. "He's willing to pay ten million dollars— electronic transfer—to acquire it."

Mac sat up. "Ten million dollars! Does he know that place is supposed to be haunted?"

Ed laughed. "I think that's one of the reasons he wants it. He's really into the paranormal—obsessed with it. His lawyer says he wants to buy it as a wedding present for his new wife. He got married a few weeks ago. They saw some item on television about Astaire Castle, so he got his people looking to find out who owns it—saw that it was you—so his people called me. What do you say?"

"What item on television?" Mac asked.

"Something today," Ed said. "I think you should accept this offer, Mac."

"Do you ever watch the news?"

Ed sighed. "Not really. I'm always afraid of seeing one of my clients on it. What did Gnarly do now?"

"He got bitten by a wolf man ... up at Astaire Castle."

"What was he doing up at Astaire Castle?" Ed's smooth cultured voice went up an octave. "The rattlesnakes avoid that place."

"Maybe because of the wolf man," Mac said. "Look, I found out about it and I wanted to see it."

"Who told you about it?" Ed gasped. "Hector. I bet it was Hector." The lawyer went into full paternal mode. "So you took Gnarly up there? I suppose the next thing you're going to tell me is that you took Archie along with you."

"No, I didn't."

"That's good," Ed said. "So what's this you said? Gnarly got bitten by a wolf man? What wolf man?"

"Is there more than one?" Mac asked.

"You know what happens to dogs when they get bitten by wolf men, don't you?" Ed asked.

"They turn into men," Mac said with chuckle.

Ed didn't get his joke. "Werewolves. They turn into werewolves."

"Ed, do you really believe that stuff?'

"I didn't until your mother decided to buy that castle … the crazy things we heard from people coming out of there …" The silence from the other end of the line seemed to indicate that Ed had paused to reflect on the stories he had heard. "But I never heard of a Wolf Man up there. That's new. And he bit Gnarly? What does happen to dogs that get bitten by a werewolf?"

"Wolf man," Mac corrected him.

"Whatever."

"If a wolf man bites a human, they turn into a wolf man," Mac said. "Gnarly isn't a human, he's a dog—" Catching himself, Mac drew in a deep breath. "Why am I talking about this like it's real? There's no such thing as werewolves and ghosts. Gnarly was bitten by a man who is psychologically ill. He thinks he's a wolf and he bit Gnarly because Gnarly had invaded what he considered to be his territory, which is Astaire Castle."

"I guess Gould saw this wolf man bites dog story on the news," Ed said, "and that was what got him interested in the castle."

"More than likely they saw the story about us finding Damian Wagner's body," Mac said.

"Damian Wagner?" Ed's voice went back to high-pitch. "Are you sure?"

"The ME needs to check the dental records," Mac said, "but we found him in an abandoned turret and he had an ax sticking out of the back of his head."

"Robin was convinced he was murdered and his body hidden," Ed said.

"Did she have any suspects in mind?" Mac asked.

"Yes," Ed said without hesitation. "Raymond Hollister, Damian Wagner's literary agent. He's a snake in the grass. Damian Wagner called him a thief. The only reason he stuck with him was because he was one of the best literary agents in the business. Robin left him as soon as her contract with him expired. Damian Wagner's contract was due to expire at the end of the year and Robin told me that he was planning to fire Hollister."

"Well," Mac said, "I've never seen a suicide where someone hit themselves in the back of the head with an ax. So the legend of this being a murder and Damian Wagner disappearing has been broken. It's a multiple murder with not only Damian Wagner being murdered but his daughter and editor. Until we can examine all the evidence, I can't sell the castle to Stan Gould."

Mac was surprised by his own relief. *Who said it? David, or was it Jeff? Robin Spencer refused to sell the castle or even rent it out to protect people. As long as she owned it, it could be controlled. What if I sell it and Stan Gould and his new wife got hurt or murdered? I'll feel responsible for having sold it to them—like David when he held a party there and his friend turned into a wolf man—like Robin did when Damian Wagner's daughter was murdered.*

"What?" Ed's voice went up even higher than before. "Are you serious?"

"I can't sell it now anyway," Mac said. "It's a crime scene. Tell Gould that his wedding present can wait. The castle isn't going anywhere."

"You don't know Stan Gould," Ed said. "He's got powerful friends and when he wants something, he tends to get it."

"I heard that before," Mac said. "While I was a detective, I was told that all the time by murder suspects—eventually they would end up in jail. I refused to let myself be pushed around when I was poor, I'm not going to start now."

Ed uttered a long groan. "I say this with all due respect, Mac. You can be a real pain in the butt sometimes." Before Mac could hang up, the lawyer said, "You are going to be around that conference call tomorrow."

"What conference call?"

"The one I emailed you about," Ed said. "You, me, and your business manager to discuss diversifying your assets. You're going to get killed in taxes next year if you don't do something."

"I never thought I would live to see the day that I was making too much money," Mac said with a sigh.

"Ten o'clock tomorrow," Ed said. "I'll call you."

After a quick goodbye, Mac tossed the phone onto the night stand. When he turned back, he met Archie's gaze. "Stan Gould, the billionaire? He wants to buy the castle?"

"Yep." Mac lay back down.

"Are you going to sell it to him?" She wrapped her arms and legs around him.

"Maybe, maybe not," he said. "Ten million dollars is a lot of money for a broken down haunted castle. Robin refused to sell it for a reason." With a deep sigh, he grasped her and held her close. "In any case, I can't sell it while it's a crime scene."

She gazed up into his face. "While you're thinking about it, I'll dig more into its history."

He kissed her. "That's my girl."

ᘓ ᘕ ᘓ ᘕ

Mac couldn't believe how easily Archie would fall asleep. Snuggled against him, her face tucked into his neck, her breath brushing across his chest, she would fall asleep as easily as a baby in his arms—a beautiful , sexy, sassy, grown-up baby.

As always, after she had drifted off to sleep, she rolled over onto her side to face away from him. Mac then rolled over and pulled her back so that they could sleep like a couple of spoons fitted together. Now, on his side, with one arm tucked under the pillow under his head, he would be able to fall asleep.

As usual, Mac woke up at three o'clock in the morning with a rumble in his stomach. He was in need of a little snack to hold him over until morning. He pictured the unopened pack of bologna in the lunch meat drawer in the fridge. It seemed to be calling to him from down in the kitchen.

When he got out of bed, Mac saw the moon beam shining through the skylight to illuminate the closed bedroom door. He followed the beam to look up at the moon—big and bright and full.

Full moon. Time for the werewolves to be out.

Mac looked over at the bed where Gnarly's two rear paws usually stuck out from where he had burrowed into his makeshift den.

They weren't there. Mac knelt down to peer under the bed. Gnarly wasn't there.

The sneak. He's down on the loveseat sacking out.

Wanting to sneak up on Gnarly to catch him in his dirty nocturnal hi-jinks, Mac crept to the top of the stairs. Down below, he saw that the loveseat was empty.

Mac made his way down to the living room. Across the room, down in the dining room, he saw a light shining under the kitchen door. The bang of a drawer closing and movement revealed that something was in the kitchen and not trying to be quiet about it.

That hog is in the fridge again! He'd better not be stealing my bologna!

More than once Mac had caught Gnarly stealing food from the fridge. He had even managed to close the refrigerator door behind him by swinging his body around and hitting the door with his hip and butt.

On his toes, Mac made his way down into the dining room. He wanted to catch Gnarly red pawed in the act of chowing down on whatever he was stealing from the refrigerator … and it had better not be the bologna.

At the door, Mac gently pushed it in and peered inside.

The sight took his breath away. His heart felt like it was going to beat out of his chest when he saw the big hairy beast at the kitchen counter—on his hind legs—standing several feet up so that he was a head taller than the refrigerator—at least ten feet tall—slapping slice after slice of bologna and cheese on the bread neatly placed on a plate. With his broad chest and back, he was as wide as the fridge. His long tail swayed gracefully behind him.

When he stepped away from the counter to go to the fridge, Mac saw that the package in which the bologna was kept was now empty.

That werewolf is eating the whole thing!

Gnarly was taking the jar of mayonnaise out with his right paw—with his dew-claw acting as an opposable thumb, when he saw Mac frozen in shock in the doorway.

Mac's eyes met those of Gnarly, standing several feet taller than him, with fangs at least six inches long.

On his hind legs, Gnarly walked towards him. He huge head towered over Mac. He looked down on him, his face so close that he could feel his hot breath in his face. It smelled like peanut butter.

That beast ate all of the peanut butter, too! What a hog!

"Yeah, that's right. I'm a werewolf," Gnarly spoke in a voice that sounded eerily like that of Vincent Price. "So what are you going to do about it?"

"Bad, werewolf! Put that bologna back where you found it!" Mac screamed at him while springing upright in his bed.

Archie jumped up from where she was sound asleep and grabbed for the lamp on the night stand to use as a weapon.

Beneath them, Gnarly banged his head on the underside of the box springs and yelped.

"What's going on?" Archie rolled back to him in the bed.

"Gnarly's up to his old tricks again." Mac switched on the light and hung down over the edge of the bed to look under it. To his relief, Gnarly was blinking at him with a touch of disgust about being woken up. He was the same size he had been the day before.

"Did I hear you say 'bad werewolf?'" she asked.

Mac sat back up in bed and turned off the light.

"What were you saying about bologna?" Archie asked while he pulled up the covers to cover his shoulders. "Were you dreaming about werewolves and bologna?"

"Gnarly was raiding the fridge again."

"Oh, is that all?" She rolled over and wrapped her arms around him. "What's so bad about that dream? He does it all the time."

"He ate all the bologna," Mac said.

"It's okay, honey," she squeezed him. "If Gnarly eats all the bologna, I'll buy a new pack just for you."

They settled back into bed, but Mac wasn't able to close his eyes. The feeling of Gnarly towering over him, as broad as a refrigerator, with six-inch fangs, eating the whole pound of bologna, was still too fresh in his mind. The beating of his heart refused to slow down.

Mac threw off the covers and jumped out of bed.

"Where are you going now?" Archie sat up to ask.

Mac shrugged into his bathrobe. "To check on the bologna."

Exasperated, Archie plopped back down onto the bed.

A moment later, she heard a scream from down in the kitchen. "That bologna-sucking werewolf! He did eat the whole thing!"

From under the bed, she heard Gnarly utter a long guttural groan.

Chapter Eight

It was during Gnarly's six o'clock check of the perimeter that David came out of his cottage and closed the door. Under his police chief's winter coat, he was fully dressed in his uniform and heading out to go on duty.

Overseeing Gnarly's patrol from the back deck, Mac felt a twinge of jealousy. While David was digging into Damian Wagner's murder, he was going to be on a conference call with his business manager about how best to diversify his earnings since his inheritance. Surprisingly, Mac discovered that he had quite a talent for making investments. Since he had inherited two-hundred-and-seventy million dollars, his investments had made his worth increase twenty percent. His worth was now well over three hundred million.

He'd give away every penny to be back on duty and delving into Damian Wagner's murder case. "You're up early," he called over to David before he turned the corner of the cottage to take him to the garage.

After halting, David turned to the back deck to see where Mac was concealed by the early morning darkness that had yet to lift with the rise of the sun. He followed the sound of Mac's voice to where he was waiting in his bathrobe for Gnarly's return from securing the estate from Otis and other trespassing squirrels gathering nuts for winter.

"I have a lot of work to do," David said. "I have to dig out the case files for the murders at Astaire Castle and see what could have been missed to help us find out who killed Damian Wagner, Genie, and the editor."

"Didn't Bogie say something yesterday about a housekeeper?" Mac asked.

David nodded his head. "She found the bodies."

"Is she still around?"

"That's something I need to find out," David said. "I've got a lot to do. I found Riley's sister, Chelsea, last night. She's working for the state attorney general's office in Annapolis. I gave her a call."

"I thought you were going to have Tonya do that."

"I figured it would be better her hearing it from me," David said with a shrug of his shoulders. "Chelsea has to make a few arrangements in Annapolis, but she'll be out here as soon as possible."

"You'd think she'd be coming out here ASAP," Mac said. "I didn't even grow up with you, but if someone called to tell me that you've spent the last decade living in the woods like a wolf, I'd be flying out on the first flight."

"Most people don't have a private plane available to take them anywhere at a moment's notice."

"I don't have a private plane," Mac said.

"You also don't have a boss to answer to," David said.

"What do you call him?" Mac pointed at Gnarly who was clawing at the door to signal that he was now ready to go inside for his breakfast.

"I don't have time to judge Chelsea," David said. "I've got three murders to solve."

"And only a small staff to help you." Mac wanted to offer his help but didn't want to overstep his bounds. Like a racehorse that had been retired and put out to stud, he resigned himself to being forced to enjoy his life of leisure while the younger race horse got to go for the glory in the big race. While the life of leisure was nice, it wasn't for Mac Faraday.

"True." Patting his service weapon on his utility belt, David turned around and crossed the deck to head out to his cruiser.

Longingly, Mac gazed at his back as he walked away.

David stopped at the corner of the deck. Without turning, he called out, "Mac, are you coming?"

Mac rushed to the deck doors to go inside. "I just need to feed Gnarly and get dressed. Don't leave without me."

☙ ❧ ☙ ❧

In the upscale resort town of Spencer, Maryland, where many of the town's residents were listed in Marquis Who's Who in America, the small police station resembled a sports club. Located along the shore of Deep Creek Lake, the log building that was home to the police department sported a dock with a dozen jet skis and four speed boats. Its fleet of police cruisers was top of the line SUVs, painted black with gold lettering on the side that read: SPENCER POLICE. For patrolling the deep woods and up the mountains trails, they had eight ATVs. Like the cruisers, all of the vehicles were black with gold lettering and trim.

It was the first time Mac had been to the Spencer police station before it opened for business. He had forgotten that small town police stations usually closed their doors after business hours. Coming from Washington, Mac was used to the metropolitan police stations that never closed.

Small resort towns don't have the budget or manpower to keep their offices open twenty-four-seven. The police force worked in shifts. Only two officers would work the graveyard shift, with each of the officers in the department taking turns.

Police Chief David O'Callaghan and Bogie, his deputy chief, were on call twenty-four hours a day, seven days a week, including holidays.

On their way to the station, David stopped at the local bakery for a box of donuts for his officers and two coffees for him and Mac to hold them over until the first pot of the morning was brewed. They also picked up a croissant for Gnarly, who was stretched out across the backseat in David's cruiser. Threatening to come through the barricade between the front and back of the cruiser, Gnarly insisted on getting his croissant immediately, instead of waiting for them to reach the station.

"You'd think after a pound of bologna that he'd be full," Mac told David.

Gnarly practically vacuumed up the back seat while sniffing the cushion in search of any crumbs that may have escaped his attack.

"Have you ever known Gnarly to get full?" David asked with a laugh.

"True."

It was a surreal experience for Mac to follow David into the station and wait for him to switch on the lights, unlock doors, and check for messages on the voice mail. He had never seen a police department so quiet.

"Doc Washington left a message," David called out to Mac, who was preparing the coffee. "Dental records were a match. The corpse was Damian Wagner."

"Which means we have a triple homicide to solve, but then, we already knew that."" Mac punched the button to set the coffeemaker in motion.

By the time David had finished taking down the messages and putting them on each officer's desk, the coffee was brewed and Mac freshened both of their cups.

Gnarly was already asleep in his bed, which Tonya, the desk sergeant, had brought in for him to use during his visits.

The file room was located on the ground floor. Rows of shelving contained white file boxes for each of Spencer's cold case files, those cases not yet solved. David had no trouble finding the three boxes for the murders of Genevieve Wagner and Bill Jansen, and the disappearance of Damian Wagner—which was now officially a homicide.

David pushed a box in Mac's direction while taking one for himself. "You take Genevieve Wagner," he said.

"Is that because you slept with her?" Mac asked with a grin.

"I'd appreciate it if you could keep that information to yourself." David's cheeks turned pink.

"I'll do my best," Mac said while taking the lid off his box, "but there's no guarantee that it won't come out, considering how I found out about it."

A silence fell over the police station while Mac and David became absorbed in their respective cases—even though they were shared. Upstairs, they could hear the station coming to life. Officers were arriving and checking in—Sergeant Tonya being the first.

She came halfway down the stairs to greet them. Gnarly was by her side. When she stopped, he sat down on the step next to her feet to study them. When she returned up the stairs, Gnarly followed. He was confident that she would be giving him a donut after his plea of starvation.

"Here's something I didn't expect to find." David broke the silence that had fallen back over the table. "Bill Jansen wasn't hacked to death."

"Was the COD stabbing?" Mac asked.

"No," David said, "Poison. They found evidence of strychnine poisoning. Forensics was able to uncover that in his remains. He was already dead when he was dismembered and then burnt."

"That's strange." Mac referred to the autopsy report. "Genevieve was stabbed. They found evidence of blade marks on her ribs that are consistent with a butcher knife." He tapped the top of his pen against the report. "Why two different CODs? This was meant to look like a madman run amuck."

"Maybe that's why the killer tried to burn the bodies," David said. "To cover up the poisoning."

"Why poison Jansen? Why stab Genevieve, but not Jansen?"

David opened his mouth to make a suggestion, but when he came up with no answer, he shut it and shook his head. "If the killer didn't have the stomach to stab Jansen, then he wouldn't have had the stomach to stab Genevieve."

"Maybe Genevieve escaped the poisoning and so the killer had to improvise," Mac said. "I had a murder case like that once. A wife tried to poison her husband, but he wouldn't eat her meatloaf. Said he was full from lunch. So she had to find another way to kill him."

"What did she do?"

"Burnt down the house after he went to sleep," Mac said. "She was furious when the fire fighters saved him."

"He didn't die?" David asked.

"Nope," Mac said.

"How did you end up with the case?"

"She killed the psychic who told her that her husband was going to kill her," Mac said.

David was still digesting that news when his cell phone rang. From where he sat across from him, Mac could read the caller ID, even though it was upside down. Randi. Her smiling face filled the screen.

"She's calling early." Mac noted the time was nine-thirty.

Excusing himself, David took up the phone. "Hey, Rand. How's it going?" As the conversation continued, David's grin fell from his face. The topic shifted from conversational to serious—directed from her end. "Yeah, I can talk." He got up from his seat and moved across the file room.

"I'm going to go get some more coffee." Grabbing both of their cups, Mac went upstairs to give him privacy.

As Mac expected, Gnarly was eating his second donut. Tonya had sent most of the officers out on patrol. Hanging up the phone, she held a message sheet out for Mac to see. "The wolf man's sister, Chelsea Adams, called and left a message for the chief."

Setting down his coffee cup, Mac took the message sheet to read while she reported, "She'll be leaving this morning and expects to be here later on this afternoon. She's coming to the station and would like to meet with the chief to discuss her brother's case."

"Why doesn't she go to the hospital to see her brother?" Mac asked.

"Because the news has been reporting that Damian Wagner's body was found, and that a crazed wolf man was captured there," Tonya said. "I saw it on the news this morning. They're already speculating that this crazy wolf man, a deranged obsessed fan, killed the king of horror fiction, which included a lot of werewolves, his daughter, and his editor."

"And was sane enough to hide Damian Wagner's body so everyone would think he did it?" Mac asked with a shake of his head. "I don't think so. Who's the leak?"

"No one here," Tonya said with an air of insult at the suggestion. "Most likely the hospital. It isn't every day they get a real wolf man. I feel sorry for this Chelsea. She sounded stressed out. Here she's been thinking her brother was dead—I remember when that happened. Their mother died of a broken heart. David felt responsible. And now poor Riley gets found, and they're calling him a man-eating wolf man."

As if in response to her assertion, the phone rang. She read the caller ID. "That's the newspaper," she groaned.

"Riley Adams didn't kill those people," Mac said.

"Tell them that." She nodded to the ringing phone.

Leaving her to the tough job of handling the media, Mac refilled their cups with hot coffee and went downstairs, where he found that David had finished his phone call and returned to leafing through the case file for Bill Jansen's murder.

After murmuring a thanks for the coffee, David said, "I compared the ME reports for Jansen and Genie. His body showed signs of being in the fire longer than hers. The burns were more extensive." He closed the folder. "He was killed first, dismembered, and then put into the fire. Genie was killed at a later time, dismembered with the ax, and put into the fire pit. The killer then left shortly before Rafaela arrived to discover the murders."

Mac sat back in his chair to enjoy his coffee while envisioning the scenario. "When was Damian Wagner killed?"

"That's going to be hard to determine," David said. "Rafaela Diaz, the housekeeper, stated that she saw no sign of him when she arrived or while she was there. The question would be, was he killed before Jansen and Genie were killed, between those two murders, or afterwards?"

"Maybe they were killed to cover up his murder and not the other way around," Mac said. "Think about it. If he was alive, what would he have been doing while people were being poisoned and stabbed and hacked up and set on fire? He had to have been dead already."

"That's a thought." David sat back to drink his coffee.

In silence, Mac watched him sip his coffee.

Finally, David cleared his throat. "What I predicted would happen, happened."

"What?" Mac asked.

"Long distance relationships don't work," David said.

"She's only been gone one day."

"Last night, Randi went to a diner next to the complex where she's leasing her apartment," David said. "You'd never guess who she ran into."

"Who?"

"Butch."

"Who's Butch?"

With a chuckle, David looked up from his coffee cup. "Randi's ex-husband."

"I thought he was in Alaska."

"Was," David said. "He's in training in Quantico. They ate dinner together. One thing led to another and she ended up at his place. By morning, they decided to give reconciliation a try."

Mac searched for the words to make David feel better. He wanted to say Randi was in the wrong, but in his heart, he felt that marriage was a sacred institution. He was never crazy about how David and Randi had plunged into their relationship so soon after her marriage had ended. If there was a chance for her to save her marriage, she should at least try.

Yet, David was his brother and friend. He didn't like to see him hurt.

"I'm sorry," was all Mac could think of to say. "Are you okay?"

"Why wouldn't I be?" David sat up and opened the folder. "I think we need to find Rafaela Diaz. Unfortunately, she's not still in the area. According to Dad's notes, she had requested to return to Brazil shortly after the murders. They let her go."

"There has to be an address in the file." Mac craned his neck to see the folder across from him. "They wouldn't let her go without insisting on contact information for where she was going."

"There is." David made note of the address. "I'll try contacting her."

"Maybe over the years," Mac said, "she'll remember something that she didn't mention before."

"Like a wolf man being on the scene?" Bogie asked from where he was coming down the stairs. "Because you'll see in her statement that she swears she saw the wolf man leaving the scene. She'd seen him more than once at Astaire Castle."

Mac leafed through his case file in search of the housekeeper's statement.

"At the time," the deputy chief continued, "we didn't take her too seriously because she didn't seem to be too credible. She was from a small village in Brazil—practiced voodoo—very superstitious—believed in zombies and werewolves and all types of creatures. Heck, she was a creature herself with hair all over the place—all these medallions and tattoos all over her. She swore Astaire Castle was cursed and couldn't wait to get back to her high priestess in Brazil to purify her of all the evil that she'd picked up there." He concluded with, "Good luck finding her. I told your father when he gave her permission to leave that we'd never get her back in this country again, unless we hog tied her and threw her into the trunk of a car."

Mac wanted to continue the conversation, but the cell phone on his hip was buzzing. When he checked the ID, he saw that it was Hector, who was not one to call Mac for idle conversation.

"You'll never guess who just checked in here at the Spencer Inn," Hector said by way of greeting.

"The President."

"Be serious," Hector laughed.

"I was. The Spencer Inn is a five-star inn that has been frequented by celebrities from all walks of life. Why wouldn't the President visit?"

"Because Gnarly can't get cleared by the Secret Service," Hector chuckled. "I'm talking about Raymond Hollister."

"Raymond Hollister?" Mac stood up. In response to David and Bogie's questioning looks, he asked Hector, "He's at the Spencer Inn right now?"

"Just checked in without a reservation and made a fuss when the desk clerk told him that no suites were available—only regular rooms. He's in the spa now getting a massage from Laynie."

"I want to talk to him." David stacked up the files and returned them to the case boxes.

"We're on our way," Mac told Hector.

When she saw David heading across the squad room, Tonya threw up her hand and waved a message at him. "Before you go, Chief. Chelsea Adams will be here later on this afternoon and she wants to meet with you."

David halted so fast that Mac, who was gesturing for Gnarly to come, collided into his back. "Why is she coming here? I told her that Riley was in Oakland."

"She wants to see you," Tonya said. "I told Mac all about it."

Snatching the message out of her hand, David turned to Mac with yet another angry glare in his eyes.

"I forgot and I'm not your secretary," Mac said.

"There's nothing more I can tell her that the hospital won't."

"It's easier hearing it from a friend," Mac said. "You did grow up with her."

"Who told you that?" David asked.

"You grew up with Riley," Mac said. "Chelsea is his sister. Is it that big a jump to say you grew up with her, too?"

"Spoken like a detective." Tonya smiled.

"This day just keeps getting better and better," David said with a groan before opening the door and rushing out.

With Gnarly in the back, David hit the accelerator to make the cruiser fishtail before shooting out into the road and heading up the mountain to the Spencer Inn.

"Care to talk about it?" Mac grabbed the armrest to brace himself.

"I'm having a bad week." David glared out the windshield.

"I can tell," Mac said. "What is it about Chelsea?"

"Nothing."

"David, I've met you. I can now tell when something is bothering you. What bothers you about Chelsea Adams?"

The clenching of David's teeth and his silence gave Mac his answer.

"Seriously?" Mac gasped. "Who have you not slept with?"

"It's not the way you think."

"What do I think?"

"Chelsea was different."

"How is she different from all the other women you've been with?" Mac asked forcibly. "Katrina. Yvonne. Randi.—"

"Chelsea was my first—that's how she's different."

To this, Mac had no response.

Even Gnarly seemed to be staring at David with a hint of sympathy.

David pounded the steering wheel with his fist. "She was my first and I screwed things up royally. That's why I don't want to see her. I didn't realize at the time what a big mistake I'd made. Now I know, but it's too late."

"So she's the one you were talking about yesterday … who you're too ashamed to face," Mac said. "How did you screw it up?"

"I was seventeen years old." David glanced over at Mac. "You know how it is. Think back to when you were seventeen?"

"Seventeen was a long time ago for me," Mac said. "What happened with Chelsea?"

"My hormones were raging," David said. "Chelsea was my first serious girlfriend. We were in love. Maybe it was more lust on my part, but she was in love at least." He fell silent.

Sympathetic to the pain of past mistakes coming back to the forefront, Mac asked, "What went wrong?"

"Katrina went wrong," David said. "Chelsea was a nice girl. Katrina wasn't. Katrina had breasts. Chelsea didn't. Use your imagination." He shook his head. "By the time I grew up and realized what a good thing I'd thrown away, Chelsea was long gone." He swallowed. "The last thing she said to me was, 'Thank you for ruining my life, David.'"

They were coming up over the rise. The overlook provided a sweeping view of Deep Creek Lake and the valley far below. As always when he saw it, Mac was amazed by the beauty before him.

Turning his concentration back to David's dilemma, he asked, "How did she sound when you called her last night?"

"Polite," David said. "What happened was years ago. Of course, we didn't talk about it. But I didn't expect us to spend that much time together. I expected her to come see Riley, have him committed and be gone. I didn't expect to—"

"Face her?"

"Not really."

"You know," Mac said, "my mother, my adopted mother, used to say that things happen for a reason. Maybe Randi's ex coming back, her dumping you, and us finding Riley to bring Chelsea back now, is to give you a second chance to make things right with her."

"Or maybe it's her chance to slap me alongside the head," David said.

"Opportunities are what you make of them," Mac said with a shrug of his shoulders. "You'd be surprised how much mileage you can get out of the two little words 'I'm sorry,' especially when you mean it—and I think you do."

Chapter Nine

When David pulled his cruiser up to park in front of the Spencer Inn, they found what resembled a royal procession entering through the main entrance. A full stretch limousine took up much of the curb at the end of the red carpet leading up to the front doors. A crowd, including paparazzi and men in suits with ear pieces, buzzed along the carpet like bees entering a hive.

"Who's that?" David asked. "Is it the senator?"

"Stan Gould," Mac said, when he saw the short slender man in a gray suit step out of the back of the limousine. "He wants to buy Astaire Castle." He was surprised that such a powerful man could be so short. He was a full head shorter than every member of his entourage.

David's head jerked around to look at Mac. "You're not going to sell it to him, are you? Robin said it was never to be sold or occupied again."

"I said no," Mac replied, "but Stan Gould is the type of man who insists on getting what he wants."

"There's a saying. 'Look out for what you wish for.'" David threw open his driver's side door. "'You might just get it.'"

One of Gould's entourage reached inside the back of the limousine and helped out a statuesque redhead.

Keeping Gnarly tightly leashed, Mac and David slipped into the lobby ahead of the entourage, where Hector Langford was waiting with three members of his team. As always when VIPs were on the premises, they were wearing their communication ear pieces.

Hector told Mac, "Gould's people made their reservations at midnight last night, when he decided at the last minute to fly in from Italy, where he and his wife were honeymooning. He wasn't happy about not getting to reserve the castle and having to settle for one of the Inn's luxury vacation rentals. It only has three master suites, a private swimming pool, spa, and tennis court."

"I don't care," Mac said.

They took note of the horde surrounding and following the slightly built man with thinning hair and wire-rimmed glasses across the lobby. He had a baby face that looked like it was incapable of growing any hair. By his side, the redhead stood a full head taller than him in her stiletto heels.

Stan Gould made a beeline for Mac and stuck out his hand. "Mr. Faraday. Stan Gould. I'm glad to see that you saw fit to personally welcome me."

With a curl of his lip, Mac refrained from telling him that it was a coincidence that he happened to be there when the business mogul arrived. He saw the redhead licking her lips while giving David an up and down look. Her fingers were curled around the crook of her husband's arm.

"I'd like to introduce you to my wife, Lacey." Stan wrapped his arm around her waist. "Just Lacey. No last name."

"Nice to meet you, Lacey No-Last-Name." Mac shook her hand, which she offered in a limp grip. "This is David O'Callaghan. He's the chief of police here in Spencer." He went on to introduce Hector Langford, the chief of security and his team.

David paused when Lacey offered her hand to him. "Excuse me for staring ... but I could have sworn we met—"

She shot him a seductive grin.

"That happens a lot," Stan Gould interrupted her answer. A smile of pride crossed his face. "Lacey is a famous lingerie model from France. I'm afraid men all over the world have seen my wife in her underwear—and lusted over her."

"Must be," David said before turning to Mac. "While you take care of business here, I'm going to go locate Raymond Hollister."

Leaving Mac trapped with Stan Gould, David rushed off to find and interrogate a murder suspect. As the wealthy owner of the Astaire Castle, Mac's duty was to conduct business with the world-famous billionaire. Sometimes life can be so unfair, he thought while watching David jog over to the reception desk.

Even Gnarly, who had parked himself between his master and Gould's entourage, peered around Mac to watch David leave them.

"I assume you're here to discuss the offer that I told my people to put forward to yours." Stan captured Mac's attention. "I'm afraid there was some sort of miscommunication. My people told me that yours declined my offer. Of course, that can't be right. So I came out here to see the castle in person and close the deal."

"I'm sorry you made the flight from Italy for nothing," Mac replied. "The castle isn't for sale."

Stan blinked his small eyes. "Excuse me?" he said in a tone similar to that of a parent to a child who has disobeyed them out of nothing more than spite.

The attitude alone made Mac want to decline the offer, even if it was for ten million. He had no desire to have this man so close to his Inn's employees and guests. Over Stan's shoulder, he could see Hector smirk. The Australian loved nothing more than seeing his boss put arrogant guests in their place.

"One," Mac said, "right now, Astaire Castle is a crime scene. A decomposed body identified as Damian Wagner was found there yesterday and the police are investigating. Now is not a good time to sell it."

"That's not acceptable," Stan replied.

"It is to me," Mac replied. "It's my castle and I have no problem with the police taking their time to find out who killed this man."

Stan Gould's eyes narrowed. "Do you know who I am, Mr. Faraday?"

"Yes, I do, Mr. Gould. Your problem is that I don't care."

Seemingly too enthralled with his accomplishments to have noticed Mac's lack of interest, Gould said, "I own the most successful company in America. I have estates in four countries, two yachts, both of which have swimming pools on them, two private jets, and I'm making millions of dollars a day!"

The mogul's nostrils flared in tune with his temper. He went on to list more of his holdings. Before Mac's eyes, Stan Gould morphed from a respected and feared businessman into a spoiled child outraged by the less privileged child who had the bike he wanted.

"Now, all I want to do is give my new bride here something that she has always wanted—a castle—a haunted castle—Astaire Castle." Stan softened his tone to reach over to caress Lacey's face.

Her eyes fell.

In the flash of a second, Mac caught what appeared to be repulsion by the touch. *Oh, yes, she's a classic gold-digger all right. How long will she stay married to him before taking him for all she can get?* His mind flashed back to her checking David out.

The billionaire's tantrum continued. "I would like to get this business taken care of now so that we can renovate the castle in time for our Halloween night a gala."

"Halloween is days away," Mac said.

Stan Gould chuckled. "When you have the resources I have, Mr. Faraday, anything can happen. We're going to have to build a helipad in order to have my friends flown in for what will be the biggest party that this burg has ever seen."

"Ain't happening," Mac said.

"Yes, it is," Stan said.

"No, it's not, because I'm not selling Astaire Castle to you."

"Oh, I get it." A wide grin crossed Stan Gould's face. He dropped Lacey's hand. Now it was serious business. "Listen, Mr. Faraday, I have played hard ball with the biggest balls busters in New York, Washington, and LA. Bring it on. What has to happen in order for you to sell that castle to me?"

Mac stepped forward. He glared down into the little man's face. Gould resembled a creature that he had seen in The Lord of the Rings movies. "No."

Stan Gould's entourage stood with their jaws dropped open. Mac guessed no one had ever said, "No," to the mogul before.

Laughing out loud, Hector slapped Jeff Ingles on the shoulder. The manager had come over to welcome the distinguished guest, only to see the Inn's owner enrage him. All color drained from Jeff's face.

His eyes still on Mac, Stan Gould stomped his feet. "Kyle! Call The Wisp. Tell them I want to book the whole hotel!" He scoffed at Mac. "No way in hell am I ever giving even a penny to the Spencer Inn again. You just wait. Within the next fifteen minutes, my people will spread this atrocious treatment all over the Internet." He pointed a finger at Mac so hard that it threatened to poke him in the face.

Gnarly reminded everyone of his presence with a loud bark and growl, and Stan Gould and his entire entourage jumped back a full three feet.

"I'm afraid I'm going to have to teach you a lesson the hard way about messing with me," Gould said. "You mess with the big dogs and you're liable to get bit—hard!"

"If you want to compare dog bites, bring it on," Mac said with a laugh while stroking Gnarly's head.

"You're going to be surprised by how far I can reach and how much I can take from you—things you really care about."

"Is that a threat?"

"Yes."

Mac laughed. "Take your business elsewhere, Mr. Gould. I don't want you and your type here. It's contaminating our atmosphere of hospitality."

With a wave of his arm, not unlike that of a monarch, Stan Gould ordered his entourage to turn around and leave as a single unit.

"Mac, what have you done?" Jeff came running over to him. "Do you have any idea what you did?"

"Mac just told Gould and his group to take their business elsewhere." Hector sauntered over. "I think he was great. Robin Spencer would have done exactly the same thing."

"Mac?" Jeff gasped out. "Stan Gould is big."

"No one is too big to have basic manners," Mac said.

Jeff glared at Mac. His eyes dropped down to Gnarly. "You've been hanging around Gnarly too long."

"Gnarly didn't do anything this time," Mac said.

"Actually, Mac did everyone here a favor," Hector said. "Stan Gould is a demanding, arrogant, cheap jerk. He quibbles over everything, including the bill, and is the cheapest tipper on record—anywhere. It's all over the Internet. There are nasty postings about him from hotel and restaurant employees everywhere he goes. Everyone in that entourage is an employee of his because he has no friends. He even has to pay hangers-on to make him look like a big wheel. I'm glad Mac threw him out. He's a twerp."

"He's a rich and influential twerp," Jeff said.

"Which goes to prove what I've always thought," Mac said.

Disgusted with the exit of his most wealthy guest, Jeff asked, "What is that?"

"Money," Mac said, "and I'm talking about extreme wealth, doesn't really change who you are. It only makes who you really are more extreme."

Hector laughed. "Like you were intolerant of decadent SOBs before you became rich. Now you're more so."

"Now you hurt my feelings, Hector." Mac frowned. "Because I have the money to do whatever I want to do, I don't have to compromise my beliefs or feelings by playing political games to stay employed or to move up in the police department anymore. If I don't like the attitude of some arrogant jerk in this hotel, which I happen to own, then I can throw him out."

"Even though he has the resources and power to announce his displeasure to the whole world in less than thirty seconds," Jeff said with a grumble.

"You can take a jerk," Mac said, "dump billions of dollars into his bank account, put him in the longest stretch limo the auto assembly lines can build, put him in a tailored suit, attach a super model to his arm, and surround him with a dozen body guards wearing dark glasses, but in the end, you still have a jerk—just a flashier, louder, and more obnoxious jerk." For Jeff's benefit, he added, "And most of those billions of people reading his Internet gripes can see it, too."

With a jaunty salute at Jeff and Hector, Mac took Gnarly to search for David and Raymond Hollister.

Hector asked Jeff, "How many times have you predicted the Spencer Inn would close after Mac, or in a previous life, Robin Spencer, pulled one of their stunts?"

"I've lost count," Jeff said. "Sometimes it's weekly. Why?"

Hector glanced around the lobby at the steady flow of guests coming through the door and the busy reception desk. "And how many times has it shut down?"

"In every business, there has to be one naysayer." Jeff mopped his sweaty brow with his handkerchief. "That's me. Chief Naysayer." He turned on his heels, and hurried back to his office to fill in their public relations specialist.

ᘓ ᘕ ᘓ ᘕ

Mac almost collided with a tall, slender, silver-haired man exiting the Inn's salon and spa through the double doors. After holding the glass doors open for the older man, Mac was closing it when David turned the corner at the end of hall and waved for Mac to stop him. "That's Hollister."

Mac raced through the doors to practically grab him by the elbow. "Mr. Hollister."

The man turned to Mac. A puzzled expression crossed his face when he noticed Gnarly sniffing his leg. His small dark eyes shot a glare at both of them. "What is this? A drug-sniffing dog? I assure you I have no drugs on me."

"I'm Mac Faraday." He offered him his hand, which Raymond Hollister ignored. "I'm working with the police department in their investigation of the Wagner murders."

David caught up with them. "I'm Police Chief David O"Callaghan, Mr. Hollister. May we have a few minutes of your time?"

Raymond Hollister regarded David with disdain. His eyes narrowed. "O'Callaghan? Any relation to Patrick O'Callghan?"

"He was my father."

"Your father was like a dog with a bone on that case," Hollister recalled. "Him and Robin Spencer—"

"David takes very much after his father," Mac said.

David rested his hand on his service weapon as if he was considering using it. "My father didn't make accusations without reason."

Aware that they were standing in the middle of a busy corridor with guests entering and leaving the salon, Mac suggested that they go to the lobby to sit in front of the fireplace. "We can talk more privately there."

Raymond Hollister shot David a look, as if he considered refusing, but instead followed Mac and Gnarly down the hallway. David brought up the rear.

When they returned to the lobby, Mac noticed that the stretch limo was still out front with some of Gould's men milling around. "What's going on?" Mac paused to ask Hector, who was chuckling over something. Everything amused the Australian.

"Ms. Super Lingerie Model had to go to the head."

With a roll of his eyes and shake of his head, Mac led Raymond Hollister over to the sitting area in front of the fireplace, which had a fire ablaze. Mac sat in one of the chairs while Hollister took the sofa facing the lounge and the small corridor down which the rest rooms, phones, and service entrance leading back to the kitchen were located. Sitting at attention, Gnarly faced the subject of their interview.

David chose to stand over them. "Mr. Hollister, can I assume you didn't come to Spencer for the spa, but because Damian Wagner's body was found at the castle yesterday?"

"That's exactly why I'm here," the literary agent said. "Damian Wagner was more than an author, he was my friend."

"Not to mention the goose that laid the golden eggs," Mac said. "Do you have any idea who would have killed Wagner, his daughter, and editor?"

"They say insanity sometimes runs in the genes," Hollister said. "Anyone who read Damian Wagner's books—"

"I've read all of them," Mac said. "Damian Wagner wasn't insane. He had a brilliant imagination. To say that he was insane is like saying my mother, Robin Spencer, was a homicidal maniac."

"Robin Spencer was your mother?" Raymond Hollister turned to look Mac straight in the eye. "Oh, yeah, you're *that* Mac Faraday, Robin Spencer's love child."

"Yes, I am."

"I was her agent when she first started out," Raymond said. "She dumped me as soon as she hit the big leagues. Damian Wagner knew the definition of the word loyalty."

"I guess it's all a matter of perception," Mac said. "You did petition the courts to have Damian Wagner declared legally dead so that you could inherit his estate."

"I know what you're both thinking." Raymond Hollister gestured with his finger to point from Mac to David and then back again.

"Tell us what we're thinking," David said.

"I had the biggest motive for killing Damian Wagner and his daughter," the agent said. "Yes, we had a legal agreement, a standard legal agreement that a lot of authors have with their literary agents."

"I'm not an author," Mac said. "So fill me in. What was this standard agreement?"

"I inherited the copyrights for Damian Wagner's books upon his death," Raymond Hollister said. "Since his daughter, his only heir, was murdered as well, then there's no one to make a claim to the rights for his books."

"His books are still selling world-wide," Mac said. "You must be making millions."

"Yes, I've been doing very well," Raymond Hollister said with a grin. "And, seeing that you are both very smart men, I won't pretend. When Wagner's last book is located, it's mine. Every publisher in New York will be making bids to publish it—we're talking millions of dollars. And, with the publishing of that book, sales on Damian Wagner's previous books will skyrocket."

"And you will be even richer," Mac said.

"Yes," Raymond Hollister said. "Did you find Damian Wagner's book?"

"No," David said.

"That's bad for me."

"Could that be why you killed him and his daughter?" Mac said. "So that you would inherit the rights to his book and get rich off of his work?"

"I didn't kill Damian Wagner or his daughter."

"You pointed it out yourself," David said, "with Genie dead, there's no one to fight you for those rights."

"Damian Wagner's life was a tragedy," Raymond said. "After his wife was killed in that unfortunate car accident, in which he was driving, he blamed himself and gave up custody of Geneviève, who was fourteen years old at the time. It was a miracle she wasn't killed. She was in the back seat when he rammed into that utility pole. He wallowed in self-pity for a couple of years and then got sober. By the time he got out of rehab, he read in the media that Geneviève and her grandparents were killed in a ferry boat accident up in Canada. Damian stopped writing and all of his money was gone. His publisher was about to cut him loose because he didn't believe there was going to be a last book to complete the series. On the off chance that the reports of Genevieve's death were wrong, I hired a private investigator to find her—and he did. It was a miracle. When Genevieve came back into Damian Wagner's life, suddenly, he was able to write again."

Mac grinned. "Which was good for you because you made how much from his royalties?"

"Fifteen percent at that time."

"Now, you get one-hundred percent," David said.

"That's right," Raymond said without shame. "Look, I'm not the monster here. I supported Damian for years when he was producing nothing. Bill Jansen was young and hungry. He was just starting to get a reputation as an editor. I got him the job to work for Wagner."

"And Wagner's daughter—" Mac shot a glance in David's direction. "What about her? You found her and brought her to Spencer to be murdered."

"I reunited a family." Hollister hung his head. "Do I feel responsible—yes, but it wasn't my fault. None of it was supposed to happen like that." He looked up at them. "Damian was my friend and I thought that with the right motivation ..." He turned to look up at David. "I was only—" He stopped speaking. His eyes grew wide and his face pale. He looked ill.

"What happened, Mr. Hollister?" David asked him. "What were you only?"

"It wasn't my fault," he said in a low voice.

"What wasn't your fault?"

"If you think—" he stammered. "All these years ... I know who you are. I know what you did and you aren't going to get away with it."

"Get away with what?" Mac asked.

Hollister raised his voice. "If you think for one minute I'm going to take the fall for what you did—you are sadly mistaken. You have no idea who you're dealing with."

"Mr. Hollister, are you threatening me?" David asked.

"I may have set the wheels in motion to get them killed, but I certainly wasn't the one who did it. I'm not responsible and I'm not taking the blame." He pointed his finger up at David. "I'm personally going to make you pay for what you did."

David stepped up to stand over Raymond Hollister. "You have no right to talk to me like that."

Mac joined in. "This is the chief of police you're talking to, Mr. Hollister."

"I wasn't even in the country when they were killed," David said. "I had no reason to kill Genie, Jansen, or Wagner. Now I want to know who killed them."

"Am I under arrest?" Raymond Hollister rose to his feet.

He had moved so fast that Gnarly jumped between him and David, stopping Raymond Hollister's movement. He paused long enough for Mac to grab his arm.

"You just said that you had set the wheels in motion that led to Wagner's murder," Mac said. "That sounds like a confession to me."

"But I didn't kill him or Jansen." Hollister turned back to David. "I want the animal who did punished, and I intend to do everything I can to help. But first, I need to make a couple of phone calls."

"You can call from the station," David said.

"Do you have any evidence to prove I killed them?" Hollister asked.

David looked over at Mac. He may have been the chief of police, but Mac had this conversation countless times. He knew best how to play it. Knowing that the only evidence they had was circumstantial, Mac slowly shook his head. They couldn't even prove Raymond Hollister was in the area at the time of the murder.

A smirk crossed the agent's face. "Tomorrow morning," Hollister said. "I'll come to your office tomorrow morning with the name of your killer."

Before David could object or order him to go to the station with them, Raymond Hollister hurried across the lobby to the elevators and practically knocked a couple out of the way to get up to his room.

Mac turned to tell David. "Now that was weird."

"Very."

On the other side of the entrance, Mac saw Stan Gould's limousine pulling away. He also saw Hector sighing with relief. Next to the security manager, Jeff Ingles was mopping his sweaty brow.

Chapter Ten

A white sedan with Maryland state government plates was in the parking lot when David pulled the chief's cruiser into his reserved spot at the Spencer police department. "Who else did I tick off?" he asked.

"Look at it this way," Mac said. "It can't get any worse."

In the back seat, Gnarly's hackles were up. He clawed at the door for someone to let him out. When David opened the door, the shepherd shot out like a bullet shot from a gun.

"Did Fletcher order pizza again?" Mac spilled out of the cruiser and gave chase.

As soon as the station door opened, Gnarly scurried across the reception area to greet the intruder. He charged with such force that the other dog yelped while diving for safety behind her master, causing her to become entangled in the dog's leash and tumble.

Bogie caught her in his arms before she hit the floor. "Gnarly, behave yourself!"

Mac grabbed Gnarly by the collar and held him back. "That's no way to treat a guest."

Deciding the visitor was friend and not foe, Gnarly sat down with a whine.

"Friend, Molly," the white German Shepherd's owner said. Patting her dog on the head, she gazed up. "Bogie didn't tell me that the Spencer police department had a K-9 unit." Seeing David, she locked her steel blue eyes on him.

In the moment of silence between them, the electricity was palatable.

Mac couldn't imagine David being with a woman who wasn't gorgeous. With his blond hair, blue eyes, and athletically slender build, the police chief had his pick of women. What red-blooded man in his position wouldn't choose the most attractive beauties?

Chelsea took striking to a whole new level.

She was exceedingly slender—and flat chested as David had mentioned. Her platinum blonde hair, same shade as her brother's, fell in a single wave to her shoulders. Her fair features seemed to border on albino, down to the lightest blue eyes that Mac had ever seen.

"Hello, Chelsea." Noting Molly's service vest, David said, "I didn't know the Attorney General's office had K-9s, either."

"Molly doesn't work for the Attorney General," Chelsea said. "She works for me."

"Well, Chelsea, if everything is taken care of, I'll be on my way," a man in a suit called out as he came down the hall from the rest rooms. He was a tall, muscular, handsome man.

Seeing the man who was obviously with Chelsea, David stood up tall and took on the stance of a man ready for a battle.

"Roger," Chelsea said, "This is David O'Callaghan, he's the chief of police and …" Realizing she didn't know who Mac was, she paused.

"Mac Faraday." Mac offered the man his hand. "And you are …"

"Roger Bennett," he said. "I'm a friend of Chelsea's. I happened to be going to WVU for a seminar and gave her a ride." He turned to her. "Do you need a ride to the hospital?"

"I'll give her a ride," David said so quickly that everyone was startled. A glance from Mac told him that he had spoken too sharply. "I'm going there anyway to check on Riley, so I can drive her."

"That's okay," Chelsea countered. "Roger can drop me off at the hospital. It's on the way to Morgantown anyway."

"Your message said you came *here* to the police station because you wanted to see me," David said.

"That's done and over with." Chelsea turned to Roger. "Let's go."

David's hands were now on his hips. "Why'd you come out here—"

"Bogie told me everything that I needed to know about Riley," Chelsea said. "Besides, you're busy investigating the Damian Wagner murders."

"I'm going out to the hospital anyway." David bit off every word.

Mac could see Chelsea's friend Roger becoming increasingly nervous by the police chief's agitation.

"After leaving the hospital I need to go find a hotel to stay at until I decide what to do about Riley," Chelsea said.

"I can take you to a hotel," David said. "No problem."

"Then it's settled," Roger said. "I can go." He turned to go to the door.

"No!" Chelsea said. "Stay!"

Like a little boy in trouble, Roger froze in place.

"Roger will take me to the hospital and I can take a cab to a hotel," Chelsea said. "That way I won't be any *embarrassment* to you."

Judging by the emphasis she had put on the word embarrassment, everyone sensed that Chelsea had just ripped a bandage off an old wound.

Roger waved his hand like a child trying to get the teacher's attention. "I'd really like to leave now."

"Go!" David ordered.

"Stay!" Chelsea said.

David stepped up to her. His eyes locked on hers. "I'm driving you and that's final."

"I'm not going to impose on you," she said through gritted teeth.

"You're not," he said. "I *want* to drive you."

She shrugged. "If you insist."

"Can I go now?" Roger asked.

"Yes," David and Chelsea said in unison.

Not taking any chance on them changing their minds, Roger ran out the door and slammed it on his way out.

David gazed down into her face. "Good to see you, too, Chelsea. You look great."

"You're so full of it, David O'Callaghan," she said.

Aware of all the eyes in the room watching them, David stepped back out of her space. "You don't drive anymore?"

"The police told me I shouldn't," Chelsea said. "I was in a car accident seven years ago and was in a coma for four days. Since then, I have seizures. Not all the time. My last one was well over a year ago. But when they hit … That's why I have Molly. She can sense when I'm going to have a seizure before it happens so that I can take my medication to stop it. Unfortunately, she can't drive."

"All Gnarly can sense is the arrival of food." Mac noticed that while Chelsea was stroking Molly's head, Gnarly was licking her ear. Patiently, Molly accepted the ear cleaning. "Gnarly, stop that."

With a loud whine, Gnarly collapsed at Molly's feet.

"I can drive you anywhere you need to go," Mac said, "unless David objects." He smiled at the blush that came to David's cheeks.

"How about a motel?" In response to Mac's shocked look, she laughed. "I meant for me to stay at while I'm here."

"What about your house?" David asked.

"I sold that after Mom died," she explained. "I had Riley declared dead three years ago and I had assumed he was. All of my Deep Creek Lake roots are gone."

"Since you have Molly and you probably don't know how long you need to stay," Mac said, "how about if you stay at the Spencer Manor?" He ignored the glare that David shot in his direction.

"Spencer Manor?"

"Mac is Robin Spencer's son," Bogie said, "in case you didn't know."

"I'd take him up on that if I were you," Tonya said. "It isn't every girl who gets invited to stay at a mansion on the shores of Deep Creek Lake."

Chelsea still looked uncertain.

"You'll be safe," Bogie assured her. "Mac's taken."

"Very taken," Tonya said. "He's engaged to Archie."

"Archie?" Chelsea asked.

"Archie is a girl," Mac explained. "We have plenty of room and I don't think Gnarly is going to let Molly go."

They found that Molly had lain down, and Gnarly had a paw draped across her shoulders and his head resting on her neck.

"She is fixed, isn't she?" Worry crept into Mac's tone.

"I hate to disappoint Gnarly, but she is," Chelsea said.

ଓ ଛ ଓ ଛ

Since he had ridden to the station with David, Mac was stuck with going along with them to the hospital to visit Riley. Molly had to go wherever Chelsea went, and Gnarly wasn't about to let the new love of his life out of his sight. Mac was delegated to the back seat of the cruiser with two large dogs. At least Gnarly let him have the window seat on one side, and, a true gentle-dog, let Molly take the other window seat.

The on-duty working dog, Molly refused to display if the feeling was mutual or not.

Gnarly's panting was steaming up the right side of Mac's face.

"How did Riley look when you found him?" Chelsea asked once they were on the road running along the lake's shore.

David and Mac were quiet.

"Surprisingly good for someone who has been living off the land," Mac said. "I think he's incredibly lucky to have survived all those years by himself."

She looked over at David. "The news said he was eating garbage?"

"We found dead animal carcasses in the garage where he seemed to have holed himself up."

"Then it's true?"

"What?" David asked.

"Riley was living at the castle," she said, "hiding out in the same place where Damian Wagner and those other people were killed. Did Riley do it?"

"No."

"That's what the news shows are saying," she said.

"I don't go by what a bunch of talking heads say," David said. "I go by the evidence."

"Well, if Riley was there..." she said, "and he disappeared before Wagner was there, then where was he when the murders happened—"

"He could be a witness," Mac said. "The MOs of the murder don't jive with how Riley would have killed them."

"They found dead animals," she said tearfully. "He must have killed them. How much of a jump is it, if he's crazy, to imagine him killing—"

"They had broken necks or bite marks on them," David said. "He killed them with his bare hands—not the same COD as Damian Wagner. If anything, Riley's a witness."

"That's what I wanted to hear you say."

In the back seat, Mac caught her sneaking a look over in David's direction. When David turned his head to check the traffic in her direction, she jerked back and looked in the opposite direction.

This is going to be fun. Mac smiled to himself.

☙ ❧ ☙ ❧

David groaned when he pulled the cruiser up to the hospital to find the media camped out front.

"They all want to see my brother—the Wolf Man," Chelsea said.

David drove on past the crowd and turned the corner. "We'll go in the back employee entrance."

Mac leaned forward in his seat. "Does Molly go everywhere with you?"

"She goes everywhere I go." Chelsea turned and tilted her head toward Molly's red service vest. "She's certified, so the hospital won't have any problem with her going inside. They'll see her vest and know that she's a service dog."

"I'm thinking about Riley," Mac said while David parked the cruiser. "He attacked Gnarly. Since he thinks he's a wolf, he may try to attack Molly if you take her into the room."

"They have him tied down," David said. "He's also heavily sedated. Maybe he won't notice her."

Mac stayed with Gnarly in the cruiser. Gnarly watched David and the white shepherd escort Chelsea inside. When the door shut, he let out a whine.

"She'll be back." Mac patted him on the head.

Gnarly's ears perked up. Both Mac and the dog looked over their shoulders to see a man wearing a green jacket came around the corner and into the parking lot. He carried a red box with the logo of the local fried chicken takeout down the road. Between his arm and side, he clutched a takeout soft drink.

Licking his chops, Gnarly stomped his front feet and pressed closer to the window.

As he passed the dumpster, the man tossed the box inside, wiped his hands on the front of his coat, took the drink container, and sipped away while making his way to the hospital's service entrance to go inside.

With a sigh, Mac sat back in his seat and closed his eyes to catch a nap, which Gnarly refused to let happen. Whining, Gnarly gazed at the dumpster and then back at his master to tell him telepathically to let him out to get the discarded fried chicken bones.

"No," Mac said, when he received the message.

Gnarly continued to stare at him.

"I said no."

Gnarly stomped his feet.

Mac answered with silence.

Gnarly pawed at his arm.

"Lie down."

Gnarly answered by charging forward and slamming into Mac's body. Incensed, Gnarly stomped and pawed at him until Mac threw open the door in order to escape the attack. He rolled and landed face down on the pavement. Now free, Gnarly ran across the parking lot and hurled himself at the dumpster, only to discover that it was too tall for him to jump inside.

Still on his knees, Mac laughed at him. "Serves you right!"

A van rolled into the lot and parked next to the dumpster. Recognizing Mac, who was climbing up to his feet, a tall bleached blonde with dark eyebrows descended on the man who, according to their sources, owned the castle where the wolf man had been staying and was the one who had found him. She stuck her microphone into Mac's face. "What was your first thought, Mr. Faraday, when you found a wolf man living in your castle?"

Behind her, the camera operator focused in on Mac's face.

"I have no comment." Mac turned around to see Gnarly circling the van and the dumpster.

His lack of comment was not an acceptable answer for the journalists. Like a pack of wild hyenas who spot an elk separated from the herd, they stayed on him. "You had to have been aware of the bizarre history of supernatural occurrences at the Astaire Castle," the journalist said. "In light of this latest incident, what are your plans for the castle?"

"I plan to help the police find out who killed Damian Wagner and his daughter and editor." With a wave of his arm, Mac gestured for Gnarly to come to him so that they could get back into the cruiser.

"Does that mean you have ruled out the wolf man as a suspect?"

Forgetting about Gnarly, Mac turned to her. "He's not a wolf man," he said with force. "You make him sound like some creature. He's a man—just like any of us—only he's sick—and keeping in mind that he is a man—a human with family who care about him—he and his family deserve your respect for their privacy while he gets treatment and becomes well again so that maybe—just maybe he can help us find out what happened that night when Damian Wagner was killed."

The journalist jumped on his statement so fast that her dark eyebrows jumped up into her bleached blonde bangs. "Then you consider him a witness?"

"I have nothing more to say."

The camera operator burst out laughing.

The journalist turned to the camera. "What's so funny?"

"That dog climbed up onto the car parked next to us and then onto the top of our van and dove into the dumpster," the operator laughed, "and I got it all! I can't wait to load this onto YouTube. Guarantee—this will go viral in no time!"

"You were supposed to be recording me!" she yelled.

"Aw, man!" Mac ran for the dumpster where Gnarly was digging through the trash with both paws. "I should teach you a lesson and just leave you there for the garbage truck to haul away."

Chapter Eleven

Gnarly let out a long mournful cry from in the rear compartment of David's cruiser.

"I don't want to hear it," Mac said to him from the back seat while holding his nose. "This is what you get for dumpster diving. You're lucky David wouldn't let me leave you there."

In the front seat, David smiled over at Chelsea.

"Do they always argue like that?" she asked him.

"Today's a good day." He was glad to see the corner of her lips curl.

Chelsea had sobbed when she saw Riley, who, even in a medicated state, strained against his restraints to try to get at Molly. He growled and snarled until a nurse took Molly out of the room.

Still, Riley, who didn't recognize his sister or childhood friend, refused to calm down. He seemed to have forgotten how to speak—communicating only with barks and growls.

A psychiatric specialist was traveling in from Boston to better diagnose his condition and recommend treatment. Until then, the hospital doctors were keeping him sedated and restrained.

When Chelsea asked about her brother's chances of ever returning to mainstream society, the doctor gave the standard, "We need to know more before we can determine that."

When he had escorted her out the back door, David found Gnarly in the dumpster and Mac threatening to leave him there while a news crew filmed it all. Chelsea sobbed in the cruiser while David chased away the media and Mac hauled Gnarly out of the dumpster.

Hanging his head over the top of the back seat, Gnarly cried out again. Even Molly seemed to inch closer to the window to escape the foul odor of garbage permeating from his pelt.

"Was it worth it?" Mac asked him. "Were those chicken bones worth it? When you throw them up, which you always do when you manage to steal some out of the neighbor's garbage, will that be worth it?"

Gnarly uttered a sound that resembled, "Umph!" and plopped down in the back of the cruiser.

"I think he said it was worth it," David said.

"Not to me," Mac said. "I'm the one who has to clean up after him." With a mixture of snarl about Gnarly's latest misdeed and disgust about the future mess coming, he slumped in his seat.

David glanced over at where Chelsea was staring out the side window. She was deep in her own thoughts. "When do you have to go back to work?"

"I can have as much time as I need," she said. "Emergency family leave or liberal leave—they'll work it out."

"The government can be pretty understanding about situations like that," David said. "What type of lawyer are you at the attorney general's office? Criminal?"

"I wish." She gave a hollow laugh. "I'm not a lawyer. I'm a paralegal. I do all the boring grunt work."

"Last I heard you were in law school," David said.

"I was," she said. "I was in my second year. My mom's life insurance only paid for one year's tuition. I took out a student loan for the next and had been approved for the third year when some cheerleader texting her BFF went through a red light and creamed me. It took me a full year to recover."

"Couldn't you sue the girl that hit you to pay for that year you missed of school?" David asked. "She went through a red light while texting."

"It was an accident and she was a kid," Chelsea said quietly. "I only took what the insurance company paid out and they covered my medical bills. If I went for blood it would have meant the girl couldn't have gone to college and I couldn't do that to her—not for making a mistake that I know she'll never make again."

"That's very admirable of you," Mac said. "It's rare to meet people who know the true meaning of forgiveness."

"She's a physical therapist now," Chelsea said. "She would come to the hospital to help me when I was in physical therapy and decided to study that. She now works at the same hospital I stayed at after she plowed into me."

"But you're not a lawyer," David pointed out. "Why didn't you go back to law school?"

"I was so far in debt when I was in that accident—by the time I was back on my feet, I knew that if I went any further into debt I'd never get out," she explained. "So I got certified as a paralegal and went to work for the attorney general."

With a whine, Gnarly rose up from where he laid in the back and offered a pleading look in Mac's direction.

"You're not getting any sympathy from me," Mac said. "I want you to think about your behavior and attitude."

With a glance at the back of Molly's head, Gnarly whined and dropped back down. They could hear a deep sigh from the dog.

ଔ ୭ ଔ ୭

"I hate it when women do that," David told Mac when he came out of the kitchen and climbed the three steps up from the drop-down dining room.

"Do what?" Mac was only paying half-attention while reading a copy of a report on his computer tablet from the medical examiner.

David handed Mac one of the two sherries he had poured for their after-dinner drinks. "Stop talking and stare at me when I come into a room."

"David, I never figured you for the paranoid type." Mac grinned up at him.

"Even Gnarly and Molly stopped whatever it is they were doing to watch me." David dropped down into the chair across from Mac.

"Be grateful."

"For what?"

"Archie couldn't stand the last house guest we had. You do remember how that ended up, don't you?"

"So it's either Archie bonds with the guest and they form a conspiracy against me," David asked, "or she ends up shooting them? Isn't there something in between?"

"Not when it comes to women," Mac said. "I like Chelsea. I think you were a fool to let her get away."

"You're only saying that because she cleaned up Gnarly's bone puke."

"There's no faster way for a woman to work her way into my heart." Mac lowered the tablet. "What was Hollister talking about when he said he knew who you were and what you did?"

"I have no idea," David said. "Why do I have a feeling we made a mistake letting him go?"

"He's staying at the Spencer Inn," Mac reminded him. "Hector and his people have him under tight surveillance. Last report from Hector was that he hasn't left his hotel room, even to go to dinner. He had room service sent up."

"What's he doing?" David asked. "He said he needed to make a couple of phone calls ..."

"Get his affairs in order before confessing?" Mac asked.

"Why didn't you suggest I bring him in?"

"It was your call," Mac said. "You're the chief of police."

"But you've been investigating murders much longer," David said. "I rely on your experience."

"We had nothing to hold him," Mac said. "He knew that. He confessed to setting the wheels in motion that led to Wagner's murder. Sounds to me like he knows the jig is up and he's ready to roll on who killed them. If we play nice, he may roll willingly."

"He accused me of doing it," David said.

"Is that why you're paranoid?" Mac asked with a smile.

"You'd be paranoid too if Hollister was pointing at you when he said that he wasn't taking the blame for what you did."

"Does he know about you and Genevieve?" Mac asked.

"If you mean did she ever take me to the castle to meet him, no. I never laid eyes on Hollister until today and he never saw me."

Mac slowly shook his head. "Weird." He closed the cover over his tablet. "Doc emailed that she found something peculiar in going over the reports for Genevieve and Jansen's autopsies and is going to run some tests."

"What kind of peculiar?" David asked.

"She didn't elaborate," Mac said. "She did say it could be nothing. She wants to do some further testing to find out. She'll let us know." Hearing the girlish laughter coming closer to the kitchen door, he glanced over his shoulder. "I think we're getting company."

Archie was carrying a silver serving tray with a black cognac bottle on it. The bottle was surrounded by three cognac snifters. She came up into the living room. "Have I got a treat for you guys. Hennessey XO, extra old cognac. " She set the tray in the middle of the coffee table and sat down next to Mac.

Taking a seat in the wing-backed chair across from David, Chelsea opted out on the cognac for a cup of tea. Always at her mistress's side, Molly sat at attention by her feet.

Seeing the bottle, Mac sat up. "I thought you were going to break that open for the formal announcement of our engagement—after I bought you the ring."

"I got tired of waiting," Archie said with a sly grin. "Besides, David and Chelsea haven't seen each other in years, Riley is alive—"

"Not well," Chelsea interjected.

"But alive," Archie said. "Where there's life, there's hope."

While Archie was opening the bottle of cognac, Gnarly trotted down the stairs with his favorite toy clutched in his jaws. It was two tennis balls joined together by a rubber bone to make for a bouncy, chewy bone. He made a beeline for Molly and dropped the toy at her paws.

Molly jumped up and pressed back against the chair.

Archie stopped uncorking the bottle to swoon. "Ah, Gnarly is sharing with Molly. For him to offer that toy is big."

Yelping, Gnarly dropped down at Molly's feet and gazed up at her. He nudged the toy closer to her. Turning to Chelsea, a questioning expression crossed Molly's face.

"It's okay, Molly." Chelsea picked up the toy and held it in front of her nose. "You can take it. Gnarly wants you to have it."

Molly sniffed the toy. Gnarly's eyebrows rose up to the top of his forehead. His gaze never left her face. Everyone held their breath waiting for her decision.

"Take it, Molly," David said. "Gnarly will be crushed if you reject him. He's very sensitive."

That seemed to do it. Molly took the toy into her mouth. The uncertainty on her face was replaced with pleasure. She lay down to enjoy the toy. With caution, Gnarly inched forward to take one end of the toy while she enjoyed the other.

Archie swooned again. "Isn't it romantic?" She handed a snifter to Mac and one to David before taking up one for herself. "To reunions." She held up the snifter in a toast. "Happy endings—Riley being found, and new beginnings—new friendships and fresh starts on old friendships."

Mac noticed Archie casting an eye in David's direction. David was staring down into his snifter as if he expected it to jump out of the glass to slap him across the face. Seeing that Chelsea had filled Archie in on her side of the story, Mac softly grinned into his snifter. It was clear what Archie was hoping would happen during Chelsea's stay at the manor.

He saw that his summation was correct when as soon as Archie had drained her snifter, she set it down on the tray and yawned. "Well, it's been a long day. We're tired."

"We are?" Mac asked.

She took his snifter, which was still half-filled with expensive cognac, and set it on the tray next to hers. "I hope you don't think we're rude if we leave you two alone and go to bed."

She took Mac by the hand and urged him up from the sofa. Gazing at the expensive cognac that she was pulling him away from, as well as the glass of sherry that he hadn't had time to drink, Mac gave in. He wondered how it would appear if he were to pour both drinks back into their bottles with a funnel.

"Mac …" Archie tugged on his arm. "Let's go to bed."

"I guess we're going to bed." Mac couldn't tell if David was amused or frightened with the prospect of being left alone with Chelsea.

"Good night," Archie sang out merrily while leading Mac up the stairs to the master suite.

From the top of the stairs, Mac looked down to see David still staring into his snifter while Chelsea turned her attention to Molly. Curiosity made him wish he could be a fly on the wall.

"Well …" David began after he heard the door to the suite close up above them. "You've had a long day. I'm sure you're tired, too."

"Kind of," she said. "But I don't know if I'll be able to sleep." She stood up. "I need to let Molly out before I go to bed. Gnarly probably needs to go out, too."

Hearing the word "out," Gnarly and Molly jumped to their feet. Gnarly led the way across the back deck and through the gardens. Outside, Molly sprang to life. She was taking a break from her on-duty job to chase Gnarly. Upon being caught, he would turn and chase her back. Excitedly, they barked at each other.

Seeing Chelsea hugging herself against the cold night wind blowing in off the lake, David grabbed her coat from the hook inside the kitchen and brought it out to drape across her shoulders.

Startled by his touch, she jumped before turning to him. In the light from the outside lamp, her face was filled with a mixture of excitement and fear. "Thank you." She hugged the coat tighter. "I forgot what a gentleman you could be sometimes."

"Sometimes," David murmured with a shrug.

"Mom always liked you," she said. "I think you broke her heart as much as you did mine."

"I know," David said.

"Not really." She kept her gaze on the dogs. "I don't think it was possible for anyone's heart to be as badly broken as mine."

"I'm sorry, Chelsea," David said. "I was too young and hormonal to realize what a stupid thing I was doing."

"Which is why parents and grown-ups kept telling us to not get so involved," she said. "We were too young and dumb to listen or know any better." She laughed at Molly rolling Gnarly over onto his back. "Go get 'im, Molly!"

"Not we," he said, "Me. I was the jackass."

"I know," she said with a smile. "I was there. Remember?"

He took her by the shoulders and turned her to him. His gaze held hers until she was forced to look at him. "I am so very sorry for hurting you."

Her laughter caused him to let go of her. "Get over yourself, David."

Speechless, he peered at her. *Where is she coming from? Is this girl for real?*

Chelsea cocked her head at him. "Yes, David O'Callaghan, you ruined my life. I had plans—big plans for us. Do you remember them? I do. We were going to get married. You were going to college ROTC and then serve your time in the military as an officer. I was going to be an officer's wife. I was going to go to law school. After you got out of the military, you were going to the police academy. By the time you were a police officer, I would be a prosecutor. After your dad retired, you would take over as Spencer's chief of police and catch the bad guys and I was going to put them away forever as Garrett County's county prosecutor. We were going to live on the lake and have two children, a boy named Justin and a girl named Caitlin." She squinted at him. "Do you remember that?"

David swallowed with guilt. "I don't remember our planning two children and picking out their names."

"I may have neglected to tell you about that part of our plans." A slow grin crossed her lips.

"I fulfilled my part of the plan," he noted. "I'm Spencer's chief of police—just not the way I planned it to happen."

"Like either of us had a clue about anything when we made those plans," she said. "Neither of us had ever been out there, David. We had no idea of how the world worked. How can you save the world if you don't know how it works? Who goes to fix an oven without figuring out how it works first?"

"I've never fixed an oven," David said.

"I have," she said. "Because I've learned how to take care of myself." She laughed. "*You* taught me that—by sleeping with Katrina and dumping me—you forced me to grow up and for that I can thank you."

Laughing, she grasped him by the arms. "David, before you dumped me, I couldn't get my hair cut without getting at least five opinions—yours holding the most weight—and then taking votes. Overnight, I had to stand on my own two feet. If things had gone according to my plans, I never would have been strong enough to handle Riley's disappearance and Mom's death."

"So you don't hate me?" David held his breath. *Is this a trap? Is she drawing me into a false sense of security to shoot me? Is she armed?*

"I did," she confessed. "For the longest time, I hated your guts. I hated the very sight of you. But then, when I had my accident, and I was lying alone in bed all those months, I had a lot of time to think about my life and I saw how it all happened. By you betraying me the way you did, you forced me to grow up—it made me strong enough to survive and make me who I am today—a pretty cool chick if I must say so myself."

He grinned at her. "You are pretty cool."

Flashing him a grin, she placed her hands on her hips, wiggled her shoulders, and looked down at her bosom. "Even if I am flat-chested?"

David felt his cheeks turn red. She had a good memory. He joined in her laughter.

To his surprise, she took his hand and leaned in to whisper into his ear. "Thank you for ruining my life, David O'Callaghan."

Her eyes met his. The electricity between them excited him. The old feelings he had for her were still there and they were as thrilling as they had been before.

When he moved in to bring his lips to hers, she jerked away to turn her attention to the dogs. "Molly, come! Time for bed." Instantly, the white German Shepherd was at her side. Together, they went inside.

David whirled around to face her before she could close the door. "I hate the name Justin."

"Then I guess you got lucky with Katrina in more ways than one." She closed the door.

Gnarly touched his cold nose to David's hand and uttered a whine.

"Looks like you got left out in the cold, too, Gnarly."

ଔ ଓ ଔ ଓ

"I need you to find someone," Mac was telling Archie, who was reading a book on her side of the bed. With a pleading look, he laid his head on her shoulder and gazed up at her.

Enticed by the prospect of a job in his investigation, Archie quickly set the book aside. "Who?"

"Rafaela Diaz," Mac said. "She was the Wagner's housekeeper. She'd found the bodies. She was so freaked out that Pat O'Callaghan allowed her to go back to Brazil."

"Now you want to find her," Archie said. "Since this is an active case, isn't that Bogie's job?"

"Bogie's looking," Mac said, "but he doesn't think there will be much luck. She's from a small village in Brazil—according to the file, a primitive village where they are big into voodoo."

"Which means they probably don't have much in the way of paper trails." She cocked an eyebrow in his direction.

"They had enough for her to make her way to America and Deep Creek Lake," Mac said. "She was legal and had a passport at the time. After the murders, she went running back home."

"What about Riley?" Archie asked. "Do you think he witnessed the murders?"

"That's very up in the air," Mac said. "I've had witnesses like him in the past."

"You never told me you encountered wolf men before." With a giggle, she looked down at him.

"I mean mentally ill," Mac said, "never to the degree of Riley, but out there. I don't hold out much hope that he can be any help to us, let alone prove that he didn't kill them. I'm hoping Rafaela can help us catch the real killer."

She picked up her book and returned to the page she had been reading. "Well, without a road trip to Brazil, it'll be a challenge finding her."

He grinned back up at her. "And you love challenges."

"That I do."

Mac noticed a book in her hand. "What are you reading?"

"One of your mother's books."

"Have I read it?"

"Doubt it," she said. "This is one of her later books. Mickey Forsythe and Diablo are working on a case of a murdered horror writer …"

"Sounds familiar." Mac squinted to read some of words on the page she was reading.

"There's a missing book that the writer is hiding from his crooked publisher so that he can't get his hands on it until after their contract expires. You see once the contract expires then the writer can take it to another publisher. I just read where Diablo found it."

"Diablo?" Mac buried his face into her neck and breathed in her scent. "The dog?"

"Yes," she giggled. "Guess where he found it?"

Taking the book out of her hands, Mac did not answer. He tossed the book to the floor.

"Does that mean you don't want to know where he found it?" Seeing the look in his eyes as he rolled over to pin her down onto the bed, she said, "I guess you aren't interested in talking about great works of literature right now."

With a wicked grin across his face, Mac shook his head.

"Oh, I love it when you get that twinkle in your eye." She reached up to turn off the light.

Chapter Twelve

Something was wrong. Mac felt it as soon as he woke up. It was still dark outside, as it had been since the onset of autumn. That added an even more ominous tone to the start of the day when he woke up with the feeling that something wasn't right.

Gnarly. … Gnarly isn't jumping up and down on my chest. Mac glanced over at the clock. 06:05 am. *Where is that dog?*

The bedroom door was open. Mac threw the comforter aside and slipped into his lounging pants. After picking up his bathrobe, he knelt to peer under the bed where Gnarly made his den. He wasn't there.

Gnarly would wake me up if something was going on … unless he couldn't.

The thought crossed Mac's mind that something had happened to Gnarly. He couldn't remember hearing the shepherd come to bed. With a glance over at where Archie was curled up under the comforter, he recalled that he was too preoccupied to notice. Mac put on his robe and slipped the handgun he kept in the bed stand drawer into his pocket.

At the top of the stairs, he heard a soft voice drifting up from the kitchen below. As he made his way down the stairs, he recognized it to be singing. A soft smile came to his lips when he remembered how his adopted mother used to sing in the kitchen. Recognizing Chelsea's voice and the scent of fresh brewed coffee, Mac relaxed and pressed the kitchen door open.

Fully dressed in a running suit complete with jacket and cap, Chelsea was sitting at the kitchen table with a German shepherd on either side. "Oh, did I wake you?" She tossed a couple of capsules into her mouth and washed them down with cranberry juice.

"Actually, Gnarly not waking me up is what woke me up." Mac hurried over to the coffee maker to pour a cup of coffee. "Good morning. How did you sleep?"

"Great," she replied in a cheerful tone. "I'm going to go running. Do you want to come?"

The thought of going running during the sunrise made Mac laugh. "Are you going with David?"

She laughed. "I didn't think he'd be up this early."

"Don't be so sure." Before Mac could explain, David was knocking on the kitchen door. Like Chelsea, he was dressed in a running suit.

Seeing David, Gnarly jumped to his feet and ran to the hook where his leash hung. Taking the end of the leash into his mouth, he yanked it down and trotted over to the door when Mac opened it.

"David takes Gnarly with him when he goes running in the morning," Mac explained while inviting him in. "That's why I thought the two of you were running together." He told David, "Chelsea is going running, too."

"Be serious." David took the leash from Gnarly.

"What's that supposed to mean?" Chelsea asked.

With a smile, David knelt to clip the leash to Gnarly's collar. "Back in school," he told Mac, "Chelsea refused to do anything that would make her sweat."

Her eyes narrowed to almost transparent slits. She stood up from the table. "School was a long time ago. I start every day with a run now."

"How far?" David laughed. "Half a block?"

"Five miles." She sauntered up to him. "And now nothing turns me on more than a good hard sweat." She pushed through the kitchen door. "Come on, dogs. Let's show him."

Molly and Gnarly, with his leash trailing behind him, galloped out after her.

"I think you just got challenged," Mac said.

Gnashing his teeth, David hurried out after her.

"Ah, young love," Mac mused while pouring a second mug of coffee to take upstairs to Archie. "I prefer a different type of exercise on a chilly morning."

☙ ❧ ☙ ❧

"Want to race?" David caught up with Chelsea outside, where she was stretching in the circular driveway in front of the manor. Sitting with her legs spread out in front of her, she was lying practically flat out in between them. He didn't recall her being so limber.

"Do you find it uncomfortable—my being here I mean?" she asked.

"No, do you?"

"To tell you the truth, I wouldn't have taken Mac up on his offer if I had known you lived in the guest cottage. You'd think it would be awkward."

"Like you said last night, what happened between us was a long time ago," David said. "You're not the same person you used to be, and neither am I." He turned to prop his foot up on the top step of the porch and stretched out to touch his toes. He could feel her gaze on his back. "You even like to sweat now. That's big."

Her blonde eyebrows almost met in between her eyes. Her eyes narrowed to slits. "Why is Mac so nice? Why does he let you live here?"

David considered revealing their familial relationship as half-brothers, which would have revealed his father's early relationship with Robin Spencer. Uncertain, he shrugged. "Mac used to be a homicide detective. He understands what it's like. That's something we share." He swallowed. "Mac's my best friend. We've got each other's back."

Her lips curled into a smirk. "I'm glad. I like both him and Archie. It's good to have people who care about you."

"Do you have friends like that in Annapolis?" David bent over to touch his toes.

"Kind of."

David stood up. "What do you mean by 'kind of?'" Watching her, he took a chance to ask, "What about Roger?"

Chelsea laughed. "He's my boss and you scared the daylights out of him. I'll be lucky if I have a job when I get back."

"He shouldn't scare so easily."

"David," she said, "you were packing a gun. Roger wasn't."

"I wasn't going to shoot him," David said.

"He didn't know that," she said.

He smirked. "I know."

"You like that. You've always liked doing that."

He turned to her. "Like what."

She stepped up to him. "Intimidating people. Playing mind games with them. The only reason you want to race is to put me in my place by humiliating me like you always did before." She poked him in the chest. "It's not going to happen. I'm not the immature, insecure little girl who let you win because I was afraid I'd lose you."

"You never let me win at anything."

"Huh! Lot you know. Every chess match we used to have …"

"Never!"

"If I wasn't such a wuss," she chuckled, "I would have checked your mate at will every time."

Molly had a look of pride as she sat at attention while watching her owner smirk at the male human who dared to challenge her.

"Like you could beat me in a race?" he asked. "Remember, I was an officer in the Marines."

"Desk jockey."

"No, special forces," David countered with his hands on his hips. "And I'm still in the reserves."

"I run three marathons a year just for fun." She stepped up to lock her glare on his.

"I could beat you with one leg tied behind my back."

"Wanna bet?"

"Bet," he said."Loser takes the winner out on a date—winner's choice." He pointed to the bridge in the distance. "We run to the bridge, cross the lake and come back. First one back here wins. That's four miles."

A slow grin crossed her face, starting at one corner of her lips and crossing over to the other side. One eyebrow cocked up to form an upside-down "V". She spit into the palm of her hand and stuck it out. "Deal."

David glanced down at the spit-covered hand. In a flash, he recalled when she was eight years old and he was ten. Chelsea demanded to be allowed in his and Riley's boys' club. In an effort to dissuade her, David offered a challenge. She had to eat a whole bowl of cold brussel sprouts. To seal the deal, David spit into his hand and offered it to her. That time, she closed her eyes and cringed before shaking it. Without hesitation, she ate the whole bowl and they were forced to accept her into their club.

She surprised him then. *Why wouldn't I expect her to surprise me again? Chelsea Adams is a woman full of surprises.* "Deal." David grasped her hand.

After they shook, David and Chelsea picked up each of their dog's leash.

"You should tie your shoe before we start." She pointed to his feet. "Hate for you to trip."

David knelt down to check his laces, at which time she shoved him over onto his side in the grass before sprinting off with Molly by her side.

Equally incensed by the dirty trick, Gnarly strained against his leash so hard that he threatened to drag David on his stomach until he got up to his feet to catch up with her.

In the time it took for David and Gnarly to run through the stone pillars marking the entrance to Spencer Manor, Chelsea and Molly were a third of the way down the Point. David and Gnarly sprinted down the road. With all of the residents being well-to-do millionaires who didn't have to leave their homes to work in the morning, the road was deserted.

In the fall, after the colorful foliage had fallen and before the ski season started in late November, Spencer was practically a ghost town except for the few year-round residents who, like Mac, were retired, or were worker-bees like David.

It was for this reason that David, after falling into step with Chelsea when they turned right onto Lakeshore Road, noticed a silver sedan coming up behind them.

Both runners moved over off the road to allow the car to pass them. When it didn't, David's instincts told him that this was not good. He slowed his pace to allow Chelsea to sprint on ahead while waiting for the car to move on. When the car slowed down almost to a halt, David whirled around while pulling his gun out of his pocket. The pause he took to ascertain the danger behind the wheel gave the driver ample time to surge forward while firing at him.

"Gun!" he shouted a warning to Chelsea.

While two shots were fired through the passenger window at him, David fired off three shots at the moving car. One bullet took out the front windshield, the second took out the rear passenger window. The last took out the rear window when the car surged on past. While the car sped away, David stepped out into the road and fired two more shots while running up to where Chelsea was lying in the ditch on top of Molly.

Gnarly's barks could be heard to the end of Spencer Point. Undeterred by his leash flapping behind him, he charged after the vehicle with every intention of catching it.

"Are you okay?" David helped her to her feet. He could feel her hands shaking.

"What was that about?"

"I don't know." David knelt down next to Molly who was pawing at Chelsea. "What about Molly? Did she get hit?" Noticing that his own fingers were trembling, he rubbed his hands on his pants.

"No." She hugged the dog. "We dove for the ditch before the car got up here."

David noticed red blotches in Molly's white fur. "Are you sure?" He ran his fingers through her fur in search of the source of the bleeding. More blood appeared. "I see blood."

Noticing the drops of blood, Chelsea searched her dog for a wound, but Molly, who was licking her face, wasn't acting hurt in any way.

His legs feeling numb, David knelt down. "Where's the blood coming from?" He saw that his hands were covered with blood.

"David! It's you! You've been shot!"

Her voice sounded like she was in a tunnel calling to him. Grabbing her by the arm, he fought to stay upright, but was losing the battle.

"Oh, David!" she sobbed while holding onto him. "Stay with me. Don't die."

"Call … emergency." David sucked in as much breath as he could, which made the pain ripping through his side more intense.

"David, no!" Chelsea yelled. "No! Not now! Not after … I love you. I've always loved you. I thought I hated you but when you called the other night all of those old feelings came rushing back. Even with Riley in the mental ward, you were all I could think about. That was why I had to see you, David. I love you but I'm scared and—"

"Chelsea!" David gasped out in a sharp tone.

Clutching both of his hands, slimy with blood, into hers, she swallowed. "Yes, David?"

Grimacing, David gazed into her light blue eyes that were filled with tears. "Now's not a good time to discuss it. If I live, we'll talk later. If I die, it won't matter."

His last vision before he lost consciousness was Chelsea pleading for him to stay with her.

Chapter Thirteen

Gnarly's barking was loud enough to wake up the residents of Spencer Point. Used to his barking at squirrels, birds, and low-flying aircraft; everyone had grown to ignore the protective shepherd. Yet, the frantic tone this morning brought some curious residents to their front porches when Gnarly, with his leash dragging behind him, ran past on his way to Spencer Manor.

Shrugging into his bathrobe, Mac threw open the door when Gnarly slammed into it. Tying the belt to her bathrobe, Archie was right behind him.

Instead of running in, Gnarly whirled around and ran back out into the driveway. When he saw that Mac had only come down off the porch, he ran back and jumped up to tag him hard in the chest.

"David's not with him," Mac said to Archie. "Something happened to him and Chelsea."

She had already run inside.

"Call Bogie!" Mac yelled as loud as he could while running after Gnarly.

He didn't get far before David's cruiser, its lights and sirens going, pulled up alongside to him. "Get in," Archie called to him out the window.

That was when Mac realized he was in his bare feet and wearing only his bathrobe. There wasn't enough time to change. He saw when he climbed into the passenger seat that Archie was also in her bathrobe and barefoot.

"You know it's illegal to steal a police cruiser," he told her while they tailed Gnarly down the point, across the cove, and along the lake shore.

"So arrest me." She slammed on the brakes when they came upon the scene. "Oh, dear, God!"

Chelsea was on her knees bent over David. Her leash dragging behind her, Molly ran up to Mac when he got out of the cruiser. Whining, she pawed at him before leading the way back to her owner.

"He's been shot!" Covered in blood, Chelsea had taken off her jacket, folded it up, and was holding it against David's side. It was already soaked with blood. She held it against David's stomach with one hand while holding her cell phone to her ear with the other. "The police and ambulance are on the way."

Mac knelt on David's other side and pressed his hand on top of hers to stop the bleeding. He didn't want to lift the coat to look at the wound for fear of allowing more blood to seep out. Glancing back at the cruiser, Mac saw that Archie was already on David's radio. He could hear the sirens announcing the arrival of cruisers from both directions and an ambulance from across the lake. They were growing louder by the second.

A black cruiser tore around the corner from up the road and screeched to a halt in front of them. Shouting orders into his radio, Bogie jumped out of the cruiser and ran to them. "What happened?"

After assuring the emergency operator that officers were on the scene, Chelsea hung up her cell and tossed it to the ground next to her. "It was a silver Cruze. Late model," she said while applying pressure to David's wound. "There was a car rental sticker on the rear bumper. Maryland plates. David shot out all of its windows." She pointed up the road. "It went that way in the direction of the bridge."

Bogie went back to his radio to relay the information.

"Good girl," Mac said.

"I wish I got the plate number or saw the driver," she muttered with tears in her eyes.

Mac grabbed her arm. His hand was covered with blood—David's blood. "You got more than most people in this situation. Every little bit helps."

The ambulance pulled up next to Bogie's cruiser. Mac stepped back to let the EMTs get to work. He didn't like that David was unconscious. *That's not good—not good at all.*

When ushered away, Chelsea let Archie lead her back to David's cruiser where Bogie and Mac were waiting. Gnarly and Molly were in the backseat where Archie had gathered them up to prevent them from contaminating any possible evidence.

"What happened?" Bogie asked Chelsea again. "Tell me everything."

"The car came up behind us." She folded her arms across her chest. "David and I were running with the dogs. David was ahead of me and suddenly he dropped back behind. I remember at the time thinking he was letting me win—"

"Win?" Bogie asked.

"We were racing each other." She swallowed. "I had noticed the car come up behind us but wasn't really paying attention. David must have gotten suspicious when he didn't pass us. I didn't think about it at the time. David slowed down and I sprinted on ahead. Suddenly I heard all these shots—"

"How many?" Bogie asked.

"Seven," she said with certainty. "David's got two gunshot wounds in the side." She pointed at the side of the road where Archie had parked. "This is where it happened. When the shooting started, I tackled Molly and dove into the ditch. When the car sped off, David came running up to me to see how we were. He didn't even know he'd been shot. He thought it was Molly's blood. When I realized it was him, he collapsed." She looked at each one of them. "Who did this?

"David's put a lot of people away," Bogie said. "He's got more than one enemy."

"Hollister," Mac said. "He threatened David yesterday afternoon. I was there."

"Raymond Hollister?" Bogie asked. "He gave Ol' Pat a real hard time because Pat accused him of having something to do with the murders."

"He told David that he wasn't going to put him away for these murders," Mac said. "I'm going to talk to him."

"I'm going with David." Chelsea shoved Mac out of the way to run to the ambulance where they were loading David into the back. Molly jumped out of the open window to go with her. When Gnarly tried to follow, Archie blocked the window with her body to stop him.

Mac climbed into the driver's seat of David's cruiser.

"Hold on, Mac." Bogie grabbed the door to stop Mac from closing it.

"Don't tell me that I'm not authorized to question a murder suspect, Bogie," Mac said. "I'm on contract with the Spencer police department. This is an attempted homicide. So I'm allowed to question Hollister. As for not putting him through a wall, I know how to control myself. If you want to monitor me, Bogie, then you're more than welcome to come along. The question is, who's going to stop you from putting Hollister through a wall."

"I wasn't going to say that," Bogie said.

"Then what?"

"I was going to tell you go home and get dressed," Bogie said. "Hollister might respect your authority more if you were wearing pants."

☙ ❧ ☙ ❧

Back at Spencer Manor, Mac changed into a sports jacket over slacks. As Bogie had pointed out, he wanted to exude authority when trying to capture whoever it was that tried to kill David.

When he came out of his changing room, Mac found Archie sitting on the edge of the bed. Gnarly was lying on the bed with his head in her lap. There were tears in her eyes while she stroked Gnarly's head.

"Hey," Mac said in a gentle tone.

Aware of his presence, Archie wiped the tears from her eyes with the back of her hand. Gnarly sat up.

Mac knelt in front of her. "David's going to be fine. He's a fighter."

She forced a smile to cross her face. "Shouldn't I be telling you that?"

"I know it," he said. "I've worked with people like David my whole life. They don't go down that easy."

"Someone tried to kill him." She squinted at him. "David. Your brother. My friend. *Our* friend. Why?"

"Like Bogie said," Mac shrugged, "David's put a lot of bad guys away. Whichever one it is, we're going to get him."

Archie grasped his shoulder. "I want to be there when you do."

"Hey, Mac!" Bogie called from downstairs where he had let himself in after getting his officers working on the scene of the shooting.

Mac and Archie followed Gnarly down the stairs. Mac sucked in a deep breath when he saw Bogie holding his cell phone. He had just taken a call. "Any news on David?"

"Chelsea called from the hospital," Bogie said. "One of the nurses told her that David wasn't hit twice. It was a through and through. The bullet went in at the front of his waist on the left side and went out the back. Five bullets are missing from David's gun."

"Chelsea heard seven shots," Archie said.

"Shooter shot twice," Bogie said. "One went through the chief, so it's still out there. That's two slugs from the perp's gun that we need to find. Our people will be looking for them while I'm with you, Mac. I've got to make sure you don't kill our chief suspect."

"Would I do that?" Mac asked.

"I'm not so sure I wouldn't," Bogie replied.

ଓ ജ ଓ ജ

Hector Langford and Jeff Ingles were waiting for Mac and Bogie in the lobby of the Spencer Inn. Their greeting was brief before Jeff asked about David's condition.

"Still no word," Mac said. "What room is Hollister in?"

"Four-eleven," Hector said. "I've had my people doubling their surveillance of Hollister ever since you called." He escorted them to the elevator. "According to his registration, he was driving a rental car, a silver Cruze."

Mac smirked over at Bogie. "It's him."

"Now don't do anything rash," Jeff warned Mac. "The guests get upset when you beat up fellow guests."

The elevator doors opened. Mac and Bogie stepped onto the elevator while Jeff held the door for them.

"The car isn't in the garage." Hector stepped onto the elevator and pressed the button for the floor. "But Hollister is in his room. I'd like to think we would have noticed if he had left the Inn since we were keeping an eye on him."

"He couldn't exactly drive it into the garage all shot up," Bogie said. "He could have ditched it down the road and walked in a side entrance."

"We're checking the security footage now," Hector said. "Room service delivered breakfast to him twenty minutes ago."

Jeff's tone was pleading. "Mac, please don't go in there like a bad-ass and shoot up our guest. It's not good for the Inn's reputation when people staying here get killed by the owner."

"Am I allowed to shoot back if he shoots first?" Mac asked.

"How about if you fire a warning shot first?"

"Warning shot?" Mac chuckled. "Do you have any idea how expensive bullets are nowadays? I don't fire warning shots. In my book, murderers aren't worth the cost of wasted bullets."

Raymond Hollister was wearing his bathrobe when he answered the door. Recognizing Deputy Chief Art Bogart from years before, the silver-haired businessman stood up tall and stuck out his chest. He sucked in his lips to form a thin straight line. "Why do I have a feeling this isn't a social visit?"

"It's not," Bogie said. "May we come in? We have a few questions."

Raymond Hollister made no move to invite them inside. "Your police chief questioned me yesterday. I told him that I would come by the station this morning with the name of his killer. Obviously, you bunch of incompetents are too impatient to give me a chance to get dressed." He tightened up the belt to his robe.

"Attempted murder has a detrimental effect on a man's patience," Mac said.

"Attempted murder?"

"Someone shot Chief O'Callaghan this morning," Bogie said. "That's what we want to talk to you about."

Hollister opened the door wider and stepped back into his room. They followed him inside. Hector closed the door behind him.

"I've been here in my room since I spoke to O'Callaghan yesterday." Raymond Hollister sat down at the table where he had been eating his breakfast of three eggs over easy, pancakes, and bacon, plus a tall glass of tomato juice that stood half-empty. "You can ask around. It isn't like there's a lot to do in this boring little resort town." He resumed shoveling hungry forkfuls of egg into his mouth. "Besides, why would I want to kill Chief O'Callaghan?" he asked with his mouth full.

"You tell us," Mac said. "You did threaten him yesterday."

"I did not," Hollister scoffed.

"Yes, you did." Tempted to grab the man by the front of his bathrobe, Mac stood over him. "I was there and saw you."

"Clearly, that was a misunderstanding." He drained the glass of tomato juice and wiped his mouth with a napkin before continuing. "Why would I want to kill the man who had the power to arrest the person who murdered my most successful author?"

Jeff gently pushed Mac away from the guest. "First of all, I would like to say that we are very sorry for any inconvenience we're causing you by this interrogation. I only hope you understand how important any information you can supply us can be. If you didn't try to kill Chief O'Callaghan, which I really don't think you did, maybe you know who did."

With a forkful of eggs poised to toss into his mouth, Hollister said, "Probably the same person who killed Damian Wagner." He shoved the eggs into his mouth. After withdrawing the fork, he used it to attack the pancakes.

"Care to share this person's name with us?" Mac asked with a sarcastic tone.

"Of course," Raymond Hollister said with a choked voice.

"Who?" Bogie asked.

Raymond continued to cough. His face turned red while he tried to form words.

"He's choking!" Jeff yelled.

"On eggs?" Mac asked.

Hector grabbed Hollister in a bear hug and tried to apply the Heimlich maneuver with no success. In seconds, Raymond Hollister turned blue and collapsed to the floor.

Bogie and Hector laid him on the floor while Jeff dialed for emergency. "We need an ambulance at—"

"He's dead!" Bogie announced.

"Maybe it was a heart attack," Hector said.

"I don't think so," Mac said.

"Has the world gone mad?" Jeff yelled while holding his cell phone up. "No, we have a dead body up here in four-eleven—not the parking garage."

"Parking garage?" Mac turned from the dead man on the floor to Jeff, whose eyes were huge. His face was drenched in sweat. "What is it?"

"The emergency operator said that they're already sending an emergency unit here to the Spencer Inn to answer a call for a dead body found in the parking garage."

The cell phone on Hector's hip rang. While they all watched, he answered it. "Hello," he asked in a hesitant tone. "Yeah, I know. Any idea who… I'll be right there." He hung up.

"Two deaths here at the Inn?" Bogie asked.

Hector nodded his head. "Our people found her while searching for the car. Her body was hidden in a maintenance closet—looks like she was strangled. Her clothes, hotel ID and security pass were all missing."

Mac looked over the uneaten food on the table. "How much do you want to bet that our shooter killed her to steal her clothes and ID to get access to Hollister's breakfast to murder him?"

Chapter Fourteen

"Jeff, you were there," Mac reminded the hotel manager. "I didn't touch him. Even when he was dying, I never laid a hand on Hollister. So this wasn't my fault."

"No, Mac." Jeff patted him on the arm. "I know it's not your fault."

Relieved that Jeff didn't blame him for Raymond Hollister's death and the resulting chaos at the resort, Mac grinned.

"It's your karma." With a shrug of his shoulders, Jeff wiped his face with his sweat-soaked handkerchief. He eyed a media van that cruised by the front entrance. "You inherited it from Robin Spencer. It's in your DNA. Wherever you go, trouble follows."

They watched a string of crime scene investigators, clad in jackets with FORENSICS emblazoned across the back, gather in front of the elevators. Bewildered-looking guests stepped off the elevator before half of the group stepped on to go up. The rest boarded the next elevator to go down to the garage.

Jeff sighed deeply. "If you'll excuse me, Mac, I need to go call my therapist." With a dazed look in his eyes, he went back to his office.

From the opposite hallway leading back to the security offices, Hector came jogging out. By the bounce in the security manager's step, Mac could see that he had good news. "We got the bitch's picture," Hector said. "One of the security cameras on Hollister's floor picked her up getting off the elevator with the room service cart, and then another camera picked her up wearing Sue's uniform after using her access card to enter the employee section of the Inn."

"I want to see it." Mac checked the time on the clock over the registration desk. It was quarter after eight o'clock. "What time did she take breakfast up to Hollister?"

"Forty-two minutes ago," Hector said. "It's optimistic to think so, but I sent out the picture to all of our security people's phones. They're searching the Inn, out-buildings and grounds. Maybe we'll get lucky. I sent her picture to your phone, too."

Mac took his cell phone off his belt to check the picture. She was a plain looking woman with short dark blonde hair. Her features were thin, almost gaunt looking.

Seeing the cell phone in his hand, Mac was reminded of something Raymond Hollister had said the day before—a reason why he wanted to wait before telling them the name of the killer. Mac studied the face of Hollister's killer without seeing it.

Noticing the blank expression on Mac's face, Hector asked, "What is it? Do you know her?"

"Hollister told us he had to make a phone call," Mac said. "Yesterday, when David and I questioned him, he told us that he would make a couple of phone calls and then he would give us the name of our killer. That's why he was killed." He turned toward the elevator. "We need to check his phone records to find out who he called after talking to us."

The elevator doors opened and Bogie stepped out. "What's the saying? Everything happens in three?"

"We've had our three and then some," Hector said.

"Not today," Bogie replied.

"Yes, we did." Mac ticked off on his fingers. "David was shot. One of my servers was murdered and Hollister was poisoned."

"I was counting the server and Hollister as one," Bogie said, "since the killer took her out to get to Hollister."

"A murder two-fer?" Mac asked. "I hope the jury that convicts our killer doesn't see it as that because I don't, and I don't think Sue's family will see it that way either."

They paused to listen to the increasing sound of the fire engine sirens approaching the Spencer Inn.

"What's that?" Mac asked.

Jeff Ingles came running out of his office. "Now what?" He glared at Mac. "What did you do now?"

"Fire engines," Bogie said. "Call came in while I was upstairs. Astaire Castle is on fire."

☙ ❧ ☙ ❧

Warning her to be careful of the hot coffee that she had poured in the hospital cafeteria, Archie handed the takeout cup to Chelsea and eased into the chair next to her. Picking up on her master's concern, Molly's brown eyes in her white face reflected worry. The German shepherd was almost invisible where she lay motionless at Chelsea's feet in the waiting room.

Nothing like Gnarly. Even when Gnarly is being still and good, everyone notices him. Maybe it's his stare and size that commanded attention. The red smears of blood stood out against Molly's white coat to remind Archie about what had happened. *So much blood.*

"You and I must be the same size." Archie noted that the fresh clothes she had brought for Chelsea to change into, fit her perfectly—maybe a bit loose. Covered in David's blood, Chelsea's running jacket and suit had been taken into evidence along with David's clothes.

"It isn't every day that I meet women my age who are my size," Chelsea said. "In school, I was embarrassed about how small I was. Now, women envy me."

"Things have a way of sorting out." Archie took a sip of her coffee.

"Did you ever date David?"

"No." Archie saw that she was studying her for her response. She looked right into her eyes so that she could see she was telling her the truth.

"It's okay if you did," Chelsea said. "I was just wondering. A lot of my friends had crushes on him back when we were in school. He never knew it, though. Only Katrina had the bad form to act on it. The only reason she seduced David was to prove she could. That was who she was. She played with people like they were toys. I think she was the closest I ever came to hating anyone." She sighed. "I wonder what ever became of her."

"She was murdered," Archie said in a matter-of-fact tone.

Chelsea almost jumped out of her chair. "I have an alibi."

"You don't know when or where or how it happened." Archie giggled at her reaction.

"Doesn't matter. I know I have an alibi."

Archie patted her hand. "Her murder was solved and the case closed. So you don't have to worry."

Chelsea sighed with relief.

Deep in their respective thoughts, the two women and dog sat next to each other, staring straight ahead without seeing anything before them.

Chelsea broke the silence. "Do you remember your first time?"

"I think every woman does," Archie said.

"I've read in so many places and heard so many people say that it was never what they had expected," Chelsea said. "They were disappointed." She shook her head. "David ... even when our relationship was ending—" She hung her head. "He had a way of making it magical. It was special for both of us. I was convinced it had to do completely with how much we were in love with each other." Her expression changed from dreamy to realistic. She sat up straight. "But that's the way it is with first love. You have all these cloudy memories about how fabulous it was. Too bad you can't go back to those naive, idealistic times, huh?"

"Who says you can't?"

"The dew is gone from the rose, Archie," she said. "There's no going back."

"Are you sure about that?"

"David has a very special place in my heart, not just as my first love." Chelsea sniffed. "For some reason, he was able to understand Riley. As different as the two of them were, most friends would have gone their separate ways. David became popular—as popular as you could be, living in Spencer without money. Riley withdrew from everyone and got all wrapped up in horror books and movies. He read every one of Damian Wagner's books over and over again, and knew everything there was to know about werewolves."

"How ironic that he decided he was a werewolf," Archie said, "and made his den at the castle where the master in horror and paranormal was working on his last book."

"You don't think Riley killed Damian because he was obsessed with him, do you?"

"Do you?" Archie asked.

"I really don't know." She hung her head over the cup of coffee. "I couldn't see even an ounce of the brother I used to know in that creature we saw yesterday."

"David and Mac said the MO of the murders doesn't fit with Riley believing he's a werewolf."

"Wolf Man," Chelsea corrected Archie. "There's a difference."

"Whatever," Archie replied.

"Riley would say that was important," Chelsea said. "That was all I heard about when we were growing up. Riley made everyone sick of it. His friends started drifting away one by one. Even though David never had any interest in any of that, he didn't abandon Riley. He still kept coming around." A soft grin crossed her face. "I convinced myself that he was coming to see me."

"I have no doubt but that he was," Archie said.

"By the time we were in high school, David was his only friend. He stood by Riley when no one else would—even me, I'm sorry to say."

"David is a good man." Archie squeezed her hand. "He's also very strong. He's going to make it through this."

Chelsea squeezed her hand back.

When the doctor turned the corner to come into the waiting room, the women rose to their feet in unison. Even Molly stood up to hear the news.

"You're here for Police Chief David O'Callaghan?" Not knowing which woman to address, the doctor looked from one to the other and back again.

"Yes." Archie felt Chelsea squeezing her hand so tight that her knuckles hurt.

"He's out of surgery," the doctor said. "We stopped the bleeding. He was very lucky. The bullet went through his side without hitting any organs. Barring any complications, he should recover completely and be released in a couple of days."

Chelsea closed her eyes. "Thank you, God,"' she said out loud while still clutching Archie's hand.

Archie was beginning to lose the feeling in her fingers. "When can we see him?"

"He's in post-op right now," the doctor reported. "In a couple of hours, we'll be moving him into a private room. You can see him then."

"I need to call Mac." Archie extracted her hand from Chelsea's and flexed her fingers to regain the feeling in them to dial her phone.

଒ ഗ ଒ ഗ

Mac gave Bogie a thumbs-up sign at the news.

Even with her on speaker phone, it was difficult to hear Archie over the cruiser's siren while they raced across the mountain behind the parade of fire engines heading for Astaire Castle. The smoke was getting heavier as they approached.

"We'll keep a couple of our guys attached to his butt to make sure he stays that way," Bogie yelled loud enough for Archie to hear.

"Any idea yet about who did this?" she asked.

"Whoever it is, they're covering their tracks very well," Mac told her after updating her on Raymond Hollister's murder.

"It almost seems like a professional hit to me," Hector said from where he was in the back seat of Bogie's cruiser.

"David had worked in special forces in the Marines." Bogie swerved off the road to where the terrain was smoother. "Maybe it's payback for something he did overseas."

"But why Hollister?" Mac asked. "David says he never met Hollister until yesterday."

"David was out of country when the Wagner murders happened," Bogie said.

"The only connection David had with the Wagners was a fling with Genevieve," Hector said with an evil chuckle. "Maybe our killer is a ghost scorned."

"Which brings us back to 'why kill Raymond Hollister?'" Mac asked.

Archie reminded them that she was on the other end of the cell phone. "Mac, I have to go. When you get a chance, can you run by the manor and let Gnarly out?"

"Why can't he let himself out?"

"Because you get mad at him when he does," she shot back before hanging up.

It was a good thing she had. The roar of the fire company's helicopter swooping in to douse the flames would have drowned her voice out.

One of Spencer's most dependable and youngest officers, Officer Fletcher, flagged them down when they pulled up to the gate. "Any word on the chief?"

"He's going to be fine," Bogie said. "They patched him up and expect him to be out of the hospital in a couple of days."

"All right!" Fletcher pumped his fist into the air.

"How bad is it?" Bogie gestured toward the smoke pouring up into the sky from on the other side of the stone wall.

"Not as bad as we first thought," Fletcher said. "Two vehicles were torched along with the ground floor of the castle. You can smell the gasoline. A tourist helicopter spotted it and called it in before it spread to take out the mountain."

"Two vehicles?" Bogie asked. "What vehicles?"

Fletcher shrugged. "A sedan and a Mercedes SUV." He frowned. "But it gets weirder."

"Can't be any weirder than what we've already run into," Bogie said.

"What is it, Fletcher?" Mac asked.

"Two DBs," Fletcher said. "Two dead bodies inside the castle."

Bogie looked straight ahead out the windshield. "This is a record. Four murders and one attempted murder in Spencer in less than four hours."

The deputy chief parked the cruiser on the outside of the wall to allow room for the fire engines to get full access to the castle and grounds. Mac was the first one through the gates. The stone walls had protected the structure very well. Unfortunately, it did little to protect the grounds or the two vehicles parked in front of the abandoned fountain. The sedan and SUV were only smoldering shells of what they had been.

"Is that a late model Cruze?" Mac asked Bogie what he already knew.

Fletcher came up behind them. "The fire didn't destroy the plate on the Mercedes. We ran it and it's registered to Gould Enterprises."

"Gould as in Stan Gould?" Mac felt the color draining from his face.

"I don't know."

"Any ID on the victims?" Bogie asked.

"Burnt beyond recognition," Fletcher said. "We're going to need DNA or dental records to ID them."

"What time was the fire spotted?" Mac asked.

Officer Fletcher checked his notes on his table. "It was called in at eight-minutes after eight."

His eyes narrowing in thought, Mac turned to Bogie and Hector. "David was shot around six-thirty. Sue was killed a little after seven o'clock. Hollister was poisoned quarter-til-eight. This fire was started shortly after eight o'clock."

"Our killer is having a busy day," Hector said.

"Let's hope they're done."

Chapter Fifteen

"The last thing that dog needs is caffeine," Mac told Bogie after Gnarly charged up into the front seat of the cruiser. He helped himself to Bogie's leftover coffee before being dragged out and shoved into the back.

Now, on their way to The Wisp to identify what unlucky souls were caught in the fire at Astaire Castle, Mac churned over the events of the past couple of days. After running through the list, he said, "Twenty-four hours ago, I was wrestling with Gnarly in a dumpster in the back parking lot at the hospital."

"I'm afraid to ask why," Bogie said with a chuckle.

"Gnarly decided to go dumpster diving," Mac said. "He jumped up onto the hood of a car, onto the top of a van, and then dove into the dumpster to dig for chicken bones that he's not supposed to have."

Bogie laughed. "Ingenious."

Mac chuckled. "You know, last night, I offered Molly a dog biscuit. She sat there looking at me like I was … I don't know what. She refused to take it. Chelsea told me that I had to say it was okay. Once I told her that it was okay, she took it—nice and politely—almost said thank you."

"Those service dogs are very well-trained," Bogie said. "They have to be and they don't come cheap. They have to get a lot of top-notch training to get certified."

Mac squinted down into his lap before turning around to look at Gnarly, who was chewing on one of his back feet.

"Jealous?" Bogie asked.

"Maybe I'm addicted to the thrill of the unknown," Mac said. "I mean—" He stopped to form the words. "Willingham says that my net worth is now over three hundred million dollars. I could do whatever I want to do. When I was a cop, my fantasy was lying on the beach while reading a good Damian Wagner novel. Yet—"

"Here you are looking for his killer," Bogie said with a laugh. "You have no obligation to be here in this cruiser with me, Mac."

"You'd have to kill me to keep me from being here." Mac smiled back at Gnarly. "I can't help but respect a dog with a mind of his own, and I kind of like not knowing what he's going to do next. I'm addicted to the thrill of not knowing if I'm going to have all my fingers after handing him a biscuit. It's the same type of thrill I get while working a case and finding out who is behind the murders and why."

"That's what makes you a good cop," Bogie said. "To tell you the truth, even if I was retired, I'd still be here in this cruiser. You know I got a son?"

Slowly, Mac shook his head. "I thought you had a daughter and a couple of grand kids—"

"Sophie's by my second wife," Bogie said. "Her and her kids take after Marilyn's side in the looks department. Sophie's got a good man. I lucked out there."

Mac sensed a but coming. "Your son?"

"By my first wife," Bogie said. "We were young. Right out of high school and I went into the Army. By the time I got back from Vietnam, the marriage was over and my son had no idea who I was. The last time I saw Greg ..." He swallowed. "I'm closer to David than I ever was to my son." His fury was rejuvenated. "If I get my hands on whoever took a shot at him—"

"I'm with you, Bogie."

At the Wisp Resort, Mac and Bogie were instantly escorted to a conference room. At Mac's direction, Gnarly sat next to the door with his unblinking eyes aimed at the man who took charge of the meeting.

A tall, slender, dark-haired man, whom Mac recognized as Kyle, who was the one called on to move Stan Gould's entourage from the Spencer Inn to the Wisp, now stood at the position of honor at the head of the table. It wasn't difficult to see that he was in charge among the room of corporate types.

"Mr. Faraday, I believe we met briefly yesterday morning," he said without offering his hand. "I'm Kyle Finch, Stan Gould's chief vice president. I believe we have an issue that you and your people here in the Spencer police department need to take care of."

"Excuse me," Mac said with a broad smile, "but you seem to have the mistaken impression that you're in a position to give me orders."

Kyle flashed an equally wide grin at him. "I apologize if we got off on the wrong foot yesterday. We need your help. We believe something has happened to Stan Gould and his wife."

Mac turned to Bogie for his reaction to the announcement.

"Well," Bogie said, "that's very interesting, because we've found two unidentified bodies and a car that's registered to Gould Enterprises."

Bogie's announcement caused gasps from around the room. Kyle Finch dropped down into his chair.

"How did this happen?" a woman sitting near the head of the table asked. "Were they murdered? How did they die?"

"They said they were unidentified," Kyle told her. "It may not be them."

Mac and Bogie took the time to meet the eye of every executive around the table. Mac saw a new face. She wasn't among the entourage the day before. It was the woman who had gasped upon the news of the two bodies. Of everyone around the table, she was the only one with tears in her eyes at the news. Dressed in a heavy sweater and worn skirt, she did not fit in with the rest of the crowd. Her big round glasses covered much of her small face. Her long dark hair fell in a bushy bob down to her shoulders.

When Mac met her gaze, she dropped her eyes to the note pad in front of her.

"Let's get to work." Bogie broke off the staring contest. "Any thoughts on when Mr. Gould and his bride went to Astaire Castle and why? When was the last time any of you heard from them?"

"No one has seen either since yesterday afternoon," Finch said with impatience in his tone. "Look, we have some very important deals going down that we need him for. That means that if you bunch of idiots don't get your heads out of your butts and find out what happened to him, and who is responsible and pronto; then we all stand to lose a lot of money." He pointed a finger at both Mac and Bogie. "Consider this a warning. If that happens, then your whole police department will get slapped with a lawsuit to cover our losses."

Mac turned in full to Bogie. "In light of the tone of this interview, I believe this case can take a backseat to the other cases that have come in this morning, don't you, Deputy Chief Bogart?"

"I believe so," Bogie said.

"Come along, Gnarly," Mac ordered his dog to fall in behind him on their way out of the conference room.

"Wanna go pick up a donut and some fresh coffee on the way to the station?" Bogie pulled open the door.

The room vibrated with a crash when Kyle Finch slammed his hand flat down onto the table top. "Now that I have your attention, let me tell you idiots something—I can have the governor on the phone in less than a minute. Maybe he can impress on you the seriousness of this situation."

"I doubt it." Mac shrugged. "Oh, when you call him, tell him that I received his invitation to his daughter's wedding. There will be two of us coming. I'll be bringing a date—just haven't had time to RSVP yet."

Finch's eyes met his. Some of his cockiness dissolved.

"I think we need to start over," the woman in the heavy sweater said. "You have to understand, this is very unsettling to all of us." She brought both of her hands to her heavy bosom. "I'm Karin Bond. I was Lacey's assistant. I drove in from New York and only got here this morning. Lacey had texted me last night to remind me to bring her red dress and shoes. She had forgotten them. That text came at nine-thirty last night."

"Do you know where she was when she sent that text?" Mac asked.

Karin shook her head.

"Lacey didn't want any work to interfere with their romantic evening out," Kyle said. "She was adamant and insisted that Stan leave his cell phone and security detail behind."

Mac turned to Karin. "Yet, Lacey sent you a text last night to ask you to bring her a dress?"

Karin's face was blank. "I saved the text if you want to see it."

"I've never had a woman, on a romantic evening out, suddenly stop everything to send out a text about a dress." Mac turned to Bogie. "Have you?"

Bogie shrugged.

"Can we move on?" Kyle interrupted. "When we discovered this morning that they hadn't returned, our security chief, Reese Mobley went into their room. Tell them what you found, Reese."

Reese handed a cell phone encased in an evidence bag to Bogie. "That's Mr. Gould's cell. It has a text message that he received yesterday afternoon about two-thirty. It was from Mac Faraday." He smirked at Mac.

Bogie read the text and frowned before holding the phone for Mac to read: *Changed mind re sale of castle. $15 mil. Transfer funds to my off-shore account by 5 pm EST or no deal. Will send account number. U & Lacey meet me there @ 7 pm to close deal. Come alone. No lawyers. M. Faraday*

"I didn't send that."

"We didn't think so," Reese said. "So I traced the call back to the cell it came from. It's a pre-paid account. No record of whom it belonged to."

"They were set up." Mac snatched the phone from Bogie's hand. "Our killer lured them there to kill them and used my name to do it."

ᨓ ᨔ ᨓ ᨔ

"This suite has already been cleaned," Mac noted with frustration when the hotel manager let them into Stan Gould and Lacey's suite to search for clues to their murders.

To prevent any contamination of possible evidence, Gnarly was put back in Bogie's cruiser. Later, they would discover that not only did Gnarly finish Bogie's coffee, but he had also found the deputy chief's hidden stash of energy bars in the center console. Between the coffee and the energy bars, Gnarly was bouncing off the walls the rest of the day.

The Goulds had rented a penthouse with a mountaintop view. It had two levels, with the master suite on the upper floor. Finch was in an identical suite next door on one side while Karin was in a one-bedroom suite the next floor down. The rest of the employees in Gould's entourage had a whole floor in the hotel across from Spencer Mountain.

"All of our rooms are cleaned by one o'clock, unless the guest specifically requests that they not be," the manager said with pride, "not unlike your Spencer Inn. According to our housekeeping records, the hanger was left on the door giving instructions to clean the room."

"We'll need samples of both of their DNA for positive identification," Bogie told Karin who had followed them in.

"Will their toothbrushes do?" Karin asked.

"Toothbrushes will be excellent," Bogie said.

"I'm sure their overnight bags are still here."

Bogie followed Karin up the stairs to the master suite.

Mac went into the room that acted as a sitting room and office. He had only opened up a laptop he found resting on the desk when he heard Kyle Finch's voice in the penthouse foyer. "Faraday! We need to talk! Now!"

When Mac came into the entrance way, he found Bogie and Karin physically holding Kyle Finch back from coming after him.

"Listen, Finch," Mac said, "what's this about?"

"It's about the over-one-hundred mil that you stole from Gould's account," Finch said. "Like you didn't think I'd do anything about it."

Speechless, Mac could only stare at the vice president. Finally, he realized fully what he was being accused of. "What one hundred mil?"

"Gould's accountant just told me," Finch said. "You probably thought I didn't know about Gould's rainy day account."

"Rainy day account?" Bogie asked.

"Many rich men have off-shore, secret accounts that they keep hidden from the IRS," Mac said in a low voice.

"It was from that account that Gould transferred the fifteen mil to your secret account," Finch said.

"Your chief of security said that text was a phony sent from a burn phone."

"And being a detective, you know all about using burn phones, don't you?" Finch replied. "You know what I think. I think you used a burn phone and your name to make it look like someone was framing you."

"I didn't send Gould that text, and if I had fifteen million deposited into my account, which wasn't my account, I'd know about it," Mac said. "Believe it or not, I don't have a rainy day account."

"Why not?" Bogie asked.

"Don't need one. I've lived through monsoons," Mac said with a wave of his hand. "I've developed the back of a duck. Rain just rolls off me."

"To get back to the hundred mil that you stole off me—"

"You?" Mac grinned. "Now it's not Gould, but you."

Finch grit his teeth. "Gould's accountant transferred fifteen million to someone's off-shore account yesterday afternoon. Then, when he checked on his accounts just now, since we notified him about Gould's murder, he found that at nine-twenty-two last night, someone hacked into that same account and emptied it. Someone stole one hundred and twenty million dollars from me." He jabbed himself in the chest with his thumb.

"IT investigators have to be able to track the transfer," Mac said.

"It went into the same account that you gave Gould yesterday," Finch said.

"I did not send that text to Gould," Mac said, with a flap of his arms. "How many times do I have to tell you?"

"Our forensics people can track those texts to find out the location they were sent from," Bogie said.

"This theft has to be the motive for Gould's murder," Mac said.

"But what does it have to do with Raymond Hollister and David?" Bogie asked.

Mac turned to Kyle Finch, whose face was red with fury. "Did Stan Gould ever have any business dealings with Raymond Hollister?"

Kyle Finch rolled his eyes like an immature teenager. "Who the hell is Raymond Hollister?"

"How about Lacey?" Mac asked Karin, who was already shaking her head.

"Never heard of him."

"They killed them for the money, and they're going to get away with it," Finch said. "Hands-off. Not like some mugging or car-jacking. The guy hacked into the account and emptied it. He may not have even been in the country for all we know. All he had to do was get Gould to open the door to send the first fifteen million, and then he stuck his foot in and took out all the rest."

"Sounds like you know pretty well how to do it," Mac said. "And now that Gould is dead, you're not only sitting on his company, but maybe you got a nice big bonus, too."

"That thief got the money," Finch said. "It's gone and I'm not holding my breath until we track him down to get it back. If he's smart enough to get in to steal the money without even touching him, then why kill Gould?"

"Good question," Bogie said.

"One hundred and twenty million dollars," Mac said. "You know your boss, Finch. Do you seriously think he wouldn't use all of his resources to hunt down the guy who stole all that money to make him pay?"

Bogie agreed. "Dead men don't hunt. We need to contact Gould's accountant to find out exactly what happened and where that money went. We'll get the state police computer forensics people on following that money trail."

"Follow the money and it might take us to Gould's and Lacey's killer," Mac said.

With a wicked smirk, Finch said, "Like you're smart enough to catch him."

Mac's cheeks felt warm. He resisted the urge to punch Finch in his laughing face.

While Bogie was collecting the contact information for Stan Gould's accountant from Kyle Finch, Mac went back to the study to take a look at the laptop he'd found. He was wishing that Archie was with him to examine it. She would know more about what to look for than he did.

Surprisingly, the laptop didn't have a password. When he hit the enter key, the screen opened up to the home page. The image was of Lacey in royal blue satin bra and panties. He opened up the email program to discover Lacey's inbox. While it was downloading her new e-mails, Mac searched through what appeared to be her briefcase. Her cell phone, a sleek black smart phone, was on the side pocket.

Mac checked out what Lacey had on her cell phone. There were several calls made to and received from Kyle Finch. With message after message from Stan Gould's second-in-command, including pictures; the text messages were more telling..

When Mac opened one, he was so stunned that he had to juggle the phone to keep from dropping it. When he managed to regain his grip on the device, he peered at the image with only one eye while holding his breath. *Yep, that's exactly what it looks like.*

"Find anything?" Bogie came into the study.

"You might say I have." Mac held up the phone for Bogie to see for himself.

The screen was filled with a close up of an erect penis. The caller ID read Kyle. The text message: *Thinking of U.*

"Whoa," Bogie breathed.

"Whoa is right."

"Do you ever send texts like that to Archie?"

"Why send her pictures when she can see the real deal anytime she wants?" Mac chuckled. "I think we have more of a motive for Finch killing Stan Gould. But why Lacey?"

"She was going to blow the whistle on him," Bogie said.

"Something else is suspicious about this cell phone," Mac said.

Bogie's eyes narrowed. "Didn't Karin say she got a text from Lacey last night—from her cell phone?"

Mac pressed the buttons on the cell phone until he found the last text sent. "Here it is. Sent at nine-thirty-two last night. What time did Finch say that money was stolen out of Gould's account?"

"Nine-twenty-two," Bogie said.

"Ten minutes before allegedly Lacey sent this text." Mentally, Mac was forming a time line. "The message to Gould and Lacey told them to meet me at the castle at eight. If they got there and were killed at eight o'clock, then what was happening for the hour and twenty-two minutes?"

"Maybe the killer didn't kill them right away," Bogie said. "Maybe he got held up."

"Another thing," Mac shook the phone for Bogie to see. "Lacey sent the text to Karin from this cell phone—"

"How did that cell phone end up back here?" Bogie whipped an evidence bag out of his pocket and held it open for Mac to drop inside. "The killer must have brought it back here."

"And why poison Raymond Hollister and why shoot David?" Mac asked. "What do all of them have in common?"

"We're talking overkill here, Mac," Bogie said. "Shoot David. Strangle a woman who happens to be in the wrong place at the wrong time, just to get access to a man's breakfast to poison him. Whoever did this is a psychopath."

"And we're going to get him before he strikes again."

Chapter Sixteen

"Well, if it isn't the ghost castle owner." Dr. Doris Washington tittered when he came into her medical examiner's office. She rolled away from where she was sitting at her desk in the corner of her examination room and whirled her chair around to face him.

"Okay, I admit it." Mac stepped up to her. "I still don't believe in ghosts, but I am starting to believe a place can be cursed." He cast a glance in the direction of the two charred bodies on two of her examination tables. Two more examination tables contained bodies covered with sheets.

"Taking into account all the things that I've seen people do to each other, I do believe in evil—very much so," Dr. Washington said. "Many scientists make it a point not to believe in God and a divine intelligent maker. But maybe it's because I've seen the result of so much evil come through this office that I understand I can't possibly know everything about our universe and our maker. Explain this: how is it that you found Damian Wagner's body?"

"You know that," Mac said. "The wind in the turret blew the door shut and locked it so that we had to go out the other turret, which is where Damian Wagner's body was hidden."

"Really?" she asked. "I was in that turret. It was air-tight, and that door was extremely heavy. No wind could have blown it shut."

"So you think what?" Mac asked with a crooked grin. "Damian Wagner's ghost closed the door and locked it to force us through the other turret so that we'd find his body and reopen his case? I don't think so."

"Why is that so unbelievable?"

"I've investigated hundreds of murder cases, and I have yet to have a ghost for a witness or a suspect."

It was her turn to smile. "There's always a first time."

"Not this time." Mac stepped over to the examination tables. "Are they Stan Gould and his wife?"

"DNA from the tooth brushes that you picked up at the hotel says they are," she said. "They were shot multiple times with the same gun. The slugs I recovered from the bodies are from the same gun used to shoot David."

"Then they found the slugs from the shooting?" he asked.

She nodded her head. "Both of them."

"That means David's shooting is connected to the Gould murders." Mac moved over to a third gurney. He lifted the sheet to discover that it was Raymond Hollister's body. "And the car the shooter was driving was burnt up at the castle. That car was rented by Raymond Hollister, who was poisoned. Have you been able to identify the poison used?"

"Hemlock," she said. "It was chopped up and sprinkled over his eggs and stirred into his tomato juice. It resembles parsley, which is why he didn't notice it."

"First, David was shot." Mac lifted the sheet over the fourth body and frowned. She was an attractive slender woman with long auburn hair. He saw a bruise across her throat. "Sue was strangled."

Dr. Washington laid her finger on the bruise. "Whatever she was strangled with was thin and left a minute residue in the wound. It could have been a leather strap—like a belt."

"We've found no witnesses," Mac said. "In the parking garage, around shift change, with employees coming and going. Sue was killed in a blind spot in the garage where there were no security cameras."

The medical examiner's eyebrows rose up on her forehead. "Sounds like a professional. Our killer definitely knew what he was doing."

"Cleaning up loose ends from what?" Mac ticked off. "We have a shooting, a strangling, a poisoning, and a double shooting with the bodies set on fire. Why burn up their bodies?"

"The Goulds were killed last night."

"That's what I suspected," Mac said. "But the fire wasn't started until this morning. Why go back to set fire to the bodies? No one goes to the castle. The killer could have been long gone before anyone found the bodies, at which point they would have been decomposed. Why draw attention to them by setting the place on fire?"

"Maybe the killer wasn't in a position to leave," she said. "Job, family, unfinished business—like shooting David and poisoning Hollister."

"Why did the killer target all of them?" Mac asked. "There has to be a connection between David, Hollister, and the Goulds."

"It's your job to find that connection." A slow grin crossed her face, making her look like cat that had just eaten a canary.

"What else do you have to tell me?" he asked her.

"It may or may not mean anything," she said. "But since you brought in Damian Wagner's body, as part of procedure, we compile a DNA profile. At the same time, I went ahead and did a DNA profile on the other victims and discovered . . ."

When she fell silent, Mac asked, "What?"

"Genevieve was not his daughter."

"Whose daughter was she?"

"That's—"

"—for me to figure out," Mac finished while his cell phone buzzed. "I know." He checked the caller ID which read, BOGIE.

"Hey, Mac," Bogie asked, "are you coming back to the station?"

Mac checked the time on the clock over the wall. It was almost five o'clock and he wanted to see David before visiting hours ended at seven. "What have you got?"

"A possible break or a complication," Bogie said. "Hollister's phone logs shows that he called three people yesterday. First call he made on his cell was to his office manager, who happens to be his girlfriend. She called him back two hours later. In the meantime, he called an actors' booking agent. He was on the phone with him a good thirteen minutes. The third call was to a private investigator, after he talked to his girlfriend the second time. He talked to the PI for forty-three minutes. The PI called him back on his cell last night at eleven-thirty, and they talked for another seventeen minutes. I've been trying to get in touch with all of them and just got off the phone with the girlfriend."

"What did she say?" Mac asked.

"Hollister was fixated on locating Damian Wagner's last book."

"That's what he was working on when he was staying at the castle."

"But the book disappeared," Bogie said. "Yesterday, Hollister got a lead on who possibly had it."

"Well, if the book disappeared when Damian Wagner was killed, then it's very possible that his killer had it. Did the girlfriend have a name?"

"Taylor Jones."

"Who's Taylor Jones, and where does she fit into all this?" Mac asked.

"You've got me," Bogie said. "Hollister asked his girlfriend to hunt for Jones on the Internet. That's what she did until she gave up and called him to tell him that she had struck out. After talking to her, he called the PI. I'll want confirmation, but I think we can assume that after the usual route in the Internet, he stepped things up by having the PI dig deeper."

"It'll be interesting to find out what the PI uncovered." Mac went on to ask, "Have you been to the hospital to see David?"

"I stopped in but he was asleep," Bogie said. "Are you going in?"

"I'm going over now," Mac said. "I want to get there before visiting hours are over."

"Give him my best and tell him that we're all praying for him here at the station."

ଓ ஐ ଓ ஐ

Mac could feel exhaustion setting in when he pulled his SUV into the hospital parking lot. Adrenaline had held it at bay during the day, but when he saw the sun setting while he was making his way from Deep Creek Lake to Oakland, he realized that he'd been going nonstop since six o'clock that morning.

Gnarly's head hung where he sat in the passenger seat. With his eyes heavy lidded, he looked like he was about to collapse. The rush from the stolen coffee and energy bars had worn off. The German Shepherd had crashed. Leaving the window open a crack, Mac left the dog in the SUV to catch a nap while he went inside to go up to David's room.

Mac didn't realize that he hadn't eaten all day until the smells of food drifting out of the cafeteria met his nostrils to cause his stomach to churn with hunger. He was tempted to stop in to grab something to eat; but, according to the clock in the hospital corridor, time was short. If he wanted to see David, he had to hurry.

He found two Spencer officers flanking the door. One that Mac knew as Brewster checked the time on his watch. "You've got twenty minutes before visiting hours are over."

"Is Archie in there?" Mac asked.

"She and the other lady went home about ten minutes ago," Brewster said. "They took the dog with them."

The other officer, Zigler said, "That is a nice dog. Beautiful."

"Gorgeous," Brewster agreed with a nod of his head.

"Mild mannered," Zigler said. "You wouldn't have even known she was here. Sat and stayed quiet all afternoon."

"Archie bought us dinner," Brewster said. "These massive subs—stuffed us. Molly didn't even think of begging. And when we offered her a bite, she refused to take it until we told her that it was okay."

Zigler jabbed Brewster in the ribs with his elbow. "Do you remember the time Gnarly held up the pizza delivery truck and refused to let it leave the station until the guy handed over his garlic sticks?"

"Some dogs have bigger personalities than others." Mac stepped forward to go into the room, but the two officers blocked his way. They exchanged wicked grins.

"Is it true that Gnarly was dishonorably discharged from the army?" Zigler asked.

Mac's cheeks felt warm. "Yes," he answered in a low voice.

"What'd he do?" Brewster wanted to know.

"I have no idea. The army says it's classified and gets mad when anyone asks them about Gnarly." Using his hands as a wedge, Mac parted the two men blocking his access to the door and pushed his way into the room.

"I think he stole a general's lunch," Brewster said with a laugh.

When he went around the privacy curtain into the patient area, Mac found David sitting up. He was still wearing the oxygen tube across his face and up his nostrils. His eyes were narrowed to slits, but Mac could see that he was awake and had heard them outside.

Mac moved up next to the bed. "Hey, how are you feeling?" He took David's hand into both of his.

David grasped his fingers. "Like I was cut in half by a train," he said in a hoarse whisper.

"I guess that was kind of what happened," Mac said. "Chelsea just left. She was here all day for you."

A drugged smile crossed David's face. "Yeah … Chelsea."

"Things are going well?"

David took in a deep breath and grimaced. He clutched his side. "I don't know." Painfully, he turned his head to look at Mac. "She told me that she loves me … has always loved me."

"That's good."

"No, it's not," David said. "She lives in Annapolis. I can't get involved with her only to have it turn out like Randi and Yvonne. Not with Chelsea. It'll hurt too much." He let out a pained laugh. "Like anything can hurt more than this." He shook his head. "Can't do it."

"What if it didn't turn out like Randi and Yvonne?" Mac took the seat next to the bed.

David let out a long groan before asking, "Did you catch the guy who did this to me?"

Sitting back, Mac noted the sudden change in subject. "Not yet. Do you remember anything about the shooter?"

David tore his eyes from Mac's face and looked over at the equipment and monitors hooked up to him. "Chelsea told me that someone pulled up on us and started shooting. I managed to shoot out the windows."

"We found the car," Mac said. "It was burned up at Astaire Castle. Raymond Hollister had rented it when he flew in yesterday. Hollister is dead. Poisoned less than an hour after you got shot."

"Same perp?"

"We believe so. Murdered a server at the Inn to get access to his breakfast. We have a woman on a security video wearing the server's clothes and ID. She could be the killer acting alone, or maybe working with someone."

"There was only one person in the car," David said. "What's the connection between me and Hollister?"

"We were hoping you could answer that,"' Mac said. "Does the name Taylor Jones ring a bell?"

David shook his head.

"Maybe you heard the name while you were having that fling with Genevieve Wagner," Mac said. "Hollister had his girlfriend looking for her. He believed she got Damian Wagner's last book somehow."

David uttered a drugged chuckle. "Genie and I didn't talk very much."

☙ ❧ ☙ ❧

After spending the whole day with Chelsea, Archie felt she knew her well enough to tell that Chelsea was a woman with something on her mind. *Why wouldn't she? The man she loved had been shot and almost died.*

Archie had assumed that Chelsea would relax once she found out that David was going to be okay. She did see that she was relieved upon hearing that news. But then, as the day wore on, while sitting next to David's bed, with him slipping in and out of sleep, Archie sensed that anxiety had slipped back in. Driving Chelsea and Molly back to the manor,

Archie's suspicions were confirmed when she saw Chelsea staring straight ahead out the windshield. She was twirling a lock of her platinum hair around her finger.

"Bet you'll sleep good tonight," Archie said. "Now that we know David's going to be okay."

Chelsea continued staring ahead.

Molly sighed in the back seat of the SUV.

"You okay?" Archie reached over to tap her arm.

Startled out of her thoughts, Chelsea jerked and looked over at Archie. She sighed as if reminded where she was and that Archie was a friend. "I'm fine."

"You look worried," Archie said. "Are you thinking about Riley?"

She hesitated before answering. "Yes."

"No, you're not," Archie pressed her foot on the brake pedal to stop at the intersection to wait for the green light to turn right to cross the bridge over to Spencer. "What's wrong? You'll feel better if you talk about it. You've been getting antsier and antsier all afternoon."

Chelsea sighed. "I told David how I feel about him."

Mulling over what that meant, Archie missed the light turning green until the car behind her honked. She turned onto the bridge. "When did you do that?"

"After he was shot," Chelsea said. "Before you and Mac got there."

Why do women always feel compelled to discuss their feelings with their men after they've been shot while they're bleeding out all over the place? Archie fought her curiosity about the timing. Instead she asked, "What did you say?"

"That I've always loved him, and when I came to town and saw him, all of those old feelings came back—" Chelsea let out a moan filled with anguish. "What am I going to do, Archie?"

"One," she said, "David may not even remember that."

"Do you think?" Hope filled Chelsea's voice.

"Two," Archie said, "if he does remember that, don't you think it's better having your feelings out in the open?"

"No," she said in a firm, almost harsh, tone.

"Why not?"

"I can't go through that," Chelsea said. "I won't go through it. I've worked long and hard all these years to become an independent woman—not dependent on some man to make me feel whole. The last thing I need in my life is David, or any man, messing with my head and heart."

In the dark compartment of the SUV, Chelsea couldn't see the soft smile that worked its way to Archie's lips.

"I know what you mean," Archie said. "I don't need any man either." She saw doubt come to Chelsea's eyes. "Really,. I get five thousand dollars a month from a trust that Robin Spencer left me. I make almost double that a year as a freelance editor to some of the biggest authors in the world. I have permission to live at Spencer Manor for as long as I want. I have no need for any man." She giggled. "But when you get a good one, they're mighty nice to have."

"Until they break your heart." Chelsea reached around to pat her sleeping dog on top of the head. "Molly is all the companionship I need."

☙ ❧ ☙ ❧

Nothing looked more comfortable to Mac than his bed. He was unsure which he desired more: the feel of his pillow beneath his head and the feel of the satin comforter caressing his body, or the feel of Archie in his arms.

As tired as he was, he chose the pillow and comforter.

When she saw him come dragging into the bedroom in the master suite at the Spencer Manor, Archie sat up from where she was working with her laptop on what had become her side of the bed. Mac was too tired to notice that she was wearing the top to his pajamas. "Where's Gnarly?"

"Outside, eating some mums?" Mac plopped down on his side of the bed and kicked off his shoes. "I noticed Chelsea and Molly already in their room and the light out."

"They were exhausted, too. We didn't even stop for dinner. Came home and they went straight to bed." Realizing what he had said, she sat up straight. "Gnarly is eating my mums and you let him?"

"Yeah." He dropped straight back on the bed to lie crosswise. His head landed on her legs.

"Why didn't you stop him?"

"Because I don't like mums," he said with his eyes closed. "They offend me and he's very intense about it. So I decided not to waste what little energy I have left trying to save them."

"Molly wouldn't even think of eating my mums," Archie said.

"Of course, she wouldn't. No self-respecting Stepford dog would," he said in comparing Molly, the perfect German shepherd, to the perfect wives of Stepford in the thriller movie *The Stepford Wives.*

Covered in dirt and shredded flowers, Gnarly opened the door, came in, and dropped to the floor. Archie shrieked at his condition when he bellied under the bed.

To her shock, Mac threw his arm across his face and laughed. "That's my dog."

"Since when do these antics amuse you? I think you're jealous."

Mac sat up. "Jealous? Of what?"

"Molly."

"You've lost your mind," he said. "Why would I be jealous of a dog?"

"Because she's perfect and Gnarly's—" Seeing Mac's eyes narrow into a glare that dared her to continue, she shifted gears. "Gnarly is gnarly." With a giggle, she reached over to clasp his hand. "I'm glad you appreciate Gnarly and his special quirks. Did you stop to see David?"

"Yes." Mac rolled over and wrapped his arms around her. "He wasn't much help. He's happy on pain killers."

"You'd be too if you had a bullet go through your stomach," she said. "I hope we catch the guy who did this."

"We will." Nuzzling her neck, he drew in his breath to take in her scent. It was the sweet scent of roses. "They have a woman wearing Sue's uniform and using her ID to gain access to the employee section of the Inn on security video. Assuming she's the killer, we can narrow down the suspect list to fifty-percent of the population. Did you have any luck finding Rafaela Diaz?"

"Struck out," she said. "Three times at bat."

"How?"

Archie cocked her head at him. "I'm not invincible you know. Most people aren't pros at disappearing. However, it is harder to find someone who doesn't want to be found. I found where Rafaela left to go to Brazil. I found the record of her flying to Brazil, but after that, she disappeared off the face of the earth. I even managed to locate the village that she claimed to be from. It's one of those small villages where everyone knows everyone. They haven't heard from Rafaela since October 2002 and according to what they told me, she was planning to visit the family for Christmas that year—but never showed. They didn't know that she was returning in November, which is when Pat and Bogie gave her permission to go home."

"Something very fishy there," Mac said.

"Very fishy," Archie said. "I think someone got her. She wanted to get away because she saw something and didn't tell the police, but the killer wasn't going to take any chances. They tied up this loose end before Rafaela could get away."

"Our killer is very good at tying up loose ends," Mac said. "They're like a pro at it."

"We're talking about the techniques of a professional hit. Now, do we want to add a conspiracy theory to our case?" She reached from where she was balancing the laptop to stroke his face. The stubble on his jaw felt rough against her palm.

He directed his gaze at the laptop. She was on a social media page. "A conspiracy sounds good to me. Have you got one that ties everyone together?"

She explained, "I was doing a background check on Lacey, Stan Gould's lingerie super-model bride—"

"Who was murdered along with him."

"A beautiful super-model," she said. "Maybe she had a deranged fan who didn't want her marrying up. We can't eliminate the possibility that she was the prime victim."

"Good thinking." He squinted his tired eyes to focus on the pictures she had spread across the screen.

She let out a laugh. "Anyway, I found evidence of a conspiracy—or maybe you would want to call it an affair—that Gould's vice president, Kyle Finch, was having with Lacey in the weeks leading up to him introducing her, as a lingerie super-model, to his boss Stan Gould. Yet, the European fashion world never heard of Lacey, the lingerie super-model."

Mac was nodding his head. "That sex-text we found on Lacey's cell phone proves that they had something going on."

"Imagine this," Archie said. "Kyle Finch meets this sexy woman at a resort. She's gorgeous. She's to die for—literally. So he comes up with this scheme to take over the company."

"Lacey was a spy?" Mac asked.

"Totally," Archie said. "Kyle Finch fixed his girlfriend up with the boss in order to get her on the inside. They give her a cover of a super-model in order to enhance Gould's attraction to her. Based on what we know about Gould, he'd be more likely to snatch up the bait of a world famous super-model that men all over the world fantasied about than a sexy nobody."

"You're right there," Mac said. "I noticed how quickly he dropped the line about her being a lingerie super-model. He was like a high school boy trying to impress his buds by having the prettiest girl at the prom."

"Exactly," she said.

"Motive?" he replied.

"Gould Enterprises is planning to go public in the next twelve months," Archie said. "With information that Lacey was collecting from across the pillows, Kyle Finch was maneuvering to take control of the company by acquiring as many shares as possible, in order to squeeze Stan out and become CEO."

"A hundred million dollars can buy a lot of shares," Mac said. "Besides that sex-text we found, did you find any real evidence of an affair that we can use to arrest him?"

"How about pictures?" She clicked on a couple of keys. "Do you know how often you're photographed during the course of a day? I found these pictures on the Internet that she had posted from a vacation the two of them went on for New Year's—months before she was introduced to Stan Gould. They were at a couples resort in Jamaica." She adjusted the laptop for him to see Lacey and Kyle Finch in a sensual embrace on the beach. "I also have records that prove they flew to Jamaica together. They were staying together in the same room at the hotel. Kyle Finch paid for the whole trip with a company credit card."

Mac was scratching behind his ear. "What if Lacey decided she liked being married to a billionaire and threatened to blow Finch's plan out of the water?"

"Then he'd have motive to get rid of both of them," she said. "He was the number two man. With Gould dead, he's now number one. Their murders put him in the driver's seat sooner than he had originally planned."

"Finch was there when I turned Gould down," Mac said. "The text Gould received lured them to the castle by saying I changed my mind. Finch had the knowledge to have sent that text. But then Hollister and David don't fit anywhere in this conspiracy."

"Hey," Archie said, "it's something."

Mac kissed her on the cheek. "And something is better than nothing."

Chapter Seventeen

Deputy Chief Bogie had an uphill battle trying to convince Ben Fleming, the Garrett County prosecutor, that they would be able to get enough evidence to bring in Kyle Finch for the murders of Stan Gould and his wife.

"Lacey's laptop has given us the motherload," Bogie told the prosecutor during a breakfast meeting in his office at the police station. "It's all there in email and pictures and sex-texts between Lacey and Kyle Finch."

"But can you place Finch at the scene of the murders?" Ben asked.

"We have a dozen witnesses who put Kyle Finch at the Wisp," Office Fletcher reported while spilling coffee across his desk during a wrestling match with Gnarly for his donut. "He's alibied out."

Mac grabbed Gnarly by the collar to drag him over to his bed. Out of spite, Gnarly refused to take the bed and jumped up onto the sofa. He shot his long snout up into the air before dropping down.

Mac was aware of Ben's smirk behind his back while he refilled Fletcher's coffee mug. "I went to see David at the hospital this morning on my way in," Ben said. "Met his new lady friend, Chelsea, and her service dog—what's her name?"

"Molly," Bogie said.

"Nice dog," Ben said with a chuckle.

"If you like dogs like that." Mac practically slammed the coffee mug on Fletcher's desk.

Despite seeming to sometimes be on opposing sides, Ben Fleming was one of two lawyers who Mac counted among his friends. Ben was everything that Mac Faraday would expect from a lawyer, based on his encounters with criminal defense lawyers and big city prosecutors. Handsome and charismatic, Ben spent much of his time playing tennis and golf at the Spencer Inn while cutting deals with the other members of Spencer's high society residents. His wife Catherine, an heiress whose fortune came from a dozen different directions, was a leading lady on the Spencer society scene, and a huge fan of Robin Spencer … and Mac Faraday.

While Ben was part of Spencer high-society, he made his quest for justice known to Mac and the police department. Using his political connections, Ben was very good at working behind the scenes to get things done, all the while putting on a front of being a wheeler and dealer.

"The texts and emails prove that Finch was having an affair with Lacey before meeting Stan Gould," Bogie told the prosecutor.

"He had everything to gain by the murders," Mac pointed out. "If Lacey had decided to back out of their scheme to help him become CEO, Finch risked being fired and his reputation ruined. He stood to lose everything."

"Now, with Gould dead," Bogie said, "Finch is the heir apparent. He's gained everything."

"Do any of the emails prove that she had changed her mind?" Ben asked.

"No," Mac groaned.

"Maybe he decided he wanted it all sooner rather than later," Bogie said.

"Finch could very well have sent the text to lure Gould and Lacey to the castle where he had a hired assassin kill them while Finch set up his alibi," Mac said. "He was there when I turned Gould down for the sale. Whoever sent that text to Gould had to be on the scene at the Spencer Inn."

"Finch isn't the type to get his hands dirty." Bogie was nodding his head at Mac's assessment. "So much of what has happened points to a professional hit."

"Or an organized psychopath," Mac said. "I mean, we have yet to come up with the connection to David. He has no connection with Gould or any of that crew."

"The motive for shooting David could be to cut off the head of the dragon," Ben said. "David is your leader. Take out the lead man and, if the killer was lucky, you'd all be chasing your tails looking for the connection back to David."

While they digested that, the lawyer went on. "Finch has the resources for a team of top lawyers—the best of the best—coming to his aid if you try to nail him for these murders. I suggest that before you show your hand, you make sure it's a damn good one." He set down his coffee cup and checked the time on his cell phone. "I've got a meeting with the town council for breakfast. You can bring Finch in to question him, but be nice about it until you have something more."

"I'll be Mr. Congeniality," Mac said.

☙ ❧ ☙ ❧

"Do I look like an idiot to you?" Kyle Finch scoffed when Mac accused him of having an affair with Lacey.

Sitting across the table in the interrogation room, Mac didn't answer. Instead, he thumbed through the case file he had resting in front of him. He saw Kyle eying the folder with a minute hint of fear, which he masked with a heavy dose of arrogance.

"My client has over a dozen witnesses to corroborate that he was at the Wisp the evening and night of the murders," Finch's lawyer said. "He's come in here voluntarily in hopes of finding the real killer of two of his dearest friends."

"And upon their deaths, he inherited a billion dollar company," Mac pointed out.

When his lawyer tried to intervene, Kyle waved him aside. "I'm thirty-two years old and Stan Gould made me his senior VP. All of my friends from MIT, they're still paying off their student loans. Half are still living in their parents' basements. I didn't get where I am today being stupid."

"More like being ruthless," Mac said, "by killing off the competition."

"Lacey was Stan Gould's wife," Kyle said. "That made her untouchable."

"Even if you touched her first?" Mac asked.

The arrogance slipped from Kyle's face.

The lawyer jumped in. "You have no proof—"

"Yes, we do," Mac interjected while holding Kyle Finch's gaze. "There are dozens of pictures across the Internet of the two of them together months before your client introduced her to Stan Gould." He slid picture after picture of Kyle and Lacey in intimate poses across the table for him and his lawyer to see.

"That's impossible," Finch said in a low voice. "When were these pictures taken? I …"

"If he was stupid enough to be sleeping with Stan Gould's wife …"

Mac cut the lawyer off by holding up his finger. "Lacey was a spy. Her identity was a complete fabrication made up by your client."

"That's not true," Finch said.

"Seriously?" Mac chuckled. "A lingerie super-model that no one in the fashion industry has ever heard of? Like you think that cover wouldn't be uncovered during a murder investigation." He paused to observe the questioning expression on Kyle's face. "You met Lacey almost a year ago in Cancun. You hooked up immediately. It was love at first sight for her. At least, that's what she said on her pages on the social media sites."

"Lacey didn't have any social media pages," Kyle said. "She was too busy building her career to have one."

"You mean as your spy?" Mac leaned across the table at him. "You saw how irresistible Lacey was— how every man wanted her. So you decided to use her gift to your advantage. You whispered your sweet plan in her ear. She'd seduce Stan Gould into a relationship—never letting on that she was already in love with you. Once she had Gould under her thumb, she would use her influence to help you gain control of the company."

"You have no proof of any of this," the lawyer said.

"We have the emails," Mac said. "They were all on her laptop and cell phone."

"Emails!" Kyle Finch's face was red. "We never exchanged emails."' He whirled to his lawyer. "They're setting me up." He pointed at Mac. "You can't get away with this. We're going to fight it."

Mac slapped his hand down on the pictures. "Tell me this is not you and Lacey in these pictures dated last year."

"I didn't know she was—" Kyle stopped to rub his face with his hands. "Pages on the Internet? Pictures? Email? She set me up," he muttered while staring at the pictures. "I don't know how she ... she set me up."

"This interview is over." The lawyer grabbed Kyle's arm and pulled him to his feet.

While the lawyer dragged him out, Kyle kept looking over his shoulder at the folder on the table. "The bitch set me up," he murmured over and over again.

Mac continued staring at the pictures scattered across the table where he had set them out to show—and shock—Kyle Finch. They had their desired effect—only not in the way Mac had expected.

"I think you got him," Archie's voice broke through Mac's thoughts. She laid her hands on his shoulders and squeezed.

"Yeah," he murmured.

Archie moved around the table and sat down across from him. "Why the look?"

Bogie came in from where he had been watching in the observation room. "That interview looked good. You certainly rattled him."

"Kyle Finch is not the type to be rattled easily." Mac picked up one of the pictures. "She set him up."

"Why?" Archie asked. "I mean, how could she? Lacey's one of the murder victims."

"If anything, her setting him up gave him additional motive for killing her," Bogie agreed.

"Think about it," Mac said. "Finch is right. He's not stupid." He held up one of the pictures of Kyle Finch and Lacey together for them to see. "No way would he have allowed pictures of the two of them together to end up on the Internet where Gould and the whole world could see. We need to find out who took these pictures and who posted them."

"At places like Cancun," Archie said, "All you have to do is slip some money into a local's pocket and they'll be snapping pictures until you tell them to stop."

""And post them on the Internet?"

"They're Lacey's sites," Archie said. "She posted them."

"Do you know that for sure?" Mac asked.

Archie sat up straight. Her eyes flashed with offense at his suggestion of her being wrong or sloppy about her research.

"I've investigated more than one murder case where someone set up a page on a social media site under someone else's name and identity," Mac said. "It's surprisingly easy … and pretty scary, too." He stacked the pictures back into the case file. "Let's start with finding this Taylor Jones that Raymond Hollister was looking for. Lacey was posing as a lingerie model. Maybe her real name was Taylor Jones. We need to question Karin Bond, Lacey's assistant, to find out what she knows about her boss's life."

"I don't know how much help she'll be," Bogie said. "According to her statement, she's only been working for Lacey for six weeks. She came on to work for her the week before Lacey married Gould."

"That's enough time to have seen or met someone who would have reason to kill Lacey and frame Finch for it."

"Are you saying you don't think they had an affair?" Archie reached for the case file. "But these pictures—"

"I believe he had an affair with Lacey." Mac opened the file. "I even believe he set her up to seduce Gould in order to help him take over the company. What I'm beginning to doubt is that Finch would be so sloppy as to exchange damaging emails that he knows are admissible into evidence with Lacey and allow pictures to be taken of the two of them that could be very easily found."

Bogie nodded his head. "So you're thinking someone else collected all of this evidence of their affair and plan so that they could kill Lacey and Gould, and frame Finch to get away with murder."

"With the motive being to steal a hundred million dollars from Gould's rainy day account," Mac said. "Whoever did this has to have had access to know about Gould's secret account and transfer the funds. Plus, they have to have some motive for getting David and Hollister out of the way."

Tonya buzzed them on the intercom. "Hey, Bogie … Mac, Karin Bond is here to see you two."

"Perfect timing," Mac said in a low voice.

Dressed in a heavy coat and a floppy black hat with her dark hair sticking out in disarray, Karin Bond was huddled on the sofa, clutching her big purse, when Mac led Bogie and Archie into the reception area. Seeing Mac, she stood up. "Mr. Faraday, have you got any news yet about who killed Lacey?"

"We've got some leads," Mac replied. "I'm glad you're here because we were going to call you. Some questions have come up."

With her index finger, she pushed her glasses up on her nose. "What type of questions?"

"Does Lacey have any family?" Bogie asked.

"No," Karin answered quickly. "I didn't know a lot about Lacey. She was really a very private person—she could come across as almost rude and inconsiderate sometimes. It was because she was afraid of people hurting her. She told me that she was an orphan. She grew up on the streets in Germany. She was a thief for a while."

"A thief?" Archie gasped. "She told you that."

"Yes," Karin nodded. "She was only a young girl when gypsies recruited her and taught her to be a pickpocket—"

"Like in *Oliver Twist*." Archie's tone was doubtful.

"Then they found out she had other talents," Karin said. "Lacey was discovered by an agent who she had targeted for a mark. He turned the tables and made her into a star."

"Who no one heard of," Mac said. "Lacey was never a super-model. Her whole background is fake."

In silence, Karin stared at him while they studied her for her reaction. "Maybe. I wouldn't know. To tell you the truth, I didn't care what she was as long as I got paid. I'd been out of work for two years. Lacey hired me to do her clothes and make her appointments and all that crap, and she paid me good. Now she's dead and I'm out of work again. That's why I'm here. I can't afford to stay at the hotel. Gould Enterprises won't pay my bill. I have to go back to New York—today. If I give you my address and phone number, can I go home?"

Mac and Archie looked to Bogie for his reaction. Sympathy came to the deputy chief's eyes. "I'm very sorry that you've ended up in this position."

Fearing that Bogie was about to send the witness on her way, Mac interrupted, "If we could just have another couple of days . . ."

"Are you willing to pay for my room at the Wisp?" Karin's scowl caused her cheeks to push her glasses up on her face.

"No," Mac replied before cutting off her scoff. "But I'll put you up at the Spencer Inn. I'll arrange for a nice suite for you and all of the resort's facilities free of charge—including meals and the spa. Think of it as a nice vacation to help relieve the stress from the traumatic experience you've gone through."

The more he talked, the wider her eyes became.

"Your police department can do that?" she asked.

"*I* can do that," Mac said.

Bogie smiled. "That will solve all of our problems. Thank you, Mac."

"But—" Karin stopped before continuing. "I need to get a job."

"We need to find out who killed your boss," Mac said. "All we need is a few more days."

"And if you aren't any closer after I spend a few days hanging out by your indoor pool . . ."

"You can go home with memories of a great vacation," Mac said.

She gathered up her purse and closed up her coat. She regarded Mac with what appeared to be suspicion. "I can order anything I want off the menu?"

"Anything you want. Everything will be on the house."

"Can I check in today?"

"Your suite will be ready by the time you get up to the inn," Mac assured her.

If anything, she peered at him with even more suspicion. Her eyes narrowed to a glare.

"We do have some more questions about Lacey," Mac asked.

"I do want to help," she said.

"While working for her, did she ever mention or did you ever run across someone by the name of Taylor Jones?"

"No," she replied without hesitation.

"Are you sure of that?" Mac peered closely at her.

"Now that you mention it," she said slowly while tapping her lip with her forefinger, "There was a message that I took the day Lacey left to come here. It was a woman, and she was mad as hell when I told her that Lacey wasn't there. She cussed up a storm and said to tell Lacey that Taylor had called and that she was going to kill the little bitch."

"What was she mad about?" Mac asked.

"I have no idea," she said. "But I remember she gave me the name of Taylor Jones."

"How did Lacey react when you gave her the message?" Mac asked.

"Never gave it to her," Karin said. "She was dead before I could deliver it. Guess Taylor Jones wasn't kidding."

Bogie paused in where he was taking down the information. "Did you get a phone number?"

"No, she didn't leave one." She sighed heavily. "I'd really like to go home. I don't feel safe here. Wasn't your police chief shot yesterday?"

"Yes, he was," Archie said. "But Bogie is the deputy chief and they have the best security up at the Spencer Inn."

"Isn't that the Inn where a man was poisoned yesterday?" she asked.

"That wasn't the fault of the Inn," Mac said. "If you can help us catch this killer …"

"How is your police chief, by the way?" she asked.

"He's going to be fine," Archie said. "We expect that he'll be able to come home tomorrow."

"Then I guess this killer isn't completely infallible," Karin said before turning her attention back to Mac. "Do they have a salon where I can get a massage at the Spencer Inn?"

"You can get anything you want," Mac said.

A smile crossed her face when Karin hurried out of the police station.

"Is that going to be a habit?" Bogie asked Mac. "You putting up witnesses for a vacation at the Spencer Inn?"

"I'm not as nice as you think," Mac said. "Believe it or not, I have my own agenda. At the Inn, security can keep a close eye on her and report back to us. I believe in keeping suspects and witnesses close."

Chapter Eighteen

"Are you sure you should even be up?" Chelsea held onto David's arm to ensure he didn't fall. "It was only yesterday that a bullet went through your gut."

"The nurse ordered me to get up and walk." His legs feeling shaky, David entwined his fingers through hers and clung tightly to her arm while they strolled down the corridor. "The sooner I get up and about, the faster I'll heal."

They formed quite a crowd in the hallway. Molly was on the other side of Chelsea and two uniformed police officers brought up the rear. Pushing an empty wheelchair, Zigler was ready for if his chief overdid it and needed a ride back to his room.

"As long as I have to walk the halls, I might as well go over to the psychiatric wing to visit Riley," David told Chelsea. "Maybe he's remembered something useful."

"I tried to talk to him yesterday and he still didn't recognize me," she said.

"That was yesterday." He stopped at the nurses' station outside the doors that blocked off the psychiatric wing.

The nurse smiled at David while he signed the register. "Riley Adams? The expert from Boston is supposed to be here to see him tomorrow. He's a little more lucid today. He's not as violent either. But we still have him restrained. For your safety, don't loosen the restraints."

"See?" David said to Chelsea. "A lot can happen in one day. They've been adjusting his meds. Eventually, they have to hit on something that'll work." He let out a chuckle. "Look at me if you don't believe what can happen in one day. Less than forty-eight hours ago, I was beating your butt in a foot race."

The nurse gestured at the two uniformed officers. "Are they going in with you, Chief O'Callaghan?"

Leaning on top of the desk, David tried to pretend he wasn't catching his breath. "No." When both the nurse and Chelsea objected, he put out his arm to stop them. "I want to see him alone."

"What?" Chelsea turned to the officers for them to make David change his mind.

"I want to see him by myself," David said. "Man to man. Bud to bud. Maybe it'll be less stressful."

"If he remembers you."

"I was his best friend." David tightened the belt to his bathrobe. "Or maybe he'll think I'm another patient. The last couple of times we tried to see him, I was in my uniform. That could have stressed him out and made him see me as a threat." He shrugged. "Let me try this. I know what's going to happen to him at the psychiatric hospital. He'll be so pumped up on meds that we'll never be able to find out what happened to Damian Wagner. We'll be lucky if he'll ever be able to remember us. He'll be totally gone and right now, he's the only possible witness we have left. If I can get through to him, he might be able to answer the question of why I got shot and Raymond Hollister was killed."

Tears came to her eyes. "When you put it that way, I almost wish he'd been left out in the wild living like an animal.

He was probably happier there." She let out a laugh. "Riley always fantasized about being a werewolf."

"Wolf man," he corrected her with a brush of his finger across her cheek. "There's a difference. I'm going in alone."

Chelsea eyed the two officers.

"We've got your back, Chief," Zigler said. "If you need anything, you holler."

"I can take care of myself." David stepped toward the door.

The nurse buzzed the lock to open the door for him to press on through.

With effort, David refused to let them see him lean against the wall, even though the sutures in his side were screaming in pain. At the door leading into Riley Adams' room, he paused to clutch his side and take in a deep breath. Forcing a smile through the pain, he went in.

A day can make a big difference. In the two days since David had seen him, Riley had his face shaved and his white hair cut up to the bottom of his neck. While it was still long and wavy, it was clean.

The wolf man resembled the man who had been his friend—except for the ties that bound his arms and feet to the bed. He was grotesquely thin. David had noticed it before. Now, as Riley lay in the bed with his arms exposed out of the sleeves of his hospital gown, David was able to see the outline of his bones.

David swallowed the sob of sympathy for how his friend had ended up this way.

Riley turned his head and looked at him. The blank look dissolved as recognition came to his eyes. "David." He cocked his head to the side. His eyes grew wide with bewilderment. "Have they locked you up, too?"

Realizing how it appeared with him standing there in his bathrobe, David grasped the front of his robe and nodded his head. "Yeah, but only for a couple of days, though. I heard you were here and thought I'd stop by to say hey." He hugged Riley. On an impulse, he kissed his neck. He lowered himself into the chair next to the bed. "How are you feeling?"

"Weird," he said in a slow voice. "There are so many things going through my head and I can't make sense of any of them."

"What kind of things?"

"Lots of things." Riley lifted his head and looked at him. "You look older. You must have partied too hardy. You look like hell."

It took a full moment for David to realize Riley was talking about the Halloween party from which he had disappeared. "Thanks a lot," he said with sarcasm.

"Hey, that was some party, huh?"

"Yeah," David said, "Some party. Where'd you go? You weren't there when it broke up."

"I went to answer the call of the wild," he said in a whisper.

"From who? Who was calling you, Riley? Who did you go with?"

"Nigel," Riley whispered.

"Nigel who?" David asked.

"The white wolf," Riley said.

"Do you mean the German shepherd that disappeared when Hindman killed his wife and her tennis pro?"

"His spirit lives in me now. They think I'm crazy, but it's true. You believe me, don't you, David?"

"Sure," he lied. "Where did Nigel take you after you left the party? Have you been living in the castle all these years? What have you been doing?"

"Protecting our territory—the mountain."

"The mountain?" David repeated with a cock of his head.

"It's our job." Riley shrugged his shoulders and nodded his head at the same time. "That's the job of the alpha male, to protect and care for every living thing in his territory—which is Spencer Mountain. Nature only gives that responsibility to the strongest and most dedicated to keeping the balance of nature. When something comes in to disrupt the balance, it is our job to do what has to be done to get rid of it, to protect the others in our territory."

"Seriously?" David tried to comprehend what Riley was saying. "What?" He decided to try a less complicated question. "Were you there when a man, he was a writer—"

"Damian Wagner." Riley almost jumped out of his bed. "He understood Nigel's and my relationship. He didn't think I was crazy."

"You spoke to him?" David fought to keep from jumping out of his chair.

"All the time," Riley said. "He gave me food and wanted to hear all about our story and our legacy—that of wolf and man coming together as one to keep the natural order. He wrote it all down in his book. He dedicated it to me and Nigel."

Unable to form one question when he had so many, David asked, "What?" It came out as a squawk.

"He said it was important to tell our side of the story and give it an ending—or rather a beginning. His book tells the story of how Santos came to be—almost like a prequel—but it is also the ending because that was to be his last book. It's our story—Nigel and mine."

"Damian Wagner told you all that?"

Riley was nodding his head.

"Seriously?"

"Don't you believe me, David?"

David could only gaze back at him.

Riley looked hurt. "I thought out of everyone that you would believe me, David."

"I do," David said. "What about the other people staying with Wagner in the castle?"

"They wouldn't understand," Riley said. "Besides, they were evil. I don't go near evil, unless it is necessary to protect my territory. I tried to once but—" He grasped his hip.

David lifted Riley's hand and moved the blanket aside.

"Evil. I can smell it." Riley sniffed deeply while David examined his hip. "I can smell it now. It's here."

David found a long ugly scar in a straight line. It was a healed over stab wound. "What happened to Damian Wagner, Riley?"

After covering the wound again with the blanket, David realized his eyes had changed. They were no longer calm. As Riley spoke, they widened gradually to take on a wild look. "Canines have a sixth sense. She's evil, David. I never did trust her. I could smell the evil in her. I told Damian that. He didn't believe me until it was too late." He cocked his head all the way to the side, so that his head was almost sideways. "Why does no one believe me, David?"

"Not everyone is very open-minded, Riley."

"I was right," Riley said. "Damian found out that they had betrayed them. So he made sure they didn't get our book. He was going to leave and he said he was going to take me with him because I was his only friend, but she killed him. She killed them all." Tears came to Riley's eyes. "If I was stronger, if I was a better alpha, I would have killed her when I had the chance."

"That would have been murder, Riley," David said. "The right thing would have been to call the police—"

"It wouldn't have been murder," Riley said. "It isn't murder in nature. She's an animal—evil, pure and simple. When the leader of the pack kills an evil animal that's threatening the natural order—it's justice. In nature, justice is swifter and not as complicated as man makes it."

"Who is she, Riley?"

"The shape shifter." He drew in a deep breath. "Can't you smell her?"

"Shape shifter?" David had to hold his breath to keep from telling Riley to pick one horror or paranormal entity and stick to it. "Shape shifter? Are you serious?"

"She killed them all and then transformed into another shape and left." His eyes were wide and red-rimmed. He grasped David's arm tightly. His lips curled up into a snarl. "She's come back."

ଓ ୫ ଓ ୫

"Anyone here looking for a private eye?" Tonya called downstairs to the file room where Mac and Bogie were going over the case files for Damian Wagner's murder. "There's a Danny Foster on the phone. Says he's got information about Raymond Hollister's murder."

"He was on the phone with Hollister for a long time the night before he was killed." Bogie tapped Mac on the arm before hurrying up the stairs to his office.

"Foster used to work for the New York City police department until he retired and got his PI license. He's been running background checks and finding missing people for the last fifteen years or so." Bogie hit the speaker button on the phone. "Hey, Foster, this is Deputy Chief Bogart and I've got Mac Faraday, our homicide detective, here now."

"Hello, Mr. Foster," Mac said into the speaker. "Thank you for calling us back."

"Anything I can do," the deep low tone replied. "Your message told me that Raymond Hollister was killed yesterday. I'm sorry to hear that. I would have called sooner but I was on surveillance for another case."

"Hollister was a suspect in the murder of Damian Wagner," Mac said. "Back when Wagner's daughter and editor were killed in 2002, Hollister was a person of interest. Since

Wagner's body has been found, the case is hot again. Hollister immediately came running back to Deep Creek Lake, even though he was still a person of interest. His girlfriend told us that he thought he had a lead on locating Wagner's last book, and he was looking for a Taylor Jones. Is that why he called you? To locate Ms. Jones?"

"Damian Wagner's last book was always foremost on his mind," Foster said. "He about had a stroke when Wagner disappeared, and no one knew where the book was, or if Wagner had even finished it. He was hoping ideally that you had found the book, because it was legally his with Wagner dead and no heirs, or at the very least that you had found a clue to its whereabouts."

"But we didn't find it," Bogie said.

"Yeah, Hollister told me that," Foster said. "But he did find someone who he thought might know where it is."

"Taylor Jones," Mac said.

"That's who he wanted me to find," Foster said. "He was desperate to find her."

"Who is Taylor Jones?" Mac asked while Bogie dug through the files in the case boxes.

"A ghost," Foster said. "Let me explain. This wasn't the first job I did for Hollister having to do with Damian Wagner. Back in 2001, he hired me to find Damian Wagner's daughter."

"He told us that," Mac recalled Raymond Hollister claiming he had found Genevieve for the author.

"Wagner had really bad writer's block ever since he got out of rehab," Foster said. "So it was either start using and drinking again, or find a way to break through. Hollister thought that if Wagner's daughter, who was now in her early twenties, came back to him that he'd break through and start writing again. So, Hollister hired me to find her."

"And you did," Bogie said.

"No, I didn't."

Bogie and Mac looked at each other. Mac broke the silence. "Excuse me."

"Damian Wagner's daughter was killed in a ferry accident in 1998," Jenkins said. "That's what I reported to Raymond Hollister. He paid me a lot of money to keep my mouth shut. So I did."

"Why didn't you come forward when it hit the news that Damian Wagner's daughter was killed Halloween night in 2002?" Bogie asked.

"I thought that maybe she was adopted or . . ." Foster said, "it wasn't my job."

"Now help us to do our job," Mac said. "Tell us everything you know about this case."

"The other night, Hollister confessed to hiring an actress to pretend to be Wagner's daughter in order to inspire him to write," Foster said. "I tell you, I knew nothing about that at the time Wagner was killed. If I had, I would have come forward. I swear. This actress Hollister had hired—her name was Taylor Jones."

"That's why the DNA showed that the female was no relation to Wagner," Mac whispered to Bogie. "She was a phony."

"Hollister swears it worked," Foster said. "Wagner was working on the book and didn't suspect a thing. Then suddenly, everyone's dead and a bunch of money from Wagner's bank account went missing. Hollister thought at the time that Wagner had drained the account and took off after flipping out and killing the phony daughter and the editor, who must have witnessed the murder. But when Wagner's body was found and it turned out he'd been murdered—Hollister went to Deep Creek Lake to find out what had happened and see if the book was found along with his body. He struck out. But he must have gotten some lead in Deep Creek Lake, because when he called me—it was to find this actress that was playing Genevieve."

"But if she was playing his daughter," Bogie asked, "and everyone thought it was his daughter who was murdered—"

"That's all Hollister told me," Foster said.

"Did you find her?" Mac asked.

"She's a ghost," the investigator said. "The booking agent hasn't seen or heard from her since the murders. There's no record of her anywhere. I struck out completely."

"Do you have a picture?" Mac asked.

"Only the head shot that Hollister had in his records from when he hired her ten years ago."'

Mac said, "That would be a good place to start."

Foster hung up with a promise to email the head shot of Taylor Jones.

Bogie was shaking his head. "What do you think, Mac?"

"The MOs," Mac muttered.

"They're completely different," Bogie said. "Shooting, strangling, poisoning, stabbing and torching."

"On the surface," Mac said. "But look beneath the surface. We have two wealthy men. Damian Wagner—"

"Wagner was broke," Bogie said.

"Seventy thousand dollars disappeared from his account the day of the murders."

Bogie added, "And one hundred million dollars disappeared from Stan Gould's account."

"That's the motive," Mac said. "Theft, plain and simple."

"Not so plain and simple," Bogie said. "Our thief is also a serial killer."

"A cunning and smart serial killer," Mac said, "the worst kind. But I know how she did it. Do you have any pictures of Genevieve Wagner from around the time of the murder?"

"I'll have to look." Bogie stood up from behind his desk.

"Did you record the interviews with Rafaela Diaz?" Mac asked.

"I know we did that."

Mac was taking out his cell phone. "Get pictures of both women and meet me at the hotel. I'm going to Hector's office to look at the security footage."

"Of Hollister's killer?"

"Of Hollister threatening David."

Chapter Nineteen

"What are you hoping to find?" Hector asked Mac while he studied the security tapes. Over Mac's shoulder, Bogie was watching the recording.

"Taylor Jones." Mac scanned through a security video of the lobby. He was fast forwarding through his encounter with Stan Gould and his entourage. "Raymond Hollister told his girlfriend and private investigator that he saw her up here at Deep Creek Lake."

"Who is Taylor Jones?" the security manager asked.

"The actor Raymond Hollister hired to play Genevieve Wagner," Bogie said.

Mac stopped fast forwarding the video at where Stan Gould was making introductions. He slowly turned around to face Bogie and Hector. "David slept with Genevieve Wagner."

"But, according to the PI, she was Taylor Jones, an actress," Bogie said.

Mac turned back to the video. On the recording, from the angle of the security camera in the ceiling, Mac and David stood before Stan Gould and his model wife—Lacey. Mac pointed at the screen. "When Stan Gould was introducing his wife Lacey to David, his first reaction was, 'I know you.'"

Hector recalled, "To which Stan Gould said she was a lingerie super-model and men all over the world lusted for her."

"Suppose that wasn't where David remembered her," Mac said.

"Why wouldn't David have said something?" Bogie asked.

"Because he thought Genevieve Wagner was dead." Mac fast forwarded the recording. "Believing she was dead, the thought that Lacey was Genevieve never even crossed his mind. I would never have considered it."

The cell phone on his hip buzzed. With one hand, Mac answered it. A grin crossed his face. "That's what I thought. Thanks, Doc." He disconnected the call and slapped the phone down on the desk. Bogie and Hector were looking over his shoulder when he pointed once again at the monitor.

In the sitting area, Mac and Raymond Hollister were sitting across from each other while David stood with his back to the lobby area. Raymond Hollister became agitated and stood. "This is where he said that he wasn't going to take the blame for something he hadn't done," Mac recalled. "He said that he had set the wheels in motion for the murders, but he didn't do it."

"You said he threatened David," Bogie said.

"That's what I thought," Mac said. "Yet, when we confronted Hollister after the shooting, he claimed he never threatened David. Suppose he was telling the truth. Suppose during our questioning, at that moment, he saw the real killer and threatened them—the person behind David." He pointed up toward the top of the image to where a woman was standing behind David while facing Raymond Hollister.

"Lacey," Hector said. "She had come back in to use the head."

"But she was shot and killed at the castle with Stan Gould," Bogie argued.

"And her body burnt beyond recognition," Mac said. "That's why the killer set fire to the bodies, just like she did back in 2002 when she killed Damian Wagner and his editor and Rafaela Diaz."

"Wait a minute," Bogie said.

"Just got the news from the doc." Mac held up his cell phone. "The DNA from the woman whose remains were in the fire-pit in 2002 contains markers that indicate she came from a Latino background. All along, you and Pat thought your witness was the housekeeper when in reality, she was the killer." He glared at the security recording of Lacey. "She got away with it once and decided to do it again."

"But DNA proved the body found at the castle with Gould was Lacey," Bogie said.

"Who gave you that toothbrush with what was supposed to be Lacey's DNA?" Mac asked.

"Karin Bond."

Mac asked Hector, "Where's Karin Bond right now?"

Hector shrugged. "I don't know."

"She was supposed to have checked in a little while ago," Mac said. "I called to set up for her to stay in a suite—"

"And for us to watch her as soon as she arrived," Hector said. "But she's never checked in."

"She's on the run." Bogie grabbed his radio.

"Don't worry," Mac said. "I know where she went. She's got one more loose end to tie up."

ଓ ଓ ଓ ଓ

Officer Fletcher looked up from where he was reading a magazine at the door to David's room when Chelsea and Molly came out. "Going home for the evening?"

"They won't let me stay." She frowned before grinning. "But he can come home tomorrow."

"Chief is really lucky," Fletcher smiled into her light blue eyes, "in more ways than one."

"Thank you." She squeezed his hand. "He's got a great team keeping an eye over him. Thank you for taking good care of him." She gestured for Molly to follow her. "Come along, Molly."

With Molly at her side, Chelsea went on down the hall and pressed the button for the elevator.

When the doors opened, Fletcher stood up at attention when a shapely blonde in a nurse's uniform came off.

Chelsea and Molly stepped onto the elevator. Molly uttered a low growl that startled Chelsea. "Molly, behave," she ordered as the doors shut.

The nurse's long thick blonde hair was tied back into a braided ponytail that draped down past her shoulders. The top button of her uniform was undone to expose her abundant bosom. She carried a tray with a paper cup and pill cup on it. As she approached, she flashed Fletcher a broad smile that lit her face all the way up to her big blue eyes framed in thick lashes.

"Well, hello there, handsome," she said in a deep southern accent. "I haven't seen you about these parts."

Flattered, Fletcher stood up tall and stuck his chest out. "I haven't seen you on this floor."

"I've been on vacation." She pointed at her name tag pinned to her bosom. "My name is Grace, but everyone calls me Gracie." She tapped him on the chest. "You can call me anytime."

Like a flustered schoolboy, Fletcher laughed along with her.

"Is this the police chief's room? David O'Callaghan? I have orders to give him a couple of sleeping pills to help him sleep. Nasty business getting shot and all. He's been in a lot of pain. I think that's just awful—trying to kill our officers who go out there every day trying to protect the rest of us."

"Well, those of us on the front lines know it's a dangerous business we've chosen, but someone has to do it." Fletcher opened the door for her. "Go on in ... Gracie."

With a girlish giggle, she slipped on inside. David was sitting up in bed when she came around the curtain. She paused to look at him. A slight smile crossed his face when he looked at her lovely figure.

"Hello, darling. Your doctor gave us orders to give you something to help you sleep." She came up to the bed and set the tray on the bed stand.

"Oh, good." David shifted on the bed. "The pain killers are wearing off."

She looked into his face. "My, you are one good looking piece of beefcake."

A blush came to David's cheeks. "Thank you."

She handed him the cup of pills. "Down the hatch and you'll be out in no time."

David shook the pills out into his palm and tossed them back. He swallowed. She then handed him the cup of water. His eyes met hers while he gulped it down.

A slow chuckle came to her lips. "Good bye, David." She reached for the tray only to have him grab her arms.

Before she could jerk away, he had twisted her around and pinned her crossways down on the bed. "Now it's your turn, Genie," he breathed into her ear while pressing down on top of her.

"No," she laughed loudly, "it's your turn. The cyanide should take affect just about now."

"Do you mean this cyanide?" Pinning her down with his knee against her shoulder blade, David held up his hand and opened his fist. The two pills dropped down onto the bed.

"Oops, I forgot to take my medicine." He yelled toward the door. "Fletcher!"

With a scream, she grabbed the tray from the bed stand and whacked David in side of the head. When he fell back, she rolled out from under him.

When Fletcher came in with his gun drawn, she plowed into him. They both fell to the floor. The gun slid across the floor.

With her blonde wig crooked on her head, she scrambled across the floor for the gun. With a loud, high-pitched laugh of triumph, she clamped her hand onto the weapon, only to have her hand crushed by the weight of a foot slamming down on top of it and pinning it to the floor.

She gazed up the leg and body to Mac Faraday's face. "You should have taken me up on my offer to take a vacation at the Spencer Inn, Karin."

"Book her, Fletcher," Bogie ordered the officer who was already slapping his cuffs on her. "Are you okay?" he asked David who was digging through the covers. The side of his hospital gown was stained red with blood from his torn sutures.

"I have a couple of cyanide tablets for you to take into evidence," David said.

Chelsea came in with Molly on her leash. "I knew I shouldn't have left you alone." She glared at the woman in handcuffs. "Molly told me you were evil. I should have listened."

"I had it covered, Chelsea." David handed the tablets to Bogie. "She never would have made her move with you here."

"That's what you think." Karin laughed when Fletcher removed a switchblade from her pocket. "Within hours, the police would have been looking for Chelsea Adams, David O'Callaghan's scorned girlfriend who killed the chief after catching him having a fling with a nurse."

"You had all your bases covered," Bogie said.

"Not all of them," Chelsea said. "David had you pegged."

"Not always." Her laugh frightened them with its evil tone.

"The wolf man warned me that there was a shape shifter at the castle," David said. "It took me a while to figure it out. Someone wasn't who they were supposed to be and took on someone else's identity. Out of everyone, the only one who would have wanted to kill me would have to have been someone I could identify. That someone had to be Genevieve Wagner because she was the only one I had met."

She licked her lips while looking David up and down. "If anyone had to catch me, I'm glad it was you, David. You always were my favorite. That's why I didn't kill you when I had the chance before."

"Are you talking about the shooting?" Mac asked.

She laughed loudly. "No, back when we were first together." Her laughter became louder and more wicked. "You still don't have it figured out."

"You're a black widow," David said in a low tone.

Chelsea clutched him with both arms.

"Get her out of here," Bogie ordered Fletcher.

"It was a blast, my love," she cackled while the officer struggled to lead her away. "Thanks for the memories!"

"This week, it was Lacey and then Karin Bond." Mac stopped them as they went past him. "Raymond Hollister recognized you at the hotel as Taylor Jones. What's your real name?"

"No one will ever know." She was still laughing when Fletcher led her away.

Chapter Twenty

"You really shouldn't be doing this," Mac told David outside the interrogation room.

Watching David leafing through the reports in the case files, he was beginning to think the police chief didn't hear him when he replied, "It's my job."

"Mac's right." Ben Fleming made his presence known when he came down the hallway with Bogie behind him. "You're too close to the case. Not only did the suspect, whoever she is, try to kill you, but you slept with her."

"A dozen years ago," David said.

"Fresh enough in her mind to make her take a shot at you," Bogie said, "and then try to finish the job."

"She's flat-out admitted to killing almost every man she slept with," Mac said. "You and Kyle Finch are lucky … excuse my pun."

"I don't want you anywhere near her," Ben said in his tone of official capacity. "This woman is a serial killer. We need to nail her to the wall. That won't happen if you go in there to interrogate her, because her defense attorney is going to use your past relationship to their advantage to let her walk."

"Mac has the most experience with suspects like this," Bogie said. "He's been close to the case from the get-go. Let him interrogate her." He gestured down the hallway. "We've got Kyle Finch and his lawyer giving his statement. He's going to be a prosecution witness."

"Do we have a positive ID on her yet?" Ben asked.

Mac, Bogie, and David exchanged glances before Bogie said, "Her prints are nowhere in the system."

"When she was pretending to be Karin, she told us that Lacey had grown up on the streets in Germany," Mac said.

"Lacey never existed," Bogie said. "She was a character this actress created to get close to Finch."

"Was she?" Mac asked. "Was she completely fiction? She told us that Karin Bond had been out of work for two years. That was true. Actors will often use experiences from their past in order to bring realism to their performances. Why Germany? Why didn't she use a more generic country like Europe? She specified Germany."

"You're thinking that since she was that specific, that maybe it could be true," David said. "In which case, there may be a record of her in Interpol."

"I'll have them run her prints through the Interpol database." Bogie was already running down the hallway.

Mac took the case files from David's arms. "In the meantime, I'm going to nail our Jane Doe for murder."

☙ ❧ ☙ ❧

Having seen her in action, Mac was able to practically predict her next move.

He saw that his prediction was right when she was curled up in her chair, looking disheveled and pitiful, while her defense attorney, a maternal grandmotherly type, who Mac had recognized from the public defender's office, patted her hand. He recalled that her name was Marietta Bissette.

Their killer was playing the insanity card.

Having seen her play the role of Lacey, a stunning supermodel, and Karin, a dowdy, chubby assistant, and the shapely blonde nurse named Gracie; Mac was curious about what the real woman would look like.

The publicity still that the private investigator had emailed to him was of a slender young woman with wavy dark hair and green eyes. She was attractive, but there wasn't anything about her that stood out enough to propel her to stardom. She maybe didn't have the looks, but she certainly had the talent to take on various personalities to lure men to her bed, where she could strip them of everything before killing them.

The woman now sitting across from Mac was plain in her appearance. Without the benefit of wigs to change her facade, her real hair turned out to be ash-colored and cropped short. He surmised she wore such a style in order to wear wigs for long periods of time. Her slender figure made her able to pass for a model to some of her marks. At the moment, she couldn't pass for that role in the orange overalls that she had been changed into after her arrest. Her makeup was streaked. She had black blotches under her eyes where the thick mascara she had worn as Grace smeared.

She was a shape-shifter in search of her next shape.

"Ms. Doe …" Mac placed the stack of case files on top of the table.

"First of all," Marietta said, "my client intends to cooperate fully … as best she can."

"Really?"

"I think we can all agree that she's in need of medical attention," the defense attorney said. "She has no memory of anything that has happened. She can't even supply me with her name. It's obvious that she won't be able to assist in her own defense. That being the case, I am planning to plead her not guilty by reason of insanity."

Why am I not surprised? Mac cast a glance across the table.

The corner of the black widow's lip was curled up in a smirk.

Mac glanced over his shoulder at the two-way mirror. He wondered if David and Ben had caught the slip of her smile. "Your client is not insane," Mac said. "She's a cold-blooded serial killer."

"I don't even know why I'm here," she said with a sob.

Mac ignored her response. "Tell us about Karin Bond," he said. "Who is she?"

"The police report says that was the name my client was using here in Deep Creek Lake," the defense attorney said.

"She was using the name and a disguise," Mac said. "We found body padding in her room that she used to make herself appear heavier. She also wore a dark wig."

"I don't understand," the black widow said. "That was my name. … It's foggy, but I have a vague memory."

"How long have you been using that name?" Mac asked her.

"Time is hard for me to judge," she sobbed into her hands. The cuffs dangled on her wrists like dual silver bracelets. "It comes and goes."

"You told us that you'd been out of work for a couple of years when you went to work for Lacey," Mac said. "Where did you work before you lost your job?"

"I was a clerk at a video movie store," she said. "When everyone started using cable television and Internet movies, the shop closed and I ended up out of a job."

"Sounds rough," Mac said.

"I guess the stress and pressure made me lose my mind," she said. "I love movies. All the time I was alone and not working, I liked to escape into the movies and imagine myself as other people."

"Like a black widow?" Mac asked.

"I'm not a black widow." With wide eyes, she whispered, "I don't know what I am—or even who I am." The corners of her lips curled. "Who are you again?"

"As you can see," Marietta said, "my client has developed multiple personalities. Maybe one of her personalities is a killer, but she's not."

"Did I kill someone?" She sobbed. "I couldn't. I never knew what I was doing."

"You have no memory of who you are or what you have done?" Mac asked.

"Exactly," Marietta said. "This is a textbook case of insanity."

"Unless she was fully aware all the time of what she was doing," Mac said, "which can be proven with premeditation and careful planning." He turned back to the black widow. "Tell me about when Lacey died."

"I don't know about that."

"You said she had texted you."

She nodded her head. "I remember her sending me a text. It was nine-thirty the night before I came to Deep Creek Lake to meet her and Mr. Gould," she added with a choked voice, "but they were already dead."

"Where were you when you got that text?"

"At my place in New York," she said. "I live alone. It's a dumpy little basement apartment. Lacey has closets bigger than my place."

"And you were driving down from New York?"

"I left a little bit after she'd texted me to bring her red dress," she said. "So, I remember going to her and Mr. Gould's apartment and getting the dress and leaving."

"Funny," Mac said, "the doorman doesn't remember you picking up the dress that night. He does remember you picking it up the night before."

"The doorman is wrong," Mariette said.

"Could be," Mac said. "But this isn't." He took a sheet of paper out of the top case file. "We do have a record of that text being sent from Lacey's cell phone to Karin Bond's cell phone shortly before nine-thirty on the night of the murders. The Medical Examiner puts the time of death between eight and ten o'clock. So that's within the kill zone."

"And my client was in New York at the time Lacey sent her that text," Marietta said. "So she couldn't have committed those murders."

"Except," Mac pointed at the report, "the cell tower is on the very next mountain across from Spencer Mountain. When that text was sent, it bounced off the tower and went right back to Spencer Mountain. That means Karin's cell phone was in the same vicinity as Lacey's."

He caught the black widow's eye. "You sent that text from Lacey's cell phone to Karin's to make it seem as if you were in New York."

Marietta was still studying the report when Mac placed a copy of a receipt on top of it. "Gas receipt from Karin Bond's credit card. She filled up her gas tank in La Vale, Maryland, forty-one miles away from Spencer, at five-thirty. That puts her in the vicinity at the time of the murder. Not only that, but she also filled up a five-gallon gas container." Mac leveled his gaze on the woman across the table. "I have no doubt about that gasoline being used to set the fire at the castle, which points to premeditation."

"Why would I kill Lacey and then set her on fire?" the black widow said with tear-filled eyes.

Mac laced his fingers together and placed his hands on the table "Because you're a cold-blooded murderer. You killed Stan Gould for his money, Lacey. As his wife, he trusted you enough to tell you about his rainy day account. You got all the access codes you needed to make the transfer via your smart phone to your offshore account, where you have been stashing the spoils from your murders."

Mac told the stunned defense attorney. "We got a warrant to go through your client's belongings and found the smart phone with records of her accounts that show the transfers. Not only did we find over one hundred million dollars stolen from Stan Gould's account, but money from what appears to be several other victims."

He turned back to the black widow. "After killing Gould, you killed Karin Bond to cover your tracks. Unfortunately for you, fortunately for us, you made several mistakes. You're not as smart as you think you are."

"She killed … how many—" Marietta began to ask before her client interrupted with her loud insane laughter.

"You have no proof that I killed Karin Bond. The DNA report says that body was Lacey."

"Did," Mac said. "Doesn't anymore." He grinned. "You only think you're smart. You gave us Karin's toothbrush and claimed it was Lacey's. When the DNA was a match, the ID on the body was determined to be Stan Gould's new wife." He held up a finger. "But you forgot something."

He had her interest. Her eyes narrowed. "What?"

"Karin Bond has been unemployed for the last two years. She was desperate for a job. We contacted the employment agency she went through and found that she has put in numerous applications—many to employers who require a drug test as part of the hiring process." He leaned toward her and Marietta. "She peed in a cup a dozen times, and each one of those places keep samples of it—which means Karin's DNA is all over the place. One of those places sent the urine sample to the ME and—" He placed the report in front of them. "It's a match. Karin Bond is the woman whose body was found at the castle with Stan Gould." He pointed at her. "You ordered Karin Bond to meet the two of you at the castle after eight o'clock and to bring a five-gallon can with gasoline. Then, you killed both Stan Gould and Karin. You then went on your murder spree—tried to kill the police chief because he saw that you looked familiar and you couldn't take a chance on him remembering you after killing in his jurisdiction. After that, you strangled a server at the Spencer Inn to gain access to Raymond Hollister's breakfast in order to poison him because he did recognize you as Taylor Jones. Then, you went back to the castle to burn up the bodies to cover up that you had taken Karin's identity. You dropped off the cell phone you used as Lacey in order to further prove Finch's affair with her as motive for him killing Lacey and Gould."

Marietta was searching for her voice when the black widow laughed. "That's quite a story."

"It's the truth," Mac said. "You're a cold blooded black widow—a serial killer, but you're not as smart as you think you are."

"That's what you think," she said with a grin. "Okay, I confess," with a sweep of her arms, she announced, "to everything."

"My client is insane," Marietta said in a choked voice.

"No, I'm not," she said. "Go ahead. Lock me up. You'll see. I guarantee you, as smart as I am, no prison has ever been able to hold me—and never will be." She cackled while looking at him. "When I break out, I'll come visit you, Mac Faraday. Have you ever danced with a black widow?"

The confession had an abrupt ending when there was a hard knock on the door. Bogie and David were waiting in the hallway with Ben.

"What's going on?" Mac asked. "I'm getting a confession."

"Those prints I ran through Interpol's database," Bogie said, "sent up all sorts of red flags."

Mac dared him. "Don't tell me she's an undercover agent."

"No, she's an international serial killer," Bogie said. "Feds are on their way. Italy has already tried to claim her."

"We get her first," David said.

"From what little bit I got from the feds," Bogie said, "this black widow, who no one knows, has been convicted of murder both in Italy and Spain. They think her country of origin is Germany. She hooks up with wealthy men, gains access to their bank accounts, kills them, drains their accounts dry, and then escapes using a new identity right under the cop's noses. The two times she didn't get away with it, she went to jail and escaped. In Spain, she walked out dressed up as a male guard. In Italy, she killed another inmate who was due for release and walked out using her identity."

Bogie leveled his gaze on Mac. "In Italy, after she escaped, she hunted down the detective who had captured her, and castrated him before slashing his throat."

Mac felt the blood draining from his face while Bogie, Ben, and David shot involuntary glances down at his crotch.

Ben's voice was sharp. "David—"

"I'm calling in all of our officers," David's voice was sharper. "We're going to keep this woman locked down so tight she'll never see the light of day again."

Chapter Twenty-One

They had been so busy investigating murders that they'd failed to notice the date. It was Halloween night and there was a full moon. Luckily, Archie had bought candy the week before and hidden it from Mac and Gnarly. All she had to do was take it out, dump it into a dish, and keep the bowl up high out of Gnarly's reach.

With a small year-round population on Deep Creek Lake, the goblins ringing the doorbell were few and far between—which was good for Mac and Gnarly, who eyed the left-over candy for themselves.

Molly had loosened up enough to take Gnarly's love seat, which he freely offered to her. He stretched out on the floor in front of it. With the candy bowl in the room, Gnarly was torn between what to be more focused on, the beautiful white German shepherd or the red licorice on the mantle.

"Are you going to tell Archie?" David had rushed into the kitchen and bent over to whisper into Mac's ear while he was loading the dishwasher after they had eaten dinner.

After the feds had arrived at the Spencer police station, you could have cut the silence with a knife in Mac's SUV on the drive home. Considering the black widow's history, David was nervous about her being held in the tiny police station's holding cells. But that was where she was until she could be arraigned on murder charges the next day, and moved to the county jail.

While they had filled in Archie and Chelsea about the case during dinner, Mac had neglected to mention the threat the serial killer had made toward him, which prompted David's rush to ask him at the first opportunity.

Loading the dishwasher, Mac was so startled that he stabbed his hand on the point of a knife and almost broke a plate. "Can't you warn someone before sneaking up on them?" he hissed while tearing off a paper towel to wipe the blood from his hand.

"Then it wouldn't be sneaking," David said. "I noticed that you didn't tell Archie about the threat this woman made toward you."

"Because all she'd do is worry," Mac said. "No, I am not going to tell her, and neither are you."

"You can't tell me what to do."

"How many perps have you arrested who threatened to come back and kill you when they got out?" When David didn't answer, Mac slid the dish tray into the dishwasher and slammed the door shut. "That's why I'm not going to tell her. If I tell her about every threat that has been made against me, she'd never sleep at night."

"I think the fact that this woman has managed to escape big prisons in foreign countries proves that this is a viable threat."

"I disagree," Mac said. "I'm not worried, and I don't want her to be worried." He pressed his finger against David's chest with each word when he ordered, "Don't say a word."

"Don't say a word about what?" Archie asked when she and Chelsea came in with Gnarly and Molly on their heels.

"You two have been in here for quite a while. What's going on?"

"The black widow says she's going to escape and when she does, she'd going to hunt Mac down and slit his throat after castrating him," David said, before turning his attention to Mac. "You're not the boss of me."

When Archie found her voice, it was much higher than normal. "And you weren't going to tell me?"

David grabbed Chelsea's hand. "Hey, Chelsea, have I shown you the grandfather's clock. It's been shot out twice and it still keeps ticking. Amazing!" He pulled her out of the kitchen to leave Archie glaring at Mac.

By her side, even Gnarly was cocking his head at Mac with a glare in his eyes.

"I can explain," Mac said.

ଓ ஐ ଓ ஐ

In spite of his best efforts, David was unable to hide how worn out he was from the shooting. After dinner, he collapsed onto the sofa. He still had many days of recovery ahead, and was fighting the need for pain killers. He preferred to numb the pain this evening with a smooth cognac.

In preparation for a relaxing evening, Archie poured a glass of wine, which she and Mac sipped between serving treats to the trick-or-treaters.

"Damian Wagner was the first victim she didn't sleep with." After serving Chelsea a cup of hot herbal tea, Mac reported the details they had learned from the killer's confession. "He flipped out when he found out that she wasn't his daughter. To protect the scam that she and Hollister were working, she killed him. That murder wasn't planned. However, after that—"

"She already knew the taste of blood." With her glass of white wine in hand, Archie sat down on the floor at Mac's feet and stroked Gnarly's ears. Gazing with adoration up at Molly on his loveseat, Gnarly rested his head on his mistress's shoulder.

"Killing comes easy to her," Mac said with a nod of his head. "Of course, the editor would have noticed that Wagner wasn't around and start to suspect something. She seduced him, for the fun of it—then she poisoned him with poison slipped into a glass of wine. She already had her plan for escape in place. She took on the role of Rafaela Diaz. She put on a costume of Rafaela, including fake tattoos—"

"Riley must have seen that," David said. "In his insane mind, she was shape-shifting."

"He tried to intervene when she killed Rafaela," Mac said. "She told us that in her statement. She stabbed him and he backed off and ran. As the housekeeper, she told the police it was the wolf man."

"The shape-shifter points the finger at the wolf man," Chelsea noted.

"She's not a true black widow," Archie said. "She didn't kill Kyle Finch."

"Due to his own greed, he managed to escape," Mac said. "She was planning to kill Finch. That was when she established the Lacey identity and posted those sites. She was planning to frame an old girlfriend of his, who he had dumped for her in Cancun. But then, Kyle suggested they target Stan Gould. He didn't know murder was on her agenda."

"He thought she was only helping him to take over the company," David said. "He had no idea what a monster he had set lose on his boss."

"What's going to happen to Finch?" Archie asked.

"He knows he escaped a bullet," David said. "He's cooperating with us to keep her—whatever her name is—behind bars."

"While what he did was unethical," Chelsea said, "Finch did nothing illegal. However, word has spread throughout the business world about what he did. Big business is very much like a small town. Those loyal to Gould will black ball him and refuse to do business with him. No one will trust him. He'll have a very hard time building up the respect Gould had."

"Do you know yet how many people this black widow has killed throughout the years?" Archie asked.

Mac shrugged. "Over a dozen—at least. It's going to be hard since we don't know her real identity. Fleming is going to be prosecuting a Jane Doe. The FBI is trying to connect her to murder cases in the United States. Interpol is checking other countries. Not only would she kill the wealthy men, but she would kill whoever she had to in order take on their identity or to shift the suspicion elsewhere."

"Collateral damage," Archie said.

Mac looked down into the cognac in his snifter. "She's so damn smart and evil. It's a fatal combination. I can see the evil seeping out of her pores."

"You can smell it." David recalled Riley's assertion.

"As smart as she is," Archie said, "I know the killer always comes back to the scene of the crime, but why did she choose to come back here? Was it Gould's idea?"

"No, it was hers," Mac said. "She actually laughed when she admitted to it. All of these murders were a big game to her. Astaire Castle was where she got her start as a killer. To her, it would have been the crowning jewel to commit the same murder, in the same town, and get away with it once more."

"She didn't count on running into Hollister and me," David said.

Chelsea turned to him. "Did you recognize her as a woman you had slept with when you first met her as Lacey?"

"I recognize every woman I've ever been with," David said. "I remember every nuance, every curve, every scent."

Chelsea was doubtful. "So you knew instantly that she was Genevieve when she was introduced to you as Lacey?"

"Careful, David," Mac warned.

Archie jumped to his defense by changing the subject. "What's going to happen to Riley?"

"He's being moved to the psychiatric hospital tomorrow," Chelsea said. "An expert from Boston will meet him there to analyze him. The psychiatric community is very excited about him. He's going to need intense treatment for a very long time. He's convinced he's a werewolf."

"Wolf man or werewolf?" Mac asked while adding in a firm tone. "There's a difference."

"I know," Chelsea sighed. She grasped David's hand. "If he's happy living in the wild like a wolf, is there really anything wrong with that, as long as he's not hurting himself or anyone?"

"The guy thinks he's a wolf," Mac said.

"Damian Wagner believed he was a wolf man," David said.

"Really, David?" Mac asked. "Do you believe in werewolves and wolf men?"

"I believe there's a lot that we humans don't, and can't, and maybe aren't meant to understand," David said.

"Next thing you're going to tell me is that this black widow is really a shape-shifter," Mac laughed. "We found the body suit that she wore under her clothes to make her appear chubby when she turned into Karin Bond. She had extensive makeup and wigs that she wore to change her appearance. We also found the leather belt she used to strangle Sue, the server at the Inn. Riley has a mental illness that makes him believe he's a wolf or dog or a spirit dog. Those cold spots in the castle were due to drafts. Everything can be explained."

"And the crime rate spikes during full moons," David said, "like tonight."

Mac's eyes narrowed to blue slits. The two men weighed each other's beliefs before Mac gave in with a shake of his finger. "I think this is one area where we're going to have to agree to disagree."

"I think so." With effort, David moved to rise to his feet. He allowed Chelsea to drape her arm around his waist to help him up. "I'm tired. I'm going to the cottage to go to bed."

"Be careful of any werewolves," Mac called to them with a laugh, opening the door to serve yet another band of goblins.

When David opened the deck doors, Gnarly and Molly raced out into the darkness. They let the two dogs frolic in the garden among the downed leaves blowing in the frigid night wind.

"I'm not an invalid," David objected when Chelsea raced ahead to open the door of the cottage for him.

"You always have to put on such a brave face." After he went inside, she called out into the darkness. "Molly! Come!" Molly ran in with Gnarly right behind her. "Does he belong here?"

"Gnarly belongs wherever he wants to belong." David reached inside his fridge for a bottle of beer. "I'd offer you a beer but you don't drink."

"Alcohol is a bad combo with my medication," she said. "Do you need anything? I'll help you get ready for bed."

"I'm fine," he said. "I'm going to take this beer to bed."

Beyond David, Chelsea saw that Gnarly was raiding the basket in the corner of the cabin's great room. It was filled with dog toys. From the basket, the dog selected a rubber chicken that had a squeak toy inside and jumped up onto the sofa to enjoy it.

The bedroom was in a loft on the far side of the cabin with the kitchen underneath. The big windows in the cottage provided a tree top view of the lake from David's queen-sized bed at the top of the circular stairs leading up to the loft.

Chelsea called to Gnarly and Molly to come with her. While Molly obeyed, Gnarly refused. Totally enthralled with shaking the chicken by its neck until it snapped, the German shepherd shook it viciously. Frustrated by the chicken's refusal to die, he continued attacking the toy. Lying on the floor in front of the sofa, Molly watched him with unblinking eyes. It was doubtful she had ever seen such an attack on a toy before.

"Stay for a drink," David said. "I have flavored bottle water." He reached into the fridge. "Hey, I have strawberries. Where did those come from?"

"I love strawberries," she said.

"I remember that." Chuckling, he took out the bowl. "I have a feeling Archie is playing matchmaker. Well, we can't let them go to waste. I can melt some chocolate for you to dip them in."

"You sit down and I'll melt the chocolate," she ordered.

On her way to the kitchen, Chelsea paused to pat Gnarly on the head, which interrupted his attack on the rubber chicken that refused to die. Gnarly uttered a low growl with his jaws clamped down on the chicken's neck. "I think that chicken is winning," she told Gnarly.

Enraged, Gnarly shook the rubber chicken so hard that the force of his attack whirled the dog around in a complete circle before he plopped down onto the sofa with the chicken still in his mouth. A squeak from the chicken revealed that even that had failed in killing the prey. Intrigued, Molly inched in closer. She sniffed the two of them to learn more about this game. Gnarly rose up to offer the chicken's head to her. Hesitant at first, she decided to dive in and grabbed it. A game of tug-of-war ensued.

David had poured his beer into a frosted mug and her water into a wine glass and set them on the table in the dining area. He took out a bowl for the strawberries while she got a pan to put the chocolate in.

Chelsea's girlish shriek made him almost drop the bowl of strawberries. When he turned to see the cause, she rushed around him to jump up onto the table. She wielded a can of whipped cream. "Look at what I found in your fridge. If this doesn't bring back memories."

David laughed. "Remember the first time we made love? It all started with a can of whipped cream just like this." He took the can, shook it, and poured some onto her finger. He then took her hand and brought it up to his mouth.

His eyes locked on hers while he slowly stuck her finger into his mouth and licked it off. In the moment, it was clear that, as it had when they were teenagers in love, it would start with a lick of her finger and end up with so much more.

This time was different.

Instead of teenagers who could not see beyond the moment, they were grown-ups who had pasts to learn from and futures to think about.

Chelsea's face grew even paler. "I'm sorry … I should go." She moved to get around David, only to have him block her path and back her up to the table where he fenced her in with his arms on either side of her.

His breath feathered her face. "I want so much for us to go back to the way it was before. You have no idea how much I regret the way I hurt you."

"I forgave you, David," she said. "You know I love you. Damn it! I wish I didn't, but I do."

David swallowed. "You wish you didn't?"

"I am so sorry that I told you how I feel about you," she said. "The only reason I told you how I felt was because I thought you were dying. But you didn't die and now you probably think that we stand a chance of getting back together, but we don't. By telling you how I feel, all I did was complicate things." She sighed. "Actually, I take that back.

I didn't complicate things by telling you how I felt when I thought you were dying. You complicated them by not dying."

"I'm sorry my surviving complicated things."

She giggled. Her eyes met his eyes. He was smiling down at her.

"I do love you, Chelsea."

Her eyebrows furrowed. She cocked her head at him. "You're not mad?"

He shook his head.

"You understand?"

"Payback is hell, but I understand."

"It's not payback." She brushed his cheek with her fingers. "I love you, David."

"I know." He rested his forehead against hers.

She felt his hot breath feather her face as he leaned over to bring his lips close to her cheek. His lips brushed across her cheek back to her ear. Anticipating his lips kissing her ear or better yet, nipping at it the way he used to, she waited.

"I'm going to bed," he whispered with a hoarse voice into her ear.

Stunned, she remained still while he stood up, picked up his bottle of beer and climbed the staircase up to the loft.

Two yelps, followed by loud barking interrupted her thoughts when Molly charged past her. With the chicken in her mouth, Molly was pulling Gnarly behind her by her tail. She whipped around to send Gnarly, who lost his grip on her tail, sliding spread-eagle across the floor to knock over a bookcase that landed on top of him. Victorious in capturing the rubber chicken, Molly leapt over the coffee table and landed on the sofa, which collapsed under her weight.

"Don't forget to lock the door on your way out, Chelsea," David called down from the loft before turning off the light.

Chapter Twenty-Two

It was in moments like this, holding Archie tightly in his arms, Mac felt as if his love for her was going to burst out of his chest. He wondered if she could sense his giddiness when he gazed down at her. She had the dewy look of an angel, especially with her blonde hair and emerald green eyes. "I love you." He kissed her on the forehead.

"I love you, too." She smiled up at him before burying her face into his neck.

He sighed. "Do you want to get married?"

"You already asked me that and I said yes," she replied.

"Then I guess we need to set a date," he said with a tired sigh.

"Tell me the date and the time and I'll be there in my white dress."

"You got the dress already?"

"I'll buy the dress when you get me the ring." She waved her ring-less fingers in his face.

"That's right. I need to get you a ring. Don't let me forget to do that."

She pulled back and leveled her gaze on his eyes. "I have a feeling David and Chelsea are going to get married before you and I do."

"I doubt it." Mac rolled over to lie down next to her. "She's going to go back to Annapolis to her job as a paralegal as soon as Riley is set up at the psychiatric hospital."

"No, I think Chelsea is different," she said with a shake of her head. "She pretends she doesn't want him, but she does. She's going to stay. She won't admit it's for David. She'll use Riley as an excuse."

"I think David needs to slow down when it comes to his love life," Mac said. "I mean—really? A black widow? The guy actually slept with a black widow serial killer ... at least he lived to tell about it."

Without warning, Archie sat up. "The book!"

Mac sat up next to her. "What book?"

"Damian Wagner's last book," Archie said. "Certainly the black widow didn't steal it. She took the money out of his account. Where is Damian Wagner's last book?"

"I wonder if Riley took it," he asked. "He told David that he and Damian Wagner had worked on it together."

"Do you really think Damian Wagner would have left something that important with Riley?"

"Let me think about it." He pulled her back down and wrapped his arms around her. "We'll find the answer."

She turned off the lights and they settled down to sleep, only to have the phone ring next to the bed. As hard as they tried to not be jumpy, they both sat up. Mac grabbed the phone. When he read the Caller ID and it read BOGIE, he felt his heart jump up into his throat.

"No," Archie gasped while clinging to his arm.

"Bogie ..." It came out as a gasp.

"Mac, you and David need to get down here to the station."

"Don't tell me she escaped," Mac said through clenched teeth.

"No, not that bad," Bogie said. "I tried to call David but he's still on sick leave and his phone is off. Bring him with you."

Mac hung up the phone. When he moved to climb out of bed, Archie was clinging to his arm with both hands. "You're not going anywhere without me."

"I suppose you're going to bring your pink handgun with you." Mac jerked loose from her grasp and reached for his bathrobe.

"Believe it or not, I have a personal stake in you not getting castrated."

☙ ❧ ☙ ❧

It was a full load riding to the police station at one-thirty in the morning. Neither Chelsea nor Archie would allow the men to leave without them. Molly had to go with Chelsea and Gnarly would not be left alone without Molly. So they all piled into Mac's SUV with Gnarly and Molly in the back compartment.

They arrived at the police station to find it crawling with police, both local, state, and the FBI, who had arrived before Mac and David had left. Bogie met them in the reception area.

"If she hasn't escaped," Mac asked, "then what is this about?"

Bogie said, "She's dead."

Archie sighed with relief.

"Suicide?" Mac asked before shaking his head. "This woman was too much of a narcissist to have killed herself."

"Nope." Bogie shook his head.

"Are you sure it's her?" Mac asked.

"One of my people would not have killed her." David looked at the federal agents milling about with suspicion.

"It's definitely her and it's no suicide." Bogie led them through the barred doors and down a short hallway that led back to the holding cells. When they came to the last cell they found a blood covered holding cell. She was sprawled across the floor with blood splatters all over the walls and floor.

Kneeling next to her, Dr. Washington's eyes were wide while she stared at the gaping hole in the dead woman's throat and the wide-eyed look of horror in her lifeless eyes.

"What did this?" Chelsea grasped David's hand.

"To me," the doctor said, "it looks like she was attacked by an animal. These are definitely bite marks on the neck. Her jugular vein was bitten clear through and it looks like her neck was snapped."

"An animal? That can't be," Mac said.

"David," Bogie said, "you saw when you left. We had people all over this place. We had people inside the station and out. Fed and police."

"I know, Bogie," David said.

"She was asleep in her cell," Bogie said. "At twelve-thirty, the guard came out to take a break. Minutes later, we hear growling and screaming. We all came running back. Thinking it was a trap, I called on the radio for the guards outside to stay put. We came in and found her like this. The guards outside said they heard someone—or something—running into the woods."

"Did they see anything?" David asked.

"Yeah." Bogie led them back out of the cells and into the security room. "We got it recorded."

Officer Fletcher was sitting at the monitor. "Are you ready to see this?"

"Show them," Bogie said.

While David, Mac, Archie, and Chelsea crowded around the monitor, Officer Fletcher brought up the recording of the police station's darkened parking lot. The time read three minutes after one o'clock. From the direction of the station's back door, a white mist moved across the lot in the direction of the woods. Upon reaching the woods, it dissolved.

"What is that?" Mac asked.

"White shape," David said.

"Ghost?" Archie said.

"No," Mac said.

"Ghost dog?" David murmured.

"She was killed between twelve-thirty and one o'clock," Bogie said. "The hospital called after we found her. Riley Adams is missing."

"He was tied down," Chelsea yelled.

"I guess those restraints don't do much good against mists," Bogie said. "According to their security video, a few minutes after midnight, they have two shots from different angles of a white mist blowing down the hall and exiting through the front door of the hospital."

"You know," Archie stared at the paused image of the mist. "When you look at it, you can see the tail. It could be a ghost dog."

"Do you really believe Riley changed into a ghost dog named Nigel?" Mac asked her.

Her hands on her hips, Archie glared at him. "Do you have any other explanation for why security cameras at two different locations have recordings of a white mist that appears at the same time that a wolf man, claiming to have been taken over by the spirit of a ghost dog—" She held up her finger in an order to let her finish. "—a friendly ghost dog named Nigel goes missing?"

Mac turned to Bogie for help in the argument.

"I've got nothing," Bogie said.

"Why come here to break into the police station to kill the black widow?" Chelsea asked.

"He didn't break anything," Bogie said. "From the looks of it, he dissolved right through the walls."

"Why kill the black widow?" Archie repeated the question.

"In nature," David said, "justice is swifter and less complicated than man has made it."

"She could escape justice in man's world," Bogie said, "but not in nature—not where Nigel is the alpha male."

"A ghost dog disappearing into thin air at the same time that a man claiming to have become one with the spirit of that ghost dog disappears from the hospital," David said to Mac who was gazing at the recording of the white mist disappearing into thin air outside the police station. "We're all waiting to hear your reasonable explanation for that, Mac."

Before Mac could answer, in the reception area of the police station, Molly and Gnarly turned toward the mountain and howled up toward Astaire Castle.

Epilogue

Back home, Mac's sleep was not restful. Yes, the black widow was dead. No, he did not have to worry about her hunting him down to slit his throat after castrating him. Still, sleep was evasive as the voices inside his head rattled while he drifted from sleep to an awakened state:

The first voice belonged to Archie: *There's a missing book that the writer is hiding …*

Jeff Ingles interrupted, *Robin told me that he had told her that his book was done. …*

Someone stole the desk. … Mac said to which Hector replied, *The day before Wagner killed his daughter and editor, he gave his desk to Robin.*

Guess where he found it? Archie took on the last voice to tell him.

Mac woke up with a start. The full moon shone through the skylight down on him and Archie, who was asleep next to him.

Robin was right. Damian Wagner had finished his last book and she was hiding it from Raymond Hollister.

"Archie, wake up." He shook her. "I know where the book is. Where's that book you were reading the other day?" Without bothering to put on his shoes, he got up and ran from the room.

"Downstairs in the study where I got it." Archie rubbed her eyes. "I finished it. Awesome ending. Why?"

"The desk in the study used to belong to Damian Wagner. He gave it to Robin the same day he died. Do you remember Jeff saying that Robin was certain that he had finished his book?"

Shrugging into her bathrobe and shoving her feet into her slippers while shuffling to the top of the stairs, she called down to him from over the bannister. "Because he had it hidden away in the desk that he gave her?"

"I think she was keeping it away from Raymond Hollister." Mac ran back from where he had started down the next flight of stairs to the study where the desk was waiting. "In that book you were reading? Did they find that manuscript in a desk?"

"As a matter of fact—"

"She must have been trying to tell us that in the book you were reading."

"Why not just leave it in an envelope and give it to Willingham?" Archie hurried down the stairs to meet him at the bottom.

Mac grinned when the thought came to his mind. "Because she was Robin Spencer—she wanted us to earn that information." He took her hand and led her to the stairs going down to the study.

"Lucky thing Hollister didn't read her book and get the meaning," Archie said. "He may have come after her either with an ax or lawyers."

"It's a toss-up of what would have been worse," Mac said. "We need to find that book." He dropped to his knees to study the heavy oak desk that was the centerpiece of Robin Spencer's study.

Of all the rooms in the manor house, Mac felt most comfortable in Robin's study. Here, he felt the essence of the woman who had given birth to him.

Robin Spencer's famous mysteries had been penned in the most cluttered room in Spencer Manor. Built-in bookshelves containing thousands of books collected over five generations took up space on every wall. Robin had left her son first editions of all her books. First editions of famous authors personally inscribed to her, and books for research in forensics, poisons, criminology, and the law also lined the shelves. With every inch of bookshelf space taken, the writer had taken to stacking books on her heavy oak desk and tables, and in the corner. With no other place to put them, Mac let them remain where they were stacked.

Portraits of Spencer ancestors filled space not taken up with books. After two years, Mac was still in the process of learning many of their names and histories. Some appeared to be from the eighteenth century. Others wore fashions from the turn of the nineteenth century and on throughout.

The most recent portrait was a life-sized painting of Robin Spencer, dressed in a white strapless formal gown from the 1960s. She looked like a young Elizabeth Taylor. When he had first seen the picture, Mac was taken aback by how much Robin resembled his grown daughter Jessica, who was a third year student at William and Mary in Williamsburg, Virginia.

The portrait of the demure-looking author filled the wall between two gun cases behind the desk. One case contained rifles and shotguns, while the other had handguns. Some of the weapons had been handed down through the Spencer family. Others, Robin had purchased for research.

Robin had acquired other weapons during her career of writing about murder. The coat rack sported a hangman's noose and a Samurai sword hung on the wall.

In a chair in the far corner of the room, Uncle Eugene watched all the comings and goings. A first aid training dummy, Uncle Eugene had been stabbed in the back, tossed off rooftops, and strangled on numerous occasions —all in the name of research. When he wasn't being victimized, he sat in an overstuffed chair in the corner, dressed in a tuxedo with a top hat perched on his head. With one leg crossed over the other and an empty sherry glass next to his elbow, Uncle Eugene looked like he was taking a break while waiting for the next attempt on his life.

"Where was it hidden in Robin's book?" Mac asked Archie.

"It was in a secret compartment along the side of the desk." Archie crawled under the desk from the front while Mac was crawling in from the back. "There was a lever that Diablo had stepped on—" She pressed her hand on the brace between the front and back legs on the side.

Before she could finish, she heard a click followed by a yell from Mac, who fell back onto his rump where he was kneeling under the desk.

"Did you say something?" she asked Mac who was rubbing the side of his head.

"Nothing," Mac groaned.

The front corner panel on the right side of the desk had popped forward to reveal that it was a corner door panel. She had tripped the lever to pop it open when she had pressed the bottom brace between the side legs. "I opened it just like Diablo did in the book," Archie said. "It's like Robin was psychic." She giggled. "If Gnarly was here, he would have tripped it for sure."

"Where is that dog anyway?" Mac asked.

"He's wherever Molly is."

"Ah, young puppy love." Mac peered into the secret side drawer to find that it was empty. "It's not here."

"Are you sure?" Archie rushed around the desk and knelt down to reach her hand inside and slap the sides. "But according to her book ..."

"Why did Damian Wagner give Robin that desk?" He pulled himself up and sat in the chair behind the desk.

From where she was sitting on the floor, Archie gazed up at him. "Because ..." she shrugged when she didn't have an answer. "He wanted her to have his last book. He didn't want Hollister to get his hands on it."

"Why give her the desk?" Mac asked again. "Why not hand over the book to her and ask her to keep it safe for him?" He gestured at the safe hidden behind the portrait behind him. "There are no less than a half a dozen places in this mansion that Robin could have hidden it for him, and she would have."

Seeing the book on the desk's top, he picked it up and read the copyright page: 2005. "Wagner was killed in 2002. This book came out years later." He shook the book at her. "Here's what I think. Robin didn't find the book in the hidden compartment until later. When she found it, she knew why Wagner had slipped it to her."

"They were friends," Archie said. "Wagner knew Robin had dumped Hollister eons before. So she knew what a snake he was." She asked, "But why not tell her?"

"Plausible deniability," Mac said. "He didn't want her in the middle. Legally, the book belonged to Hollister. But if Robin had it and didn't know she had it, she was safe from any legal action to get it."

"You're starting to think like a lawyer," she said.

"What have I ever done to you?" Mac joked. "Remember, until a few days ago, everyone thought Wagner had run off.

So maybe the book was Robin's message to Wagner. If he was alive, she was trying to tell him that she had his book and was keeping it safe for him."

"But where?" Archie turned in a circle to examine all the walls in the study. "If Robin had found the manuscript, she would have moved it to make sure it stayed safe."

"But why not tell someone so that if anything happened, like her death, it would have been located?" Mac turned around to scour the thousands of books on the bookcases that lined the wall. It was like looking for a needle in a haystack.

"It wouldn't have been bound," Archie said. "It probably would have been loose leaf."

"*The Purloin Letter*," Mac said. "She would have put it with other manuscripts."

"Her manuscripts!" Archie ran to a cedar chest on top of which rested stacks of books. Without any attempt at organization, she tossed the books to the floor and threw open the lid. "This is where Robin kept her original manuscripts, prior to editing, going all the way back to the beginning." She dug through the books that were bound with clips and rubber bands. "Of course, most of these are collector's items."

She handed Mac an arm-load. "You look through these."

While they were searching, Archie would pause on one title after another, rekindling memories of great books she had read. More than once she declared that she had to go back to read that title again.

Mac was about to give up when she reached in to take out the last arm-load and handed it to him. On a whim, he started at the bottom, with the manuscript that would have been at the very bottom of the chest.

Damian Wagner's name leapt off the front cover at him. The title did next: *Alpha Force*

"Got it!" Mac yelled.

Archie sprang forward.

Mac opened up the page to the dedication:

To Riley Adams and Nigel—The True Authors of This Book—May They—As One— Forever Answer the Call to Maintain Nature's Alpha Force.

ꕥ ꕥ ꕥ ꕥ

"Are you sure he's up here?" Chelsea asked David.

David braced himself against a deep rut that Mac eased his SUV through on their way across the mountaintop. "This is where we found him."

"It's also where Damian Wagner found him," Mac called back from the driver's seat. "He considered Astaire Castle his home—his territory." Watching Gnarly and Molly bouncing around in the rear compartment, he made a mental note to check into purchasing a much larger vehicle if they are all going to be traveling together.

Still weak from his gunshot wound, David was little help to Mac with pushing open the wooden gate to drive through into the castle grounds.

They had forgotten that Chelsea had never been to the castle until she uttered an audible gasp upon seeing the turrets and the burnt out stone structure. "Wow," she said, "I can imagine what this was like back in its heyday."

"Before all the suicides, murders, disappearances, and fire." David opened the back to allow the dogs out.

"Riley!" Chelsea called out. "It's me! Chelsea! Are you here?" She made her way through the overgrown weeds and brush to search the garage where David had told her they found evidence of her brother living.

"Oh, Mac …" Archie fought a sob in her voice while gazing at the burnt out structure. She took his hand.

Gnarly rushed over to press against Mac's leg. His tail was between his legs. His ears lay back flat against his head.

"He does have a long memory." Mac tried to maneuver around Gnarly's large furry body to climb the steps up to the front door to look inside.

"What are you going to do with it?" Archie asked him. "It's going to be expensive to repair all the fire damage."

With her clinging to his hand and Gnarly pressed against the other side of his body, Mac gave up on going inside. He gazed up at the turret at the top of which they had found Damian Wagner's body.

"I'm not going to fix it," Mac said. "I'm going to have the whole place locked up—like Robin had done."

Archie saw a hint of sadness in his eyes. "Do you think it's evil?"

"I don't know," Mac said. "Maybe cursed? The only one who found happiness here was Riley. Everyone else ended in disaster. It's too much of a pattern to ignore."

He fought to remain on his feet when Gnarly jumped up onto his back and cried into his ear as if to beg him to leave. Wiping the dog off his shoulders, he eased him down onto all fours. "Even Gnarly doesn't like it here."

"So sad," Archie said.

❧ ❧ ❧ ❧

David led Chelsea out onto the back patio which looked out across the valley.

"Awesome," she said, "I've never seen a place that was so magnificent and creepy both at the same time."

"You should have seen it that Halloween night," David said. "It was like something out of a horror movie. It made for one wild--" Remembering her brother disappearing that same night, he stopped. "I'm sorry, Chelsea."

"Will you stop apologizing?" She shrugged. "You're making me feel bad."

"I don't think Riley's up here." David offered her his hand. "I'll keep looking for him and when I find him, I'll call you. Or, if you think that's too awkward, I can have Archie—"

She took his hand. "I'd like for you to call." She gazed up at him with her clear steel-blue eyes.

"Okay." With a squeeze of her hand, he turned to lead her around to the front of the castle.

"I think I'm going to come back to Spencer," she blurted out.

Stunned, David turned back to her. "What about your job?"

"I never did like that job," she said. "I thought that maybe I could get a job here—It's important that I be close—for Riley. I'm coming back for Riley. After all, I'm the only family he has, and I really do love him, and when you love someone, you owe them a shot at having a relationship—even if you don't really need them—but maybe a relationship with them would be nice to have."

Having no idea what she had said, David nodded his head. "You're moving back for Riley."

"For Riley." She extracted her hand from his grasp. "That's the only reason I'm moving back here." She brushed past him to head back to the front of the castle. "I'm hungry. Let's go."

Looking out across the valley, piecing together the possibilities for the future, a slow grin crossed David's lips.

"You coming, David?" she yelled for him.

"I'm right behind you." David turned and jogged to catch up with her and Molly. "Are you ready to go to dinner?" David called up to Mac and Archie who were peering through the broken out front window to the castle's interior.

"Any luck?" Archie asked them.

Chelsea shook her head. "That's okay. In a way, he was still gone even after he was found. He never did recognize or remember me in the hospital."

Mac threw open the back of the SUV. "Gnarly! Molly! Get inside!"

Instead of coming, both dogs whirled around to face the brush next to the garage. Both of their hackles rose up. Molly whined while Gnarly growled.

They turned to see what had caught the dogs' attention.

A white mist rested in front of the garage doors.

"It looks like the image on the security camera," Archie said.

"Riley?" Chelsea asked. The mist moved forward to stop in front of her. It came up to her waist.

Yelping, Molly ran around and jumped up into the back of the SUV. Gnarly was close behind.

Hovering in front of her, it floated up to brush against her face before going back down to the ground and disappearing into the woods behind the garage.

"Be safe, Riley," Chelsea murmured.

David wrapped his arm around her shoulders. "I have a feeling Nigel will take care of him, sort of how Molly takes care of you."

Gnarly let out a bark to remind them that they had forgotten someone.

"And Gnarly takes care of us," Archie said.

"Except when David needs to cover up one of his crimes." Mac slammed the back to the SUV shut and went around to the driver's side.

"You know, Mac," David stopped him as he passed, "you never did say if all of this has changed your opinion about the supernatural."

"Do you mean, do I now believe in ghosts, shape-shifters, and werewolves?" Mac asked. "I always did say I believed Gnarly was a werewolf."

David countered, "That's not an answer."

"Yes, it is." Mac threw open the door and climbed into the driver's seat.

"No it's not."

"Yes, it is," Mac said. "Get in the car and shut up."

David climbed into the back seat. "Keep it, Mac, and I'm going to have to shoot you."

The End

The Lady Who Cried Murder
A Mac Faraday Mystery
Book Excerpt

Prologue

Spencer Mountain on Deep Creek Lake, Western Maryland—Three Years Ago

"Are you ready for this?" Mac Faraday asked David O'Callaghan, Spencer's young chief of police.

The two men peered through the window at the fleet of vans and SUVs. Blocking the mountain road, a mob of journalists and their camera operators filled the small front yard of the log A-frame home built into the side of Spencer Mountain.

"There sure are a lot of them," David said in a low voice.

Mac looked over at the handsome young man. The gold police shield pinned to his chest shone. It stood out against his uniform's white shirt. Somehow, it seemed unfair that the police chief, only in his early thirties, should be baptized by the media with such a horrible case.

Baptism by fire.

"You'll do fine," Mac said. "Use your officer's training from the Marines. When you go out there, take command. They're going to try to take control from you—don't let them."

"You make it sound like I'm going into battle."

"You are." Unable to look at the horde of journalists anymore, Mac turned away.

David followed him into the front sitting room. "When you were a homicide detective in DC, did you ever have to give a statement to the media?"

"Are you kidding?" Mac replied. "I'm the last person my superiors wanted speaking to one of those vultures." Grasping David's arm, he soften his tone. "You're going to do fine. We've practiced your statement. Remember, no questions because—"

"It's an open police investigation," David finished.

"It's okay to be firm with that," Mac said. "You're in charge of this investigation. A young woman is missing. Your first objective is bringing her home to her mother safely—not playing up to the cameras."

"I almost wish I wasn't chief of police," David muttered. "I remember how much Dad despised having to do things like this. They always seemed to take one thing he would say and twist it—"

"I know." A smile came to Mac's lips when he thought about the feelings he and his birth father shared, even though they had never met. There was something to genetics.

He caught a look in David's eyes, which were identical to his own. They had both inherited their deep blue eyes from their father, as well as their tall slender build. The only noticeable difference was in David's blond hair, inherited from his mother. Mac had inherited his birth mother's dark hair, touched with gray at the temples which had crept in after he had hit his forties.

As a teenager, Robin Spencer had given birth to Mac out of wedlock. Her parents had immediately whisked him away to be adopted. While Mac's mother went on to become a world famous murder mystery author; his birth father, Patrick

O'Callaghan, had become the police chief of Spencer, a resort town located on the shores of Deep Creek Lake. Eventually, he married and had a son.

It was only upon Robin Spencer's death forty-seven years later that Mac Faraday, a homicide detective in Washington, DC, had discovered the truth. She had left him her entire estate, which included a mansion on Deep Creek Lake. She had also left Mac her journal, in which the multi-millionaire learned about his birthright. While his birth parents were deceased, his half-brother was alive.

"I'm glad you're here to help me, Mac," David said.

Mac shrugged his shoulders. "It's better than losing another tennis match to Fleming."

Arthur Bogart, Spencer's deputy chief of police, came in from outside. "The natives are getting restless out there, Chief."

"I'm ready." David picked up a clipboard with his notes from the coffee table to go over his statement one more time.

"I'll give these to our officers to pass out to them." Bogie picked up a stack of papers that contained a drawing of their suspect and handed some to Mac.

"Chief O'Callaghan?"

They looked up the stairs leading to the upper levels of the home. Florence Everest was making her way down the stairs. Archie Monday, assistant to the late Robin Spencer, was behind her.

Focusing on the case of Florence's missing daughter, Mac pushed aside the thought of how lovely Archie was. For the last four days, the petite blonde had been acting as friend and confidante to the distraught mother.

When Robin Spencer left Mac Faraday her estate worth two-hundred-and-seventy million dollars, she had further increased his good fortune by stipulating that her assistant, Archie Monday, was permitted to live in the guest house for as long as she wanted. Mac Faraday had no desire for the emerald-eyed blonde who loved to go barefoot to leave. It isn't every man who inherits a house with a live-in nymph.

Under normal circumstances, it would be difficult to gauge Florence Everest's age. She was a tall, slender woman with the presence of a movie star from the days of the silver screen or a runway model. Her presence was flawless. An interior decorator, she knew all about style and had used her talents to become successful in business, as well as high society, which was how she had risen up from a single working mother to the cream of Deep Creek Lake society.

For those on the A-list, Florence Everest was the only interior decorator in town.

Casting a fearful glance out the window at the crowd that seemed to be closing in while David's officers pushed them back, she asked, "Do I need to go out there?" Her eyes were puffy from a recent flow of tears.

"No," David said. "If you're out there, they'll be focused on you. I want them to listen to me and look at our pictures from the sketch artist."

A ruckus outside caused them to return to the window. The journalists looked like they were about to mow down the dozens of Spencer and Garrett County officers trying to hold them back when the front door opened.

A young woman and man rushed inside and slammed the door behind them.

While the woman rushed to hug Florence, her chubby companion hung back to glare at David and Mac. His penetrating gaze bore through his small dark eyes under his dark eyebrows and flabby cheeks.

"Ms. Everest, have you heard anything yet?" the woman asked. "I saw on the Internet that the police chief was going to make an announcement. Does that mean they found Khloe?"

"No, Lily," Florence said. "We've heard nothing yet."

"I wish I had insisted on Khloe going home with me." With a sob, Lily glanced over at the row of pictures that lined the fireplace mantel. "I saw that she had had too much to drink. None of this would have happened—"

"It's not your fault." Florence draped her arm around Lily's shoulders.

Everyone's eyes turned to the mantel, which contained an array of pictures of the dark-haired beauty. Like her mother, she had dark hair that fell in a thick wave pass her shoulders. Her dark eyes stood out against her alabaster skin. Many of the photographs were professional shots displaying her striking features that had won her leading roles in the few local community theater circuit.

"We're passing out pictures of the man that you saw Khloe talking to down at the lake on Friday night," David explained. "If we can get it out across the media, maybe someone will recognize him."

"That's all?" Lily's friend exploded. "You're passing out drawings of this guy? Why aren't you out there looking? Why aren't you bringing in suspects to question? She's been missing for the last three days and all you bunch of boobs have been doing is hanging around looking at the view and contemplating your navels."

"Now look here, Bevis," Bogie said, "we've been doing everything possible. You don't know—" The silver-haired deputy chief, possessing the solid build of a wrestler, was more than impressive enough to cause Bevis to back up a step to avoid contact with him.

"I know all about abduction cases." Bevis tried to avoid the imposing form of the deputy chief. "My father was a sheriff in Frederick County in the 1970s. He worked hundreds of abduction and murder cases before becoming Senator and I know all about how it works. Your handling of this case is totally unacceptable!" As if he threatened to strike David in the chest, he poked a finger in the police chief's direction. "If you morons would have listened to me three days ago, Khloe would be home now and her kidnapper would be in prison."

In addition to his nasty disposition, there was something about the smug expression on Bevis's face that made Mac want to slap it. Sometimes, Mac wondered if it was who Bevis's father was that rubbed him the wrong way. Senator Harry Palazzi had earned every bit of the reputation of sleazy politician. Every bit his father, Bevis made no bones about planning to take up his father's torch when his old man decided to retire, which wasn't likely to happen, and carry it all the way to the White House.

Mac could see by David's clenched jaw that he had the same effect on him. "Everyone is on edge right now, Bevis. So I'm going to excuse your comments as simply that."

"Spoken like a man with no balls," Bevis replied. "How did you get appointed police chief anyway?" He cast a glance in Mac's direction before scoffing. "I'm sure rubbing elbows with the owner of the Spencer Inn had nothing to do with it."

"That's enough, Bevis." Florence stepped in to cut Bogie off before he was about to grab the young man by the front of his shirt to take him outside for a little talk about respect.

Seeing Bogie coming, Bevis backed up. His legs buckled and he fell backwards to land on his rump and back on the floor.

Without missing a step, Gnarly, another part of Mac's inheritance, scurried around from where he had moved in to trip Bevis and sat down next to his master. A huge German shepherd with a mind of his own, Gnarly and Mac had a love-hate relationship. When he listened to Mac, or took it upon himself to act in Mac or Archie's defense, it was love. When he was committing petty larceny, it was hate.

At this moment, it was love. "Watch yourself," Mac told Bevis, "that first step is a doozy."

Bevis pointed at the dog whose mouth was hanging open and his tongue hanging out the side of his mouth in what appeared to be a laugh. "He tripped me on purpose."

Lily offered her hand to help him up. "Really, Bevis, he's a dog. They aren't capable of doing things on purpose. What is it with you two? You've been paranoid about him ever since you met him?"

"I don't like the way he looks at me." He smoothed his hair with both of his hands. "I know he stole my phone."

"Why would he steal your cell phone?" Lily asked.

When Mac cast a glance in Gnarly's direction, the dog scurried over to hide behind Archie.

"The sooner we get this started, the sooner we get it over with." David moved to the door with Bogie directly behind him. Mac, Bevis, and Lily fell in behind them. Archie grasped Gnarly's collar to hold him inside with her and Florence to watch through the window.

As soon as the media saw David step out of the house, a hush fell over the journalists. Cameras were poised to frame him in their shot when the police chief stepped up to the bank of microphones that they had set up on a makeshift podium in the driveway.

Bevis leaned against the porch railing with his arms folded across his chest. Mac wondered if that smirk on his face ever left it. It seemed to be permanently etched there. Behind him, Lily chewed on her pinky finger.

Bogie, Mac, and two of David's officers positioned themselves behind the police chief in a show of support when he began his statement:

"Four nights ago, on Wednesday night, twenty-one year old Khloe Everest, accompanied by two friends, went out for an evening of clubbing. During the course of the evening, she had become separated from her friends. Khloe Everest did not make it home. Witnesses have told our investigators that they had seen Khloe parked at a boat launch on Deep Creek Lake. She was seen speaking to a young man. On Thursday morning, her mother, Florence Everett, who was out of town on a business trip, received a phone call from her daughter's cell phone, in which she was screaming and crying for help during what appeared to be an attack. They were abruptly cut off. Ms. Everest immediately contacted our police department. Since that time, we have been searching for Khloe Everest. All of you have received pictures of Ms. Everest. We are still searching for the young man that she was last seen speaking to on the lake. At this time, I would like to distribute composite pictures of the young man based on witness descriptions."

"Is he a suspect?" a journalist yelled out.

"Right now, we only want to talk to him," David said. "He is wanted for questioning."

"Do you think Khloe's disappearance is in any way connected to the Amber Houston disappearance and murder in Pittsburgh, Pennsylvania?" another journalist shouted out. "They are about the same age and disappeared in the same way. Could it be the same killer?"

Another journalist agreed. "Have you checked the dumpsters belonging to motels in the area ... like the ones in McHenry?"

"We have examined all possibilities," David said. "Until we get evidence suggesting otherwise, we're operating on the assumption that Khloe is alive."

Over the heads of the journalists, Mac saw a car pull up as far as it could go on the blocked road and turn off to get out of traffic. Squinting, he could see a young dark-haired woman behind the wheel. She fluffed her hair with her hands and checked her lipstick in the rearview mirror before opening the door and sliding out of the driver's seat.

With a broad grin on her face, she sashayed up the driveway in her high heels and fire engine-red short skirt.

Mac was still trying to find the words to express his surprise when abruptly, Lily screamed, "Khloe!"

It took a full moment for the journalists to react. Cameras followed the line of Lily's pointing finger to the young woman in the driveway striking a pose for the cameras.

"What's going on?" she asked. "Has someone been killed?"

While the journalists mobbed the subject of the search, David turned to gaze at Mac in stunned disbelief.

Not only was Khloe Everest alive, but, judging by the glee on her face while posing for the cameras, she was doing extremely well.

Find out what happens next in
The Lady Who Cried Murder
Coming Fall 2013!

Please note: Changes may be made to the excerpt that you have just read during the editing stage of publishing *The Lady Who Cried Murder.*

About the Author

Lauren Carr

Lauren Carr fell in love with mysteries when her mother read Perry Mason to her at bedtime. The first installment in the Joshua Thornton mysteries, *A Small Case of Murder* was a finalist for the Independent Publisher Book Award.

A best-selling mystery author on Amazon, Lauren created the Mac Faraday Mysteries, which takes place in Deep Creek Lake, Maryland. *It's Murder, My Son, Old Loves Die Hard, and Shades of Murder,* and *Blast from the Past* have been receiving raves from readers and reviewers.

Lauren is also the author of the Lovers in Crime Mysteries, which is located in the Pittsburgh, Pennsylvania area, where she grew up. *Dead on Ice* features prosecutor Joshua Thornton with homicide detective Cameron Gates. The second book in this series, *Real Murder* will be released January 2014.

The owner of Acorn Book Services, Lauren is also a publisher. In 2013 thirteen titles written by independent authors (not counting Lauren's own titles) will be released through the management of Acorn Book Services.

A popular speaker, Lauren is frequently asked for advice about how to succeed as an author while running a business, cooking dinner, feeding dogs, and doing laundry. *Authors in Bathrobes* tells budding writers the truth about what it takes to be a successful writer today: determination, hard work, a dependable laptop, a full pot of coffee, comfy slippers, and a durable bathrobe.

She lives with her husband, son, and two dogs on a mountain in Harpers Ferry, WV.

Visit Lauren's websites and blog at:
E-Mail: writerlaurencarr@gmail.com
Website: http://acornbookservices.com/
http://mysterylady.net/
Blog: Literary Wealth: http://literarywealth.wordpress.com/
Facebook: http://www.facebook.com/lauren.carr.984991
Gnarly's Facebook Page: http://www.facebook.com/GnarlyofMacFaradayMysteries
Lovers in Crime Facebook Page:
http://www.facebook.com/LoversInCrimeMysteries?ref=ts&fref=ts

Goodreads: http://www.goodreads.com/author/show/900970.Lauren_Carr

Twitter: @TheMysteryLadie

Check Out These Other Highly-Acclaimed

Lauren Carr Mysteries!

The Mac Faraday Mysteries

The story takes hold immediately and the reader quickly identifies with Mac. The plot is well done without being overplotted. There are just enough twists and turns to keep the reader guessing. The climatic confrontation with the killer is good and the wrap up leaves you laughing and feeling good. The writing style is easy and draws the reader in effortlessly. I am looking forward to the next installment! **Reviewer: Ariel Heart, Mystery and My Musings Review**

What started out as the worst day of Mac Faraday's life, would end up being a completely new beginning. After a messy divorce hearing, the last person that Mac wanted to see is another lawyer. Yet, this lawyer looked very unlawyer-like, wearing the expression of a child about to reveal a guarded secret. This secret would reveal Mac as heir to undreamed of fortunes and lead him to Spencer, Maryland, the birthplace of America's Queen of Mystery, with her millions and an investigation that unfolds like one of her famous mystery novels.

It's Murder, My Son is Author Lauren Carr's third mystery novel. Carr's first novel A Small Case of Murder was named finalist for the Independent Publisher Book Awards. She resides in Harpers Ferry, West Virginia, where she lives with her husband and son on a mountaintop. "I love a good mystery," said Author Lauren Carr. "Growing up in a small community an argument at the corner store can become a murder by dinner. Making the story a reality on paper is a real thrill."

Behind the gated community in Spencer, Maryland, multi-millionaire Katrina Singleton learns that life in an exclusive community is not all good. She thought her good looks and charm made her untouchable; but, for reasons unknown, a strange man calling himself "Pay Back" begins terrorizing her and her home. When Katrina was found strangled in her lake house, all evidence points to her terrorist, who is nowhere to be found. Three months later the file on Katrina's murder was still open with only vague speculations from the local police department.

In walks Mac Faraday, sole heir to his unknown birth mother's home and fortune. Little does he know as he drives his new Dodge Viper up to Spencer Manor that he is driving into a closed gate community that is hiding more suspicious deaths than his DC workload as a homicide detective. With the help of his late mother's journals and two newfound companions, this recently retired cop puts all his detective skills to work to pick up where the local police have left off to following clues to Katrina's killer.

The fast-paced complex plot brings surprising twists into a storyline that leads Mac and his friends into grave danger. Readers are drawn into Mac's past, meet his children, and experience the troubling relationships of his former in-laws. New fans will surely look forward to the next installment in this great new series. **Reviewer: Edie Dykeman, Bellaonline Mystery Books Editor**

Old Loves Die Hard...and in the worst places.

Retired homicide detective Mac Faraday, heir of the late mystery writer Robin Spencer, is settling nicely into his new life at Spencer Manor when his ex-wife Christine shows up—and she wants him back! Before Mac can send her packing, Christine and her estranged lover are murdered in Mac's private penthouse suite at the Spencer Inn, the five-star resort built by his ancestors.

The investigation leads to the discovery of cases files for some of Mac's murder cases in the room of the man responsible for destroying his marriage. Why would his ex-wife's lover come to Spencer to dig into Mac's old cases?

With the help of his new friends on Deep Creek Lake, Mac must use all of his detective skills to clear his name and the Spencer Inn's reputation, before its five-stars—and more bodies—start dropping!

Lauren Carr could give Agatha Christie a run for her money! This hypnotic page-turner is a whirlwind of romance, murder, and espionage. Lots of creativity went into the unforeseen twists, and culminated in a climactic ending that tied the multi-faceted story into a nice little package. I also appreciated the special attention paid to the animal characters, which were every bit as developed as their human counterparts. This was an absolutely delightful read that is sure to be a hit with mystery readers. I look forward to reading her other books, as I am now a fan!

Reviewer: Charlene Mabie-Gamble, Literary R&R

In *Shades of Murder*, Mac Faraday is once again the heir to an unbelievable fortune. This time the benefactor is a stolen art collector. But this isn't just any stolen work-of-art—it's a masterpiece with a murder attached to it.

Ilysa Ramsay was in the midst of taking the art world by storm. Hours after unveiling her latest masterpiece—she is found dead in her Deep Creek Lake studio—and her painting is nowhere to be found. Almost a decade later, the long lost Ilysa Ramsay masterpiece has found its way into Mac Faraday's hands and he can't resist the urge to delve into the case.

In Pittsburgh, Pennsylvania, former JAG lawyer Joshua Thornton agrees to do a favor for the last person he would ever expect to do a favor—a convicted serial killer. The Favor: Solve the one murder wrongly attributed to him.

In *Shades of Murder*, author Lauren Carr tackles the task of penning two mysteries with two detectives in two different settings and bringing them together to find one killer. "What can I say?" Carr says. "I love mysteries and mystery writing. Two cases are twice the fun."

In her fifth mystery, Lauren Car brings back her first literary detective while introducing a new one. In Shades of Murder, Joshua Thornton teams up with Cameron Gates, a spunky detective who has reason to believe the young woman listed as the victim of a serial killer was murdered by a copycat. Together, Joshua and Cameron set out to light a flame under the cold case only to find that someone behind the scenes wants the case to remain cold, and is willing to kill to keep it that way.

Carr is a very gifted novelist. Her mystery novels, both the Mac Faraday and Lovers in Crime Series, are phenomenal. Her ability to keep the reader guessing, as well as her plot-lines that flow so effortlessly as they work up to the big reveal, always make her novels a fun endeavor, and I look forward to even more of her work as this year unfolds.

Reviewer: Shana Benedict, ABookVacation

In *Blast from the Past*, Mac Faraday finds himself up to his eyeballs in mobsters and federal agents.

After an attempted hit ends badly with two of his men dead, mobster Tommy Cruze arrives in Spencer, Maryland, to personally supervise the execution of the witness responsible for putting him behind bars—Archie Monday!

Mac Faraday believes he has his work cut out for him in protecting his lady love from one of the most dangerous leaders in organized crime; but when bodies start dropping in his lakeshore resort town of Spencer, Maryland, things may be hotter than even he can handle.

In this fourth installment in the Mac Faraday Mysteries, readers learn more about Archie Monday's past in a flash—as in a gun fight when the syndicate comes to town. "Readers love to be surprised," mystery author Lauren Carr says. "In

Blast from the Past, they are going to be surprised to discover the secret of Archie Monday's past, which threatens her and Mac's future."

Blast from the Past also takes the Mac Faraday Mysteries to a new level as his relationship with Archie Monday moves onto a whole new level. "I do listen to readers," Carr explains. "They have been clamoring for Mac and Archie to get together for three books."

What about Gnarly, Mac Faraday's canine inheritance? The only German shepherd to be dishonorably discharged from the United States Army? "It's not a Mac Faraday Mystery without Gnarly," Carr promises. "Let's just say Gnarly kicks things up a notch in his own way."

Lovers in Crime Mysteries

Dead on Ice

Lauren Carr's Latest Mystery Series

Lead investigator in the case was Cameron Gates, whose love interest is Joshua Thornton, a prosecuting attorney; the pairing of these two adds just the right romantic interest to "Dead on Ice: A Lovers In Crime Mystery," the first in a new series featuring them. I can't wait for the next book! Five stars, and recommended for all those who enjoy romantic suspense, as well as for fans of Lauren Carr. **Reviewer: Laurel-Rain Snow**

Dead on Ice is the first installment of Lauren Carr's new series (Lovers in Crime). It features Hancock County Prosecuting Attorney Joshua Thornton and his new love, Pennsylvania State Police homicide detective Cameron Gates.

In this Lovers in Crime Mystery, spunky Pennsylvania State Homicide Detective Cameron Gates is tasked with solving the murder of Cherry Pickens, a legendary star of pornographic films, when her body turns up in an abandoned freezer. The case has a personal connection to Cameron's lover, Joshua Thornton, because the freezer was found in his cousin's basement. It doesn't take long for their investigation to reveal that the risqué star's roots were buried in their rural Ohio Valley community, something that Cherry had kept off her show business bio. She should have kept her hometown

off her road map, too—because when this starlet came running home from the mob, it proved to be a fatal homecoming.

In her new series, Lauren Car teams up her first literary detective with a new and exciting partner. Homicide Detective Cameron Gates has a spunky personality that's a perfect complement to Joshua Thornton's logical and responsible nature.

"Readers of my first series kept asking when I would bring back Joshua Thornton," Carr explained. "However, they are going to find that single father Joshua Thornton is not in the same place since we left him in A Reunion to Die For. His children are grown. He's more independent, and he's ready for some romance and adventure. That's where Cameron Gates comes in."

With that, Joshua Thornton and Cameron Gates strike out to explore the mysteries of both murder and love!

Coming January 2014!

Real Murder

A Lovers in Crime Mystery

Fast-Paced Fun for Mystery Fans on the Go!

BEAUTY TO DIE FOR & OTHER MYSTERY SHORT

Some mysteries are meant to be read slowly and every clue pondered. Others are meant to be consumed quickly, sometimes serving to give the mystery fan a fast fix.

Lauren Carr's *Beauty to Die For and Other Mystery Shorts* is her first collection of four short stories that are are sure to keep mystery fans entertained.

Beauty to Die For features the Lovers in Crime, Joshua Thornton and Cameron Gates in a race against the Angel of Death to clear the name of a dying woman's son, who was framed for murdering Miss Pennsylvania.

In *Killing Bid*, an estate auction turns into a deadly affair after Gnarly's antics cause Mac to purchase a gem of a dress, which isn't his color.

Lauren Carr's third mystery short returns to the Lovers in Crime where Cameron and Joshua try to solve the murder of a young pregnant widow before it happens.

Last, but not least, mystery fans will see that every dog has his day, especially if that dog is Gnarly. In *Lucky Dog*, Gnarly helps Mac to solve the murder of a wealthy society girl.

As with every Lauren Carr mystery, enjoy these short, but fun-filled mysteries.